MW01105653

THE ROD OF
POWER

BOOK TWO - THE STORY
EC LARTIGUE

Book Cover Design: Tugboat Designs

ISBN: 13: 978-1508808794
ISBN-10: 1508808791

To the two women who, without fail, continue to believe in me.
My dear Mom and my precious Wife.

A special thanks to Linda, Sherry, Deb, and Michael.

Before the beginning was the Story,
But then a Lie was declared and believed.
But in the end,
Everyone will know and understand
The Story.

"For the kingdom of God is not
in words, but in power.
What do you desire?
Should I come to you with a rod
or in love and a spirit of gentleness?"
1 Corinthians 4:20-21

PROLOGUE

749 B.C

(20 Miles East of esh-Sheri'ah el-Kebireh/Jordan River)

The air hung thick in a dry hot chalk dust canopy. The sun blasted hard and high on the narrow road. A small caravan slowly made its way through a narrow pass not long after leaving Medeba.

The horses, as well as the caravan guards, felt nervous. Such confines were notorious for bandits. It wouldn't take long before their suspicions were verified.

Bandits! They came out of hiding and suddenly attacked. The hired guards reeled when the attackers rode out on horses decorated in hairy skins and horns. Animal skins and horned masks disguised the raiders. The outlaws simultaneously attacked both front and rear of the caravan. All of the guards were quickly dispatched. Then came the gruesome plunder. The attackers roamed through the caravan and randomly selected individuals making death sport of them. Their bloodlust continued for several minutes until their leader took control. He rode through a circle of his men surrounding a man they had chosen as their next victim.

The bandits collected all of the women and children and separated them from the men. They culled those suitable for the slave trade. Others were not so fortunate. The screaming sounds of death echoed along and up the narrow pass.

In all of the confusion of the attack, Hanun escaped. He wrapped his cloak around his single most important possession, a solid gold serving platter. Though only fifteen inches across, it was heavy. It was a temple artifact that would bring a handsome profit. He had spent everything he owned knowing its true value and what he would make in selling it. But now, he and his fortune were in danger.

Hanun crawled through some overturned wagons into the surrounding cliffs. He slowly made his way up through a maze of ledges. Hanun tried hard not to listen to the screams below. He knew that some of the screams were coming from friends and newly made acquaintances. He worked to steady his trembling hands. He couldn't afford the mistake of being seen or heard.

Hanun stopped and saw that he was nearing the top. He also saw that the boulders and ledges were thinning. He thought about sitting and waiting. The bandits might finish their deeds and then leave. But what if they didn't? What if they remained to divide their booty? What if they retreated back into the cliffs and waited for the next caravan? Could he afford to wait? Would they find him out?

Between his mounting fear and the relentless heat he decided he had to do something. He examined the possible paths to the top. None of them were perfect for hiding him the entire way to the top. One path appeared to be the best so he went with it. He continued his slow and deliberate climb, always making sure something blocked any line-of-sight between him and the bandits. The screams continued.

Hanun stopped. Only a fifteen-foot upward traverse remained and then he would reach the top. But there was a problem. The traverse was open to anyone looking from below. He would have to stay low, almost crawling in order to lessen his sight profile on the side of the cliff. That meant it would take longer. There was no easy way to cover the remaining distance.

So he pulled his cloak up and down on his knees he went. The maneuver was awkward. He had to hold his cloak with one hand, keep the platter covered, and maintain his balance with the other. As he moved forward, the rocky ground tore into his knees until they bled. He pressed on despite the pain as he came closer to the top.

Suddenly he stopped when a scorpion scurried out in front of him. When he did, the platter slipped from his grip. He fell flat on his face as he snatched it to keep it from slipping down the cliff. It didn't make any noise but it did something worse. The sun caught the platter at just the right angle. It reflected long enough to catch the attention of someone below.

"What is that up there?" The bandit screamed out as he pointed. Several of the bandits, including the leader, looked up.

Even lying down flat, a portion of Hanun's profile was visible.

The leader called out to three of his men, "Go!"

Hanun heard the command and knew that they had spotted him. The hiding was useless. It was time to move. He got to his feet and ran. He was quickly over the top and on the other side. The slope was much more gradual. He stopped long enough to scan for possible places to run or hide. Nothing was immediately obvious, so he took the path that would give him the greatest distance from his pursuers.

He was already down and going around a bend by the time the bandits made it to the top. They didn't see Hanun until he was going uphill a half mile away. They yelled a vicious curse as they blasted off after him.

Hanun heard the ferocity in their voice. He knew what would happen if they caught him. His lungs were practically exploding as he pushed himself up the hill and then down into a ravine. He had committed himself to this route of escape. As he ran, steep cliffs bordered both sides of the ravine. He had to get out and find another way. After running for a mile he stopped to look back. The soft dirt of the ravine had left no doubt which way he had come. He had to get to higher ground. He heard the mad calls of his hunters in the distance.

Hanun ran for another mile before the ravine opened up to

some rolling hills on his right side. It was an obvious route, but he knew his pursuers would know that as well. He had no choice.

He pressed up the hill and soon saw that the terrain opened up to better options. Hanun had a better bearing of his whereabouts. He knew in which direction he could find some villages. His problem was that he was on foot and that madmen were chasing him. He had evaded them, now he needed a place to hide. In the distance he saw Neba, the sacred hill. He remembered spotting it to the south from the caravan. He dared not use the road on the south of Neba. It was a long stretch where bandits roamed freely.

If he could make his way north of Neba, he knew he would have a better chance of reaching Medeba. There was a garrison there and the bandits would not wander close to such places. He had a plan. He knew the difficulty but had little choice.

Hanun took a deep breath and started running around and along a series of small hills. He pushed himself for about two miles before stopping to rest. Then he heard a chilling shriek from his hunters. From the direction and volume of the sound he thought he had about a mile distance on them. They were letting him know that they had not given up.

Neba was only another mile, so he began making his way north of it. The pursuing bandits let out a series of yells and then Hanun heard something else. It was the sound of horses and more yells. A group from the raiding party had found their partners in crime.

Hanun had never felt such fear. He almost wanted to fall down and give up, but the fear drove him harder to escape.

He finally reached an area just above the base north of Neba. Being a sacred area, there were many small shrines scattered along the slope. There were also several carved-in niches almost like caves. He thought about hiding in one of them but that option was too obvious. He pressed on hoping for any possibility of escape. He froze when he heard the voices.

"Stop your running foolish one. If you make us find you it will go worse for you. Surrender and your death will be swift." After that came the evil laughter. They were making the hunt into a game of torment.

Hanun fell to his knees and dropped the gold platter. He lifted up his eyes to the sky and cried out. "Oh, merciful Creator God whose name I know not. I cry out to you. Rescue me and I will serve you. From this place your holy man, Musa, once spoke to you. Hear me, I plead and I will serve you."

Suddenly the ground trembled. A few rocks and dirt rolled down the side of Neba. Again the ground moved. To his left he spotted a crack where some rocks had become loose. Light seemed to peek out from the crack. Hanun got up and walked over to where the crack appeared. There were several larger stones around the area of the crack. When he moved one of the smaller ones the light was unmistakable.

Just then he heard the bandits coming closer. He looked into the crack and saw that it was a small cave. He put his shoulder to one of the larger stones and pushed. It moved slightly. He only needed a small opening to enter and he succeeded.

He squeezed himself into the opening. He then looked for something to cover the hole. He spotted several small rocks. He piled them up as best he could, hoping it was enough.

He stepped into the cave when heard voices outside.

"Look, the fool dropped his treasure."

They laughed. "Come out from hiding, fool. We know you are around here somewhere."

Hanun stepped deeper into the cave. Without warning the light in the cave exploded with intensity. Hanun was knocked down as if the light had substance. The ground trembled again.

Some of the rocks Hanun had placed at the entrance rolled off and exposed the opening.

"Look, a cave!" The bandits had discovered Hanun's hiding place. Hanun got up and began to move further into the cave.

Just then a booming voice called out, "I warn you. Come no further."

The light became brighter. Hanun fell on his face and covered his eyes.

The bandits outside heard the voice and saw the light. Their reaction was completely different. "Let's see how brave you are when we come in for you."

Again, the voice boomed out as the bandits removed several of the stones at the cave's entrance. "Come no further. I will not warn you a third time."

The bandits were only enflamed all the more by the words. "It is you, fool, who will suffer for your boastings."

Hanun remained face down on the ground. His whole body trembled.

The bandits were in a frenzy when they finished opening the entrance. They pulled out their daggers and swords, ready to destroy the one who had warned them. They ran into the cave screaming, only to be slammed to the ground. A blast of wind and light hit them. It then lifted them and threw them out of the cave. They barely had time to open their eyes when another blast of light came out of the cave. This time it was mixed with fire. They watched in stunned silence as the flames of the fire encircled them. All at once the flames attacked and consumed them completely. When the fire dissipated, nothing remained, not metal or even bones.

Inside the cave Hanun remained face down, trembling. He had not seen but had heard. His fear was indescribable.

The voice again spoke. "Hanun, rise up and go. Learn My name and serve Me. Speak of Me but not of this place. Hurry now, go."

Hanun wasted no time. He rose up and ran out of the cave.

He was about three hundred yards from the entrance when the ground again trembled. He looked back and saw the ground moving like a wave in the ocean. He fell to the ground as the full swell passed by him. All around him the ground shook and roared. Hanun saw that the entrance to the cave was covered over and dust was rising as the rumbling wave moved across the land.

Hanun placed his face to the ground and with tears swore an oath. "This day I am rescued. This day I swear to learn the name of the God who has delivered me. I praise the God whose hand I have seen and whose name I will learn."

On into the night Hanun remained on the ground repeating the oath.

In the city of Jerusalem and in the palace of Jotham the King, the ground shook. Across Israel and as far as Damascus the earth moved greatly that day. Though many died across the land, few called upon the name of the LORD or turned to seek His face. Such is the story of man.

But some day that cave would again be opened. And in that day, people would again see the fire of God and hear the Name of the LORD.

Truly.

ONE

Out of the surrounding mountains, an early evening fog drifts toward St. Gallen. The amber glow of the city lights merged with the mist into a perfect setting for the fun loving and romantic. But out of sight from the city, sinister and unholy activities fused in the dark.

Hidden away in the forest and built along the mountainside stands a castle rarely seen and never visited by the uninvited. Atop the single high tower was a room reserved for arcane rituals. A lone figured sits lotus style in a corner. Three intertwined black candles dimly burn. In a slow guttural tone, the man moans a low rhythmic chant. The air reeks with the putrid smell of burning incense laced with a mysterious narcotic. For hours the repetitive rites continue.

After a time, the man sways to the cadenced sounds of his own voice. The rising smoke accumulates and hangs across the ceiling like a black fog.

Suddenly the man begins to tremble as a black smoke finger descends. As it moves downward, it grows. Reaching the floor it starts to take miasmic form.

The man senses a presence and opens his eyes. His mind is still dulled by the incense. And yet, he has no doubt as the phantom takes shape. Never before had such an appearing taken place. A horrid fear paralyzes him and he can't look away. The apparition forms an arm that reaches out and points to the man. And then it speaks.

The voice resonates like a low deep gong across a long tunnel. Slowly, the sound takes shape into one long stretched-out word, "Ossswaaalt."

The voice repeats it six times. Then comes the message. "Kneel before me. Listen and obey."

The man falls as if slammed to the ground.

The voice continues. "A man will soon appear as one back from the dead. He will seek to uncover an ancient power, great and mighty. You must find him and take it from him. No price is too great in order to acquire this prize. Stop at nothing. I am with you. Tell no one."

Malcolm Osgood collapsed unconscious and remained there until morning.

♦ ♦ ♦ ♦ ♦ ♦ ♦

Denying someone's death is not unusual. But how does a person process it when someone comes back from the dead, especially after fifteen years?

♦ ♦ ♦ ♦ ♦ ♦ ♦

The muted television provided the only light in the room. George Franklin sat in his favorite chair in a melancholy stupor. He flipped through his five hundred channels with an empty stare. His mind wandered, trying to make some sense of the last few years.

George had handed off his workload to some of his partners for the next week. He hoped the time off would help. He was losing his focus. He simply couldn't see any patients in his present state of mind. The idea of not regaining his footing frightened him.

And so, George sat alone in the dark, not sure what to do next.

Everything was about to change. Soon nothing would be the same for George, or anyone else.

◆ ◆ ◆ ◆ ◆ ◆ ◆

After four months at sea, the Australian Navy HMAS Melville made her way home. She was a Leeuwin class ship named after Melville Island. She and her sister ship, the HMAS Leeuwin, are tasked with a RAN Hydrographic survey of one eighth of the world's surface. Her current deployment had completed the assigned sector. Able Seaman Chad Henderson, the radar instruments operator, has just come on duty. His shift is comprised of occasional glances at the radar and an hourly report to the duty officer. With their current mission coming to an end, he has no reason to expect anything different.

Henderson pulls out a folded magazine when a peripheral blip appears and vanishes. He watched for the next area sweep. The blip reappeared. It was small but definite. He called to the duty officer.

"Sir, radar contact bearing 64 degrees, distance 39.4 kilometers."

Duty officer Lieutenant Commander Miles Agnew came alongside Henderson. "What do you have, son?"

"Looks to be a small craft ten or so meters long. It doesn't seem to have much speed. We might have a drifter."

"Alright, alert the Commander and report it to headquarters." He turned back toward the control station. "Mr. Benning, make your course 64 degrees at twelve knots. Alert the watch to be on the lookout."

"Aye sir."

"Henderson, let me know when we're within 10 kilometers. And contact sickbay. If this boat's a drifter, we might have some business for them."

"Aye, Sir."

"Let's go, people. I want full rescue protocols in operation. We practiced this, now let's put it into action. "

◆ ◆ ◆ ◆ ◆ ◆ ◆

Oliver lays sprawled out and asleep topside next to the mainsail. A tired and purring ferret lay across his chest. The rough seas of the last two nights had left them exhausted. With the rudder damaged, Oliver had completely lost directional control. Oliver was satisfied to let her drift while he rested.

When the first rays of the morning broke, a distant sound stirred him from his slumber. He raised his head wondering if he had really heard anything. It came again, only a bit more distinct. It was like a foghorn.

Oliver sat up. The ferret awoke as it slipped to his lap. Scanning the horizon, Oliver spotted a distant shape. He rubbed his eyes to make sure it wasn't a mirage. A horn sounds again. Some flares launch into the air. A vessel was about three miles out.

Oliver looked down.

"Well, Snoop, it's the third day and we've been found. Just like we were told. I shouldn't have doubted that it would happen."

"He is faithful," uttered the ferret.

"Yes He is, my friend. Yes He is." Oliver stroked the ferret as he watched the ship approaching.

◆ ◆ ◆ ◆ ◆ ◆ ◆

Commander Wyatt Cooper stood looking out from the control deck. The drifting boat was well in view.

Agnew turned to the Commander. "Sir, the deck watch reports that there is one person on board the vessel and he is acknowledging our signals."

"Very well, Mr. Agnew, all engines off. Ready the rescue launch."

"Aye, Sir."

The Commander rubbed his chin as he watched his crew go into action and prepare for the rescue. He tapped his leg and turned to the duty officer.

"It's a pretty isolated spot for such a small vessel. I wonder how this chap got himself out here."

"For someone to be alive out here, he must have some story."

"Some story, indeed," replied the Commander.

♦ ♦ ♦ ♦ ♦ ♦ ♦

George almost fell out of his chair when the phone rang. Startled, he wondered if he'd dreamed it. When the phone rang again, George looked at his watch. He wondered who would call at 11:30 on a Sunday night. He picked it up on the third ring.

The voice sounded almost mechanical. "Is this George Franklin?"

"Yes, who's asking?"

An emotionless woman answered. "I am an international operator. And you have a collect ship-to-shore call via Australia. Will you accept the charges?"

"Who in the world is calling me from Australia? I don't know anybody over there."

"I'm sorry, sir, I don't have a name. I only know that it is labeled urgent. Will you accept the call?"

"Yeah, I guess so. You said it was urgent."

"Thank you, sir. I'm putting it through."

There was a slight metallic echo in the background. "George?"

"Yes. And who is this?"

"This is O.B."

"Excuse me?"

"George, it's me. Oliver."

George looked up from the phone. "Is this some kind of joke or something? 'Cause it's not funny."

"No man, it's me. And I need your help."

George rubbed his forehead. "Wait a minute. This can't be... Are you trying to tell me that you're Oliver, Oliver Cohen?"

With a slight chuckle, "Yes George, it's me, Oliver, O.B., Ollie."

"But you're, you're…"

"Dead? Not by a long shot, buddy. I'm still among the living."

"Wait, granted you sound like him, but… it can't be. I mean, it's been…"

"Fifteen years? It's been that long, hasn't it? But here I am."

"Wait." George's mind was racing. How could he verify the impossible? "Let me ask you something. What was the name of the bartender at the Marina?"

"It's Arnie. Come on, we don't have to do this. It's really me."

"What was your wife's maiden name?"

"Ryker, Mary Ryker." The voice on the phone paused. "And George, it wasn't your fault."

George froze. A flood of memories hit him hard. He knew it was Oliver. He just couldn't imagine how.

George's voice was quieted and hopeful. "O.B., is that really you? How is it possible? Where are you?"

"First, thanks for believing me. Next, I'm on a ship about two days out from Perth, Australia."

"Australia? How did you get all the way out there?"

"It's a long story. We'll get to that later. First, I need your help."

"Sure, what can I do?"

"Well, for one thing, I don't have any ID, passport, or money. When we dock, I'll need someone there to vouch for me. Think you can get there and sort of …help me through the process of getting home?"

"You bet!" He looked at his watch. "It's 11:30 Sunday night here. That makes it what there?"

Oliver looked at the radioman standing next to him. The fellow held up his wristwatch and mouthed the word "Monday."

"George, it's 1:30 pm Monday afternoon here. How's that for knowing the future?"

"Yeah, OK. I'll start making some calls to the U.S. embassy in Australia and get things rolling. Wow, O.B., this is too much."

"Yeah, it'll take some time to explain everything." Oliver smiled as he stroked the head of the ferret sitting on his shoulder.

"Yeah, well, wow, let me get going. I've got to make some calls before things shut down for the day there in Australia." George's head was spinning. "O.B., I... it's so good to hear your voice again. I can't believe..."

George's voice began cracking up. The reality was starting to sink in. "O.B., I...I'm so sorry. I've sort of lost my way lately and now you're back. I can't believe it. I've really missed you."

What Oliver heard in his friend's voice touched him. "Me too, bud. Can't wait. Better let you go. See you soon. Thanks."

The line went dead. On either end an old bond reformed. They both wiped tears off their cheeks. George's hand trembled as he laid the phone down. Oliver reached up and took the ferret off his shoulder. He thanked the radioman as he stepped out.

Oliver walked toward his assigned quarters. He looked down at the small creature in his hands. He looked around. Satisfied they were alone he spoke to the ferret.

"Well, my friend, are you ready for all of this?"

The ferret answered. "I am always ready for an adventure. There is so much to see and learn."

Oliver patted the little fellow. "You are right about that. There is much to see and learn."

◆ ◆ ◆ ◆ ◆ ◆ ◆

Immediately after Oliver left the room, the radioman, Able Seaman Lyle Everett, began composing an email to his wife. Picking up someone lost at sea was enough to ignite all kinds of theories about the man. Now, after overhearing the man's conversation, more pieces of the man's story fell into place. This was one for the record books. A man lost for fifteen years and then found. He had to tell someone. He decided to send a discreet email to his wife. She often complained about his work and how he never had anything exciting to say about his voyages. This would definitely set her straight. What he didn't know was how quickly his wife would make use of the information.

◆ ◆ ◆ ◆ ◆ ◆ ◆

The news broke early Monday morning in the U.S. The cable news shows were the first to pick up the story. First came a teaser before a commercial break. "Man lost at sea for fifteen years found alive. That story coming up."

After the commercial, the three morning show hosts bantered about the believability of the story and then one of them led out.

"We have a breaking story out of Australia this morning. There is a report that an Australian naval vessel has picked up a man on the open sea. That is amazing all by itself. But it gets better. There is an unconfirmed report that the man has been missing for fifteen years."

A second host joined in. "Fifteen years? Is that even possible? I mean, can someone survive at sea for that long?"

The third host added. "We only have sketchy details for now, but we definitely will be following this story. Meanwhile from the Middle East, increased seismic activity has scientists concerned about what it could mean."

While the story passed with little notice, correspondents were already busy confirming details and tracking down sources. Within a few hours, they had the ship's name and its arrival time. A low-level government employee with Australian immigration saw an opportunity for some notoriety and called in with additional information. It seemed that inquiries had come from the U.S. concerning just such a person. By mid-day, the rescued man's name, a picture and biographical sketch accompanied the continuing storyline. All of the major news services were soon carrying the story. They had no idea how this story would continue to unfold.

♦ ♦ ♦ ♦ ♦ ♦ ♦

Brandon Rivers was in the Los Angeles office of A&E. He worked as a free-lance producer/director of short documentaries, cable docudramas, and a few investigative projects.

He sat across from Andros Manning, a scripting supervisor. Andros was the first of many hurdles Brandon had to get passed before he could launch any new project and get it into full production. Andros looked the part he played in the media machine. He was ponderously large. His dark beady eyes sat deep in his face. Both his grins and smiles were always forced and revealed his unashamed lack of sincerity. Andros was the person producers hated but were required to go through.

Brandon had recently completed work on an episode for the History Channel and he was ready to pitch something new. His recent works had focused along the line of the weird and unusual. He knew there was no end to people's fascination with the bizarre. It kept him busy and his agent happy.

He was about to open his portfolio when a story on the TV above Andros' desk caught his eye. The caption read, "Man Lost at Sea for Fifteen Years."

Brandon pointed to the screen. "Andros, turn up the sound. This looks interesting."

Andros grabbed the remote and turned to see what Brandon was talking about.

Behind the newscaster, the screen displayed a picture of the man found at sea. Under the picture was the name, Dr. Oliver B. Cohen.

Brandon jotted down the name and a few notes. When the news story changed, Andros muted the TV and turned to face Brandon.

"Wow, that's weird. Bet that guy has some story to tell."

"Exactly. Look, Andros, forget about what I was about to show you. I think this Cohen story has possibilities. Like you said, there's a story here. Lost at sea for fifteen years, what in the world happened to this guy?"

"Yeah, this seems right up your alley."

"Andros, I've got a feeling about this. With everything that's happening these days, this is the kind of story that could provide people with some good news for a change. We need to get in front of it. This could be big."

The shrewd and greedy mind of Andros was already calculating his cut in the deal. "Look Brandon, the Manhattan office will need more than a hunch to commit. Find out what you can and write up a proposal."

Brandon recognized the look. He had seen it before. "OK, here's the deal. The story is in Australia. That's not exactly down the street. I'll need some front money to cover travel and preproduction expenses."

Andros said nothing. He put on his poker face.

"OK, seven percent if I get the deal."

"Ten." Andros clinched his jaw.

"Nine," countered Brandon.

Andros smiled, "All right, but the expenses come out of your part if we land it."

"Andros, you're heartless."

"Heart has nothing to do with it, my friend. We all have to make ours."

Andros opened a side desk drawer and picked up a credit card. He handed it to Brandon. "It's one I keep for small projects. It's authorized up to $20,000. Remember, it's your money."

"If we get the deal."

Andros smirked, "Right, so get out of here and make it happen.'

Brandon shook his head as he took the card. "Mind if I drop in downstairs and get with the research guys? I want to find out what I can about this Cohen fellow before I meet him."

"Sure, why not. They're all hourly workers, no extra cost."
Andros smiled proudly.

"You are a piece of work, Andros, you know that?"

"I do what I can."

Brandon's mind worked story angles as he made his way downstairs. He knew which research geek to talk to . . . Martin. Brandon had always found Martin's kind came in one of two body types. There was the overweight type, which came from a lack of exercise. Then there was the wiry type, which came from a lack of nourishment. Martin was the latter. Of all the times he had met with him, he didn't even know if Martin was his first or last name. He simply knew him as Martin.

As he approached Martin's office, he shrugged at the thought. Martin was the picture of the over-active computer geek. His life and this world were too chaotic to try establishing meaningful relationships. Personal advancement without hurting others, those were Brandon's goals in life. Maybe later he would find time for relationships.

When he opened the door, Martin was waiting with a big grin.

"Andros knows you pretty well. Just got a text that said to expect you. So, what's up?"

"Here's the deal. Have you heard about the lost-at-sea guy they picked up yesterday?"

"Oh yeah, this Robinson Crusoe guy's either a hoax or he's got some story to tell. So what do you need from me?"

Brandon scratched his chin. "Let's start with some basic bio-stuff before his disappearance."

"That's easy enough." Martin's fingers flew across the keyboard.

"OK, here we go. Dr. Oliver Branch Cohen left port out of San Diego fifteen years ago. After a lengthy search he was presumed lost and then declared dead after five years. Speculation was that suicide was his intention after the death of his wife. She died in a boating accident. Her boat capsized in a storm and she drowned. A Dr. George Franklin was with her in the boat, but he survived. Seems that George Franklin was the executor of Cohen's will and was the one who had him declared dead."

"What can you tell me about this Dr. Franklin?"

After a little effort Martin had an answer.

"George Franklin, pediatric surgeon practicing in Rady Children's Hospital, San Diego. My guess, is that he and Dr. Cohen are friends."

Brandon leaned over Martin. "Got a picture?"

A few more keystrokes. "Here we go. Official ad shot from the hospital. Seems like a nice enough guy. He'll be surprised to know his friend is still alive after having him declared dead. That would be a trip."

"Yeah, really. Back to Cohen, any pictures of him?"

A few more keystrokes and Oliver's picture appeared. Martin commented. "Not a bad looking guy. I wonder what fifteen years lost out there does to a guy. He probably looks like a marooned prisoner of war."

Brandon looked at the picture. "That gives me an idea. Remember that morph-age thing you did for me on that missing person story last year? Just for grins, can we see what might have happened to Cohen?"

Martin nodded. " Sure, why not. It'll be interesting to compare him to his doctor buddy now."

He went to work. He entered a stream of data to start the process. He tweaked several known variables to fine-tune the results. Martin loved the challenge. He wanted to get close to what everyone would soon see. After about five minutes he leaned back from the keyboard.

"Ready to see what we got?"

"Let's have it."

With one click, two file photos appeared. On the right, the face started to change. The jaw-line withered into hollow cheeks covered by a gray unkempt beard. Deep wrinkles formed around the eyes and forehead. The skin looked tanned and leathery.

With the process finished, Brandon stared a minute before speaking. "Wow, fifteen years can sure make a difference."

Martin reached over and grabbed a jellybean from a jar and popped it in his mouth. "It's not just the years, my friend. It's the mileage. And I figure this guy has taken a beating out there under who-knows-what conditions. It couldn't have been a spa trip to the Bahamas, that's for sure."

"Yeah, I guess you're right. Print out what you have. Include photos of the before and after as well as his doctor friend here in the U.S."

Brandon reached into his pocket and pulled out a memory stick.

"Here, burn all the data on this for me. I'd like to have it with me. Also, email it all to me, that way I can grab it with my phone."

"Sure thing, anything else you need?"

"No, that should get me started. I'll know more once I get to Australia. Which reminds me, I need to book a flight pronto."

Martin smiled. "Well, let's get it done."

Within minutes Brandon had tickets for a flight leaving late that evening. He would have enough time to pack clothes, some gear, grab supper, and get to LAX. Brandon liked the rush of starting a new work. It was like a mystery treasure hunt. There were clues to gather and angles to cover. Most of all, there was his career to advance. He liked the control he had while putting it all together on film. His ambitions were large. Sooner or later he'd have a shot at a truly big project, one that would put him over the top. He had no idea that he was heading for the biggest story of his career.

TWO

Emma Franklin sat with several of her friends on the steps of her apartment east of the University of California San Diego campus. She had her customary mega-mug of morning coffee in hand. Everyone was enjoying the sights and smells of a cool spring morning. It was a rare Monday morning awash with fresh and hopeful feelings. They were temporarily free from the pressures and rush of class schedules. With a dead week between terms, many students had left town. Emma and some of her friends opted to spend the week doing nothing. It was a scheduled ceasefire from the brain-drain battles of their second year med school classes. They wanted nothing more than to regain a semblance of normalcy before the madness started back up.

Some humorously embellished their school horror stories, while Emma sat listening. Her attention drifted from voices to ambient noises around them. She heard a branch move. A squirrel jumped from one tree to another. It scurried across the branch and out of sight. She sighed, knowing how bad she needed this week off. She suppressed her guilt of allowing herself the down time.

Emma closed her eyes, brought her coffee mug up to her nose

and breathed in the aroma. She tried remembering better times when thoughts of home and family strengthened her and didn't pull her apart. She felt temporarily lifted remembering the feel of salty air striking her face and filling the sails of her dad's boat.

All of this ended at the sound of a car door. Emma opened her eyes and her mood immediately changed. Walking towards her was her father. Their traded looks spoke volumes. Others around them immediately sensed it. Conversations ended and her friends began to quietly exit.

Emma curled her lip as she glared at her father approaching.

"Dad, what are you doing here? I meant what I said. I don't think we're ready to talk about this yet."

George Franklin's head dropped as he stopped in front of her. "Emmy, this is important, but it's not what you think."

Emma put her coffee mug down and crossed her arms. She turned a hard stare away from her father. She fumed awhile before responding. "Go ahead, say what you came to say and then leave."

George swallowed back the pain of seeing his only child with such anger directed at him. He couldn't indulge the wounds of the past year. He took a deep breath and softly spoke.

"Emmy, you remember Uncle Ollie?"

Emma's face softened. Although Oliver wasn't a true uncle, he was the nearest thing. Memories of him were among her dearest. The times of sailing with him and his wife, Mary, were tender recollections. Their shared loss had crushed her. She turned and saw the same pain in her father's eyes.

"Yeah, why do you ask?"

"Uncle Ollie's alive."

"What? What do you mean he's alive?"

George's eyes started to tear up as he tried to hold back. Another deep breath and he continued.

"I mean, he called me last night. Someone found him at sea. He's landing in Australia in a few days."

Emma could hardly believe what she was hearing. "But that can't be, it's been…"

"Fifteen years."

"How…how's that even possible?"

22

"I don't know. We didn't talk long. All I know is that it's him and he's landing in a couple of days. He wants me to come and bring him back. I'm flying out later today. I came by to see if you wanted to go with me. I know he'd be glad to see you."

Her voice softened. She felt like a hopeful schoolgirl rather than a twenty-four year old med student. "Do you think he'd remember me?"

She saw the smile she hadn't seen in a long while. "Are you kiddin' me? You're the closest thing to a child he had. I think it would mean the world to him to have you there."

George paused before adding, "You know he doesn't have anyone else."

For a simple moment the pain of the war with her father faded with the possibility of regaining a lost joy. She felt like a little girl. She simply nodded.

George wrapped his hands around hers. "Thank you, Emmy. I mean it, thank you."

His voice cracked as he whispered in her ear.

"Emmy, I know I've been angry and isolated. I know I wasn't there for you when you needed me. I just haven't been able to shake the cloud over me."

He paused to swallow the lump forming in his throat. He pulled slowly back and looked directly into her eyes.

"But...but Uncle Ollie needs us. And I think that maybe with his return, we need him."

Emma felt the warmth of her dad's hands. She liked the feeling but didn't want to show it. She slowly withdrew her hands and looked up.

"Dad, there's so much I'm still trying to understand and work through. But, you're right, Uncle Ollie needs us."

George looked up, thankful for her undeserved response.

Something suddenly occurred to Emma.

"Dad, Australia's a long way. Is it even safe to travel with everything that's been going on?

"Emma, safe or not, we have to do this."

Emma's hands pressed against her cheeks. "Dad, how can I be ready in time? When do we leave?"

"Our flight leaves for LAX at 8:05 tonight."

"What if you can't get reservations?"

"Honey, I already have confirmed seats."

"But how did you know that I'd say yes?"

"I didn't. I was hoping."

"Presuming, maybe." The words stung and she knew it. Like all such comebacks, she wanted the words back.

"I'm sorry, Dad." She waited a few seconds. "That's a long flight and a long time to be cooped up in a seat."

Her dad snickered. "Don't worry about that. I got us seats in Business Class."

She was impressed. "That must have put you back quite a bit."

He loved seeing the surprise on her face. "Let's get you packed up. If there's anything else you need, we'll go out and get it."

Her eyes narrowed. She queued into the game they used to play. "Well, Mister, you really know how to sweep a girl off her feet."

He grinned. "It's about time I did. Now get yourself moving, girl. I'll wait for you in the car."

With that said, she got up and ran up the steps. She darted about gathering what she'd need. She was giddy with the possibility that perhaps her father's long darkness was passing. If Uncle Ollie could come back from the dead, anything was possible.

◆ ◆ ◆ ◆ ◆ ◆ ◆

It was the first morning after the HMAS Melville had picked up their unexpected passenger. Orders from the Admiralty instructed them to make for Perth with all possible dispatch. News of their passenger had spread and a quick resolution of the matter was important.

Commander Cooper was looking toward the bow where their visitor was sitting. Chief Petty Officer (CPO) Ernest Wilkins came alongside the Commander.

"The chap's been down there since early morning, sir, he and his little companion."

"What's he doing, Chief?"

"As strange as it sounds, sir, he started out reading to the little creature."

The Commander turned to the Chief, puzzled. "Reading, you say?"

"Best I could tell. Then after a bit, they both started singing together."

Now the Commander's eyes narrowed. "What do you mean, singing together?"

"Well, the man started singing a little ditty and the... weasel or whatever it is."

"Ferret."

"Yes, ferret, well, it joined in with squeaks of its own. The queer part was that the little thing followed the chap just as if it knew the tune. Strange, I tell you, almost a bit creepy."

The Commander nodded slowly. "Well, no telling how being on his own out there has affected him. I was told that after he came on board he ordered that his boat be scuttled?"

"Aye Sir. Said it had fulfilled its mission. So we scuttled it."

The Commander thought for a second. "What all did he have with him?"

"Just some food stuffs, fruit, mainly. But he left it. All he brought on board, besides the little creature, was a sort of backpack and a leather looking book or satchel sort of thing."

"Must mean something to the chap?"

The Chief cocked his chin slightly. "Sir, scuttlebutt has it that he's been lost at sea for fifteen years."

The Commander looked at his chief. "That hardly seems possible, Chief. No one could survive out here for anywhere close to that. I tell you what, let the fellow finish with his morning routine. Afterwards invite him to my quarters for lunch. I'd like to hear his story for myself."

"Aye Sir."

"Thank you, Chief. That'll be all."

The Commander remained watchful for a few minutes. He could see how someone might think that the man and the animal were communicating. It seemed like the man was speaking to the creature and it was responding. He supposed, given enough time and the right circumstances, a person could train most creatures. Trained responses, that's all it was. He shook his head and returned to the command center.

♦ ♦ ♦ ♦ ♦ ♦ ♦

George and Emma landed at LAX at 8:45 pm. Their flight for Australia didn't leave until 11:30.

"Emmy, I know it's late but between the shopping and a small snack, we haven't stopped to eat. We've got time to grab something, if you would like."

"Sure, that's fine. What choices do we have?"

They walked over to a terminal map.

"Oh boy, the best of airport cuisine. Without leaving the terminal, we have a choice of French pastry, fast food, Mexican, Chili's, or burgers. What's it gonna be?"

Emma pondered the choices before answering. "Even with business class, I don't want Mexican food sitting on my stomach. Let's do Chili's. I can grab a salad and you'll have a variety of choices."

Their time there went very much like the afternoon had gone, in polite silence. They had exchanged some playful banter when shopping, but then returned to the silence. It was like an unspoken but civil armistice. Emma waited, hoping that her father would brave the danger zone. But George didn't know how to cross the divide. So, rather than venture on an ill-equipped approach, he chose an affable repression.

♦ ♦ ♦ ♦ ♦ ♦ ♦

Oliver enjoyed the morning with Snoop. They sang and talked about the future. Oliver knew that soon the questions would begin. He didn't want to jeopardize his mission. He realized few would believe the truth about his years away. Caution and restraint seemed the best guideline.

He picked up Snoop and made his way to the Commander's quarters. Under his breath he repeated two words to himself, "wisdom" and "gentleness."

Oliver tapped on the Commander's door and a steward opened it and led them in. The Commander rose from his seat at a small table set up for a meal.

"Please, come in, Doctor." His smile was as broad as his shoulders. Though trim, the Commander was not skinny. He obviously worked on his physique and was well kept for a man in his early fifties. His deep tan contrasted nicely against his pressed white uniform.

Oliver walked in. "Thank you, Commander. No need for the 'Doctor' part, 'Oliver' will do fine."

"Very well." The Commander reached out his hand. "Wyatt Cooper."

Oliver reached out and shook his hand. "Thank you so much, Com... Wyatt."

They both smiled and took seats at the table. Oliver placed Snoop on the table next to his place. The Commander raised his eyebrows a bit as he looked at the ferret and then at Oliver.

"I've noticed that you are quite attached to the little creature. I take it you've had it a long time?"

Snoop looked up at the Commander and responded. "Oliver, why does he continue to refer to me as a creature? Have you not told him my name?"

Oliver smiled, noting that although he heard Snoop clearly, he could tell that the Commander had only heard ferret sounds, but no words. He realized the curious nature of Snoop's presence and their relationship.

The Commander's eyes narrowed as he watched the short exchange between the man and his pet. Oliver noted the Commander's expression.

"I'm sorry, Commander, I mean, Wyatt. He responds best to the name 'Snoop'."

In order to humor the good doctor, the Commander bent over, smiled large, and addressed the ferret. "Well then, Snoop," turning to Oliver and then back to the ferret, "it is very good to have you with us here today."

With that said, Snoop stood up leaning on his tail, cocked his head to one side and extended a paw toward the Commander.

The Commander drew back as his eyes went wide. He took Snoop's paw and shook it. He then glanced over to Oliver.

"Curious indeed, Sir, truly."

Snoop added in, "Truly!"

The Commander was puzzled and a bit unnerved. An awkward silence followed. Oliver chuckled and broke the stalemate. The Commander responded with his own forced chuckle.

The Commander took a moment to regain his composure. He cleared his throat.

"Well then, shall we have lunch?"

And so they did. The Commander looked on in interested silence as Oliver shared fruit and bread with Snoop. He noted how the ferret expressed what seemed like gratitude. Such interactions seemed strange with a dog, much less a ferret. The longer this continued, the more uncomfortable the Commander became.

At meal's end the Commander finally spoke up. "That's a remarkable relationship you have with.... ah, Snoop. You have trained him well."

Snoop looked at the Commander and cocked his head to one side.

The Commander tapped his fingers on the edge of the table and presented an uneasy grin. He turned to Oliver while peeking a glance over to Snoop.

"It's almost as if he knows what we're saying. Of course that's... that's ridiculous. Isn't it?"

Oliver glanced at Snoop before answering the Commander. He waited a moment.

"Well, Wyatt, it's not so much me training him as him training me."

"Yes, I suppose that's true enough. Anyway, let's talk about you. You are a doctor?"

"I was, an orthopedic surgeon to be exact."

"I suppose being a doctor helped you during this time. And how long exactly have you been missing?"

"It's been fifteen years."

The Commander pursed his lips as he continued his inquiry. "Obviously you weren't at sea for that long. So tell me, Oliver, where were you for those fifteen years?"

The Commander was courteous but there was no doubting the interrogation format. Oliver paused before he answered, repeating in his mind, "wisdom" and "gentleness."

"I was marooned on an island. My ship was damaged. I survived off what was on the island. My boat was finally made sea-worthy. I was back at sea for less than a week when you found me. And that pretty much sums it up."

"Quite." The Commander sat back and brushed his hands over his pant legs. "Well, you do seem fit for all that time alone."

Oliver reached over and stroked Snoop's head. "Well, I really wasn't alone."

"Yes, yes, of course not. It is amazing though how you not only survived but thrived on this island of yours. I expect there are many people who will want to hear your story when we get back. You do know that all of the news services are talking about you?"

"Really? I was hoping to simply slip back home."

The Commander smiled. "There's no chance of that, Oliver. If I were you, I'd prepare myself for a flood of attention when we reach port. I understand you contacted a friend and that he is meeting you?"

"Yes. Hopefully he will arrive before we do. Since I have no passport or identity papers, I asked him to work out some of the problems of my arriving in a foreign country."

"As a military vessel that won't cause a problem. But, you will need a passport to return home. There's also the matter of Snoop."

Snoop looked up before Oliver responded.

"What about him?"

"Well, Oliver, at this time, the importation of ferrets is not allowed in Australia. Quarantine may be required."

"But Commander, Snoop is very important to me. And anyway I am not importing him. At best I am simply passing through on the way to the U.S."

"Very good point, Oliver. I will contact headquarters and see what can be done. And with all the attention focused on you, I don't believe anyone wants to create problems at your arrival."

"I guess there's some benefit to all of the attention."

"Yes, quite so. I do apologize for what might have seemed like an interrogation. Well, I must get back to my duties. If there is anything you need, please let us know. We have deviated from our original course and I have reports to complete on such matters."

Oliver nodded. "It's very understandable. I'm glad you found us out there. I'm anxious to get back."

"I imagine so." The Commander noticed that Snoop was looking right at him as Oliver picked him up. The Commander could almost swear that the creature was smiling at him. As they left, the Commander couldn't shake the uneasiness of their meeting. This was one mystery of the sea he would soon have off of his hands.

THREE

After supper George and Emma wandered through some of the shops in the terminal. They each purchased some magazines and a few snacks. They arrived at their gate at 10:15 pm. Their scheduled departure wasn't until 11:30. Emma tried reading but ended up dozing off on her dad's shoulder. The initial boarding call was announced at 11:00 for First and Business Class passengers. George gently moved to wake Emma. She stirred.

"Come on, honey. They're calling for boarding. The seats on the plane are more comfortable."

Emma squinted. "What?"

"They're boarding Business Class."

Emma rubbed her eyes. "Right, I forgot. Bring on a lay down seat." She smiled as she picked up her carry-on and they got in line to board.

Brandon Rivers was behind them getting something out of his jacket pocket. When he faced forward he recognized someone. He couldn't believe it. It was the friend of Oliver Cohen, George

Franklin. He was going to Australia to meet him.

Brandon wondered if he would be sitting near him. He took his time going down the walkway and into the plane. He watched where George and a young lady were getting seated. He looked at his ticket and grinned. He couldn't believe his luck; he was right across from them. As he got situated, he deliberated how to approach the doctor. Brandon sensed that things were going his way.

♦ ♦ ♦ ♦ ♦ ♦ ♦

There was a gentle tap on Oliver's cabin door. Both Snoop and Oliver looked up.

"Hello, who's there?"

The door opened only slightly. "Pardon me, sir. Commander Cooper has sent me with a word."

"Come on in."

The young seaman wore an apron over his uniform. "Pardon my intrusion, sir. The Commander wanted me to tell you that concerning meals, you may eat in the galley or we can bring your meals to your cabin."

Oliver smiled at the courteous deference from the sailor. "What's your name, sailor?"

"Able Seaman Fisher, Lloyd Fisher, sir." Fisher looked up and smiled. "If you don't mind me saying, sir, the crew would very much like to meet you. We've picked up news from the mainland. You're quite the talk, sir."

Oliver suppressed a chuckle. "Really?"

"Oh yes, sir. There is much speculation about your coming back after so many years."

Oliver slowly nodded. "I suppose that's true."

He thought for a second " Well, Seaman Fisher, perhaps I better get used to answering questions. I think we will dine with the crew."

"We, sir?" Fisher looked puzzled.

Oliver pointed to the ferret looking at them and sitting up on his hinds. "Snoop and I. I don't go anywhere without him."

"Of course, sir. Sorry, sir. And what does the little fellow like to eat?"

"Any kind of fresh fruit will do."

"Very well, sir. We'll make sure to have some on hand. We begin serving at 1700, that's 5 pm, sir, but most of the crew are on hand at 1730."

"Then that's when we'll be there."

"By the way, sir, we're having Chicken ala Orange. Cook hopes you'll like it."

"Sounds delicious, Seaman. I can't wait."

"Very well, sir. Pleasure meeting you and Mr. Snoop." He nodded in Snoop's direction.

Snoop bounced a time or two, moving his head up and down. The seaman watched Snoop and chuckled nervously as he backed out of the cabin.

Oliver turned to Snoop. "I can already see how you and I are going to raise a lot of questions."

"And why is that, Oliver?"

"Well, showing up after fifteen years, for one. People are going to want to know what happened in all that time."

For Snoop the answer was simple. "Oliver, you must tell the truth."

"Well, I don't plan to lie. But, I will take care as to how much I say and when."

"I trust you know best, Oliver. God will lead you."

"Yes, I believe He will. But there is also the matter of us."

"Us?' Snoop cocked his head to one side.

"Snoop, unlike the Island, animals here don't talk to humans. And I can see that people are sensing that we are communicating with each other. That makes people nervous."

"Oh yes, how unfortunate."

"I think that we should limit our conversations to when we are alone."

"But, Oliver, even when I talk to you and they hear, they do not seem to understand what I am saying."

"That's true. But when I acknowledge you, people notice. And while I must admit it's amusing, it makes people uncomfortable."

"Well then, Oliver, what should we do?"

"I think that when others are around, I will not react to you. I'll try to respond to what you say by the way I speak to others. Think of it as a game we will play."

"Ah, I do like games. And this one is interesting. I think I will learn very much on this journey."

"I fear that you will learn more than you can imagine."

"Do not fear, Oliver. We are being cared for, you know."

"What do you mean?"

"Oliver, even though we have left the Island, the Maker is always with us."

"Yes, yes He is. And thanks for the reminder."

Snoop began to sing a soft, familiar tune. Oliver closed his eyes and joined in. As he sang, the anxiety lifted from Oliver's heart. The words filled his thoughts and the thoughts flavored the music. He could almost hear the sounds he remembered from the Island.

◆ ◆ ◆ ◆ ◆ ◆ ◆

They were airborne for over an hour when Brandon had his strategy for approaching Franklin. He knew that honesty with sources was paramount. Nothing turned off willing cooperation quicker than deception. Even with that, he needed a pretext to break the ice. He pulled out his computer and loaded up the information he had collected on Oliver Cohen. He peeked over at Franklin as he pretended to view the screen. Franklin dropped a magazine while putting it away. Brandon reached for it at the same time as Franklin. They looked at each other and smiled.

"Wait a minute." Brandon said. "You look familiar. I've seen you before."

"Well, pardon me but you don't look at all familiar to me."

Brandon looked at the computer screen and then at Franklin. "You're Dr. George Franklin."

George looked at the computer screen. His face was on it. "Yes I am. And why is my picture on your computer?"

Brandon reached out his hand. "Allow me to introduce myself. My name is Brandon Rivers. I work for A & E."

Franklin looked puzzled. "Arts and Entertainment, the cable network, surely you've heard of it?"

"Yes, of course. But about my picture on your computer?"

"Well, as chance would have it, I'm probably on this flight for the same reason you are. I'm here because of Dr. Oliver Cohen. His return has caused quite a stir. Our network is interested in his story. I've done research on him. And naturally, you are connected to that story. Am I right. You are going to Australia to meet him?"

"Yes I am. My daughter is with me as well."

"Off the record, what do you think about his return from the dead?"

"Well, obviously he wasn't dead. He was missing, merely presumed dead."

"I read that you were the one that had him declared dead."

"It was a legal matter to probate his estate. Just how much do you know about Oliver and his life?"

"Well, Dr. Franklin..."

"You can call me George."

"Well, George, the information I have is all public record. It's easily acquired. What people don't know are the human elements of the story. That's what we like to communicate."

George looked off. "The human element? Well, Oliver called me Sunday night. I couldn't believe it at first. I don't know much more than the fact that he's alive. He wanted me to come and help him get back. And that's what I'm doing."

"You and Dr. Cohen were good friends?"

"Best friends, that is until…"

"Until his wife's death?"

George lowered his head. "Yeah, until Mary's death. Oliver was supposed to be on the boat with me that day. I keep thinking that there was more I could've done."

"George, from what I've read, it was an accident."

"Yeah, that's what I tell myself." He looked directly at Brandon. "But I don't know anyone who's come up with a real answer for guilt, do you?"

"I guess not." Brandon's voice trailed off, thinking about his own guilt closet.

They both sat silent for a few moments. Brandon wanted more.

"So, George, what's your plan?"

"He asked if I'd help him get back. That's my plan so far. I've arranged a passport for him so we can get him back as soon as possible."

"George, you do realize that Oliver's story is big news. You're not going to be able to quietly slip in and out of Australia. Just before I left, I got word that the Prime Minister desires to meet him. You know how politicians don't miss an opportunity."

"I hadn't thought about all of that. I knew about some of the news coverage. While getting ready to come, I didn't pay attention to how much the story had grown."

"George, with this kind of story, the less people know, the more curious they become. If you try to hide, it only increases the inquisitive hounding. Best bet is to ride it out for a few days. The news cycle will move on to something else on its own."

"You seem to know a lot about this sort of thing.,"

"It's the world I live in."

Franklin rubbed his chin speculating about Oliver's future.

Brandon gave Franklin a few moments.

"Look George, I won't lie to you. I am here to do a story on Oliver. But I'm not out for a flash-in-the-pan headline or passing glance news sound bite. What I do involves more than that. I do documentaries and such. I do series stories for the History Channel that involve unanswered questions. And the way I see it, Oliver's story of survival and rescue falls into that category. I would like it to be accurate, and you can help in that. I mean, aren't you curious about what happened to him?"

"Of course I'm curious. But this is my friend we're talking about. He's had enough happen to him without people taking advantage of him or using him."

"You're right. He's not a commodity. But, his story could help a lot of people. Just think about everything the world is facing today. It's almost like Oliver has come back from the dead. His life could be an inspiration to so many."

"But, we don't know what sort of state of mind he is in."

Brandon paused before responding. "You're right. He's been through a lot of trauma and isolation. Who knows how it's changed him. That's why we all have to help him in his transition."

The thought of the isolation hit George. Oliver's request for help grew in importance. With all of the firmness George could muster, he looked hard at Brandon.

"Oliver has asked me to help him. I mean to take that all the way. No one, and I mean no one, is going to harm my friend. He's been through enough. Now, you want your story, fine. You'll get it. But it's going to cost you. You and I are going to protect Oliver. Do you understand?"

Brandon smiled. "I hear you. I admire your resolve, George. Oliver's lucky to have a friend like you."

"It's not luck, it's just life. He's my friend. I'd do anything for him. And whatever condition he's in, I'm going to help him get back some of the life he's lost."

George paused for a second. "No, let me say that over. We're going to help him...aren't we?"

"Yes, we are."

Brandon reached across the aisle and shook George's hand. The firmness of each man's grip communicated the commitment they were both making. Neither of them realized the final cost each of them would pay for their vows.

♦ ♦ ♦ ♦ ♦ ♦ ♦

Oliver walked into the dining quarters with Snoop on his right shoulder. Twelve crewmembers sat around a long dining table. An obvious place was waiting for him. In military unison, they all stood when he entered.

Oliver admired the deference these young men gave him. He smiled and responded with a firm voice.

"As you were, gentlemen."

They all caught his humor, smiled and sat back down.

Seaman Fisher approached with a tray as Oliver reached his seat. Along with Oliver's meal were sliced apples, pears, and peaches. He placed the tray in front of Oliver.

"Sir, I hope the fruit is to the liking of the little fellow?"

Snoop reviewed his meal and Oliver answered. "It will do nicely, Seaman Fisher."

"Thank you, sir." He took a seat at the end of the bench.

All eyes were on Oliver.

"Gentlemen, thank you for sharing this meal with Snoop and me."

The sailors didn't seem as interested in the food as they were in Oliver. After a brief silence, Oliver continued.

"Gentlemen, if you don't mind, it has become my custom to give thanks before I eat. I have learned that I have something to be thankful for and someone to be thankful to. So with your permission,

I would like to give thanks."

The seamen all looked at each other. They understood the request and bowed their heads.

Oliver prayed.

"Lord, Father... I sit here alive and well as testimony of Your care and goodness. Thank You for bringing me in the path of these able seamen. Thank You that they plucked me out of the sea and have given me shelter and food. Protect them in the good work they do and take us all to safe harbor. But most of all, thank You for being Who You are. Without You, none of this has any meaning. Rescue and use us all to Your purpose and honor... Truly."

Snoop responded. "Truly!"

The crewmen listened to the prayer and heard the ferret's squeak at the end. They looked at Snoop and saw him raising his bowed head. A few of them curiously grinned. Seamen Johnson was especially puzzled. He looked at Snoop and at the other men. He wondered.

Oliver reached to stroke Snoop's back. Snoop raised his head to receive the loving touch from his friend.

"Well, gentlemen, I can tell you have many questions. But, to not insult the cook, let me eat first and then I'll answer your questions. And while I'm eating, you can tell me about your ship."

One of the seamen spoke up. "Thank you, sir. I think all of us would agree that the best one to give a competent accounting of our ship and its history would be Able Seaman Henderson."

Several around the table nodded in agreement and looked over at Henderson.

Oliver spotted Henderson. "Well then, Henderson, let's hear it. Tell me about your ship."

Henderson responded true to military form.

"Sir, yes sir. You are on board HMAS Melville. She is a Leeuwin class vessel. She was launched in 1998 and commissioned in 2000. The Melville and her sister ship, the HMAS Leeuwin, enable the

Hydrographic Service to provide high quality hydrographic information of the ocean. The Melville has a compliment of forty-six, which includes officers and crew. Her equipment includes: one multi-beam medium/shallow echo-sounder, one dual frequency single beam echo-sounder, a digital hydrographic data logging and data processing system, an HF medium range differential GPS, a hull-mounted forward looking sonar, towed dual frequency side scan sonar, and three 10 meter survey motor boats equipped with shallow water multi-beam echo-sounders and a short range UHF differential GPS.

Henderson took a breath and continued. "She is also equipped with a helicopter flight deck and hanger. Currently, our helicopter is not with us. Our range is 3,500 nautical miles and our average top rated speed is 14 knots. The Melville is named after Melville Island which is just north of Darwin."

Oliver put his fork down having completed most of his meal.

Henderson took another breath and went on. "Some of our current mission specifics are classified but it took us south of the Indian coast and we were on our way back to port. I was on duty as radar instruments operator when you were spotted."

Oliver responded to Henderson. "Well done, Able Seaman. I can see why your shipmates picked you as their spokesman. And since you did such a fine job, I'll let you ask me the first question."

Henderson smiled at the compliment. "Thank you, sir. Most here have read some of the published reports on your life. And let me say for all of us, we are so sorry for the loss of your wife."

"Thank you, Seaman, I appreciate that."

"But sir, the big question is, where have you been these last fifteen years?"

"I was shipwrecked on an island."

"But sir, you set sail from San Diego. How did you get all the way out here?"

"Not long after I set sail I hit a violent storm that carried me to the island."

The sailors looked at each other. One of them spoke up.

"Pardon me sir, Able Seaman Oscar Benning. I am a navigation and steering operator. That must have been some storm! I find it a bit hard to believe that a storm could carry you out this far."

Oliver turned to Benning. "Well, Seaman, all I can tell you is that I battled my way in and through the storm. During that time I was knocked unconscious. I later woke up on the island. My boat was stuck on the reef in the island's lagoon. Eventually the boat was made seaworthy and here I am."

The seamen traded glances. A few of them wondered if the good doctor had lost more than merely fifteen years of his life. They also noticed him looking at the ferret. It was as if he was seeking an opinion on how he was answering the questions. This most certainly didn't escape Able Seaman Johnson's attention.

Another seaman asked, "Sir, tell us about your companion. You seem to have an unusual bond with it. If we didn't know better, one would think that you talk to each other."

Oliver felt all of their eyes bearing down on him. He looked at Snoop and then back at the crew. He nervously smiled. His silence hung like dead air. He realized the need for a cautious answer. He took a deep breath before responding.

♦ ♦ ♦ ♦ ♦ ♦ ♦

Virgil Yaunt tapped lightly on Malcolm Osgood's door. It was 8:00 am. It was unusual for Osgood to sleep this late. There was no answer. He touched the intercom button, "Master Osgood, are you alright, sir?"

No response came. Yaunt immediately took his communicator and contacted security. He shouted, "Get someone up here to Master Osgood's suite. He is not responding. Activate the in-room cameras. Do it now!"

He didn't even wait for a response. Diligence for Mr. Osgood's care was key to his future advancement. He loathed the man and the way he was treated. But he desired the man's wealth and power. And so he persevered, waiting for his opportunity.

Yaunt's communicator squawked. "Sir, Mr. Osgood does not seem to be in his suite. We are running a full perimeter scan. I have teams going from room to room."

Yaunt listened and then interrupted. "Have you checked the tower?"

"I'll send a team there right away. As you know, sir, by Mr. Osgood's order, there are no cameras allowed in that area."

"Just send a team there right away. I'll meet you there." Yaunt knew that if Osgood was not in his room, the tower was the most likely place for him. Yaunt was not even allowed to ask what Osgood did there. He only knew Osgood spent a great deal of time there.

Yaunt arrived just before the security team. He waved them back as he approached the heavy wooden door. What if he were inside? Yaunt knew any intrusion into his forbidden area would anger Osgood. Perhaps the old man had died in there. He had to find out. Yaunt pounded hard on the door. He began shouting, "Master Osgood, are you in there?"

The pounding stirred Osgood. Looking around, he realized that he was on the floor. The memory of the previous night still gripped him. He heard a voice shouting his name behind the door. He also heard the voice in his head commanding him. His body trembled with excitement at the thought of his mission. He had to find this man back from the dead.

FOUR

Emma turned to her father, "Dad, I've been thinking. What do you suppose it's been like for Uncle Ollie all these years out there all alone?"

"Honey, I can't even imagine."

"How did he sound when you talked to him?"

"Actually, he sounded pretty chipper."

"Really?" She looked away for a moment. "It was probably just the excitement of being rescued and all."

"You're probably right." George pulled out a photo. He held it out in front of Emma.

"I took this of Uncle Ollie and Mary on their new boat not long after they bought it." His eyes started to cloud up. The pain was coming back.

Emma saw the all-too-familiar look. She placed her hand on his arm. "Dad, stop blaming yourself. The guilt is destroying you."

"Honey, I know you're right. It's…it's just hard."

They sat in silence a moment before George turned to Emma. "When I spoke to Uncle Ollie, he...he told me that it wasn't my fault. He doesn't blame me, Emma. He doesn't."

"No one does, Dad."

George squeezed his daughter's hand. "Emmy, thanks so much for coming with me. It means a lot to me. I know it will for Uncle Ollie."

"What about Uncle Ollie, Dad?"

"What do you mean?"

"Well, fifteen years is a long time. I wonder how he's changed. What sort of toll has the time and all of this had on him?"

"I guess I hadn't thought about it. But, you're right."

"We have to just not make a big deal about it. However he looks, he's still the same guy."

"That's a very good question your daughter just asked." It was Brandon.

Brandon saw their hesitancy so he continued. "As I mentioned earlier, before coming I researched his life leading up to his disappearance."

George and Emma listened.

"About the question your daughter asked. I asked the same question. I had a file photo of Dr. Cohen processed through a program that simulates aging. I'd be glad to show it to you."

Emma jumped in, "Mr. Rivers, what makes you think this is of any interest to anyone?"

"Are you kidding me? A man is found alive after being lost for fifteen years and presumed dead? It's a great story. The media is already buzzing with the story. In fact, for your friend's sake, you need to be careful that it doesn't overwhelm him. With his possible mental and emotional condition right now, he needs protecting. I'm glad he's got good friends like you two."

George watched and listened to Brandon. "You're right, Brandon. I still wonder how far I can trust you."

44

Brandon answered right away. "You need to be skeptical. Protect your friend. But remember, I make historical documentaries not news sound bites. But, back to your friend, can I show you the aged photo I had produced?"

George nodded. "Alright, Mr. Rivers, show us what you have."

Brandon pulled out a manila folder. "Let me first explain how we came up with what I'm about to show you. We started with a file photo. We then ran it through a program used in aging photos of people who have gone missing or kidnapped. You've probably seen something like that on television?"

Both of them nodded.

"I also had the programmer add a hardship factor. Dr. Cohen has no doubt suffered some malnutrition along with the isolation. These factors have an effect on a person's face and body. Now remember, it's been fifteen hard years."

They both took a deep breath. George took the photo. As they looked at it, George moaned and Emma began to cry.

Emma's head fell on her dad's shoulder. She couldn't look at it again. "Oh, daddy, poor Uncle Ollie. He's really going to need our help."

George's hand was trembling. "Yes, baby, he is."

◆ ◆ ◆ ◆ ◆ ◆ ◆

Oliver stroked Snoop's back. The ferret raised his head back, enjoying it fully. Oliver then turned to the seaman.

"I would have to say that after fifteen years on the island with Snoop here, we've both learned a lot about each other. I can honestly say that I wouldn't have made it without him. And we do have a special way of communicating."

Several seamen shared nervous grins. Johnsen's eyes darted back and forth between Snoop, Oliver and his fellow seamen.

Seaman Henderson asked. "Sir, for someone marooned for fifteen years, you seem quite fit. What were your conditions like?"

"Well, I obviously didn't suffer from malnutrition. The conditions were very suitable for living."

"Were you ever in any danger? Were you ever afraid or lonely?"

Oliver looked and waited before responding. "Yes, to all of those."

"Then how did you get through all these years?"

Oliver smiled wide. "With the help of the Lord and my little companion here." Oliver looked at Snoop.

Snoop whispered, "Truly."

Johnsen's eyes widened while one of the seamen giggled before adding. "Excuse me, sir, but he seems a bit small to provide any protection."

Oliver stroked his chin. "Oh, you'd be surprised."

A few wondered about his response. Johnsen had other questions on his mind. After a moment, some of the seamen began eating and exchanged meal banter; all except Johnson.

Henderson had another question. "Excuse me, sir, but does the little fellow do any tricks?"

"Oh my, yes. He loves to do acrobatics and sings beautifully."

Henderson chuckled. Johnsen nervously scratched his chin.

Oliver looked over at Snoop. "Snoop, let's sing them a song."

Oliver closed his eyes and began with a soft hum that moved into a smooth melody. Snoop recognized the tune and joined in. And then they both began to sing the words.

Let me never live a day,
When my heart will fail to say,
There is no one like Him.

Even if a storm may come,
Even if my hand is weak,
There is no one like Him.

Who would You compare to Me?

Says the Holy One above.
He made the stars
And knows their names.
There is no one like Him.
No one like Him.

Oliver hummed the melody once more before fading the tune. Snoop swayed his head; his eyes remaining closed.

The seamen looked at each other without knowing what to say. Oliver had sung and the ferret seemed to squeak in unison with him. Had they heard? Had he imagined it? No. There was no doubt in Johnsen's mind. He sat stunned with a tear running down his cheek. He had heard the ferret actually singing and the song had gripped his heart deeply.

♦ ♦ ♦ ♦ ♦ ♦ ♦

Commander Cooper sat finishing up the day's paperwork in his quarters when there was a knock on his door.

He responded without looking up, "Come in."

Lt. Commander Agnew entered holding some papers. "Excuse me, Commander, I wondered if I could have a moment?"

The Commander put down his pen and looked up. With a nod of his head he smiled and answered, "Not at all, Number Two. I always welcome a rescue from paperwork. What's on your mind?"

"Well, Sir, it's about our visitor. As you know, Doc did a short exam on the chap right after he came aboard. The gent is in excellent health."

"That's good to hear. Especially for someone who's been through what he has. But that's not what's on your mind is it?"

"No, Sir. Doc filled out some general information on the gentleman. Rather than simply questioning Mr. Cohen, he searched the Internet to see what he could find. It confirms that he went missing fifteen years ago."

The Commander shook his head, "That's a long time."

"Yes, Sir, and it's about that length of time that brings up a curiosity." He pulled out a sheet from the report and placed it on the Commander's desk. It was a photo.

"Sir, this is a file photo of when he went missing."

Next he placed his mobile phone and displayed a photo. "Sir, this is a picture of Mr. Cohen that some of the crew took a few moments ago."

The Commander looked at them, "Well, it's definitely the same fellow. What's your point?"

"Sir, fifteen years has passed between these two photos. He looks exactly the same. If anything he might even appear to be younger."

Agnew looked around the cabin and spotted a photo. He retrieved it and placed it in front of the Commander. "Sir, this is you when you assumed command, which was eight years ago. No offense, Sir, but I can see how you've aged in that time. This chap has been gone for fifteen and he doesn't seem to have aged a day. Don't you see that as a bit odd?"

"Number Two, everything about this incident is odd. Fortunately, our mission isn't to solve such mysteries. Let someone else unravel the oddities."

The Commander saw that his answer had not satisfied his friend. "The sea is full of mysteries. Now you have one of your own to share with your grandchildren."

"But, Sir."

"That will be all, Number Two." The discussion was obviously over.

"Aye, Sir." Agnew reached to pick up the file.

"Leave it. I'll use it to finish out my report."

Agnew nodded and left.

The Commander looked at the file. He knew that Agnew had a point. He also knew that he needed to keep to his own advice. He placed his hand on the file and grinned.

"What exactly is your story, Mr. Cohen? Maybe you'll go home and write it for us, then everyone can know."

The Commander picked up his pen and went back to work on his reports.

♦ ♦ ♦ ♦ ♦ ♦ ♦

Oliver and Snoop hung around the dining area and chatted with some of the sailors. They each wanted to be photographed with Oliver and he obliged. One by one they left for their duty stations, all except Johnsen.

After the last of the sailors left, Johnsen came and sat by Oliver.

"Hello, sir. My name is Able Seaman Johnsen, Greg Johnsen."

"Hello, Seaman Johnsen. Good to meet you. What can I do for you?"

Johnsen was visibly nervous. "Well, sir, it's about you and Mr. Snoop there. I don't know how to explain this. But, I hear him. What I mean is that I hear him speaking words."

Oliver looked at Snoop and then back to Johnsen. "Really?"

"Yes, sir. Is it true? I...I mean, how is that possible?"

Oliver waited before answering. "Let me first ask you, Greg. May I call you 'Greg?'"

"Yes, sir, quite alright."

"Well, Greg, how would you describe your spiritual life?"

"Sir?"

"Do you believe in God and do you follow Him in any way?"

"Yes, sir. I am a Christian. My walk with God is new but is very important to me."

Snoop smiled and said, "It is as I told you, Oliver. We are not alone. The Story is still alive in your world."

Johnsen looked down at Snoop. "How is this possible?"

"With the Maker, all things are possible," Snoop answered.

Johnsen put his hand over his mouth.

Oliver smiled and extended his hand toward Snoop. "Greg, meet Snoop."

Snoop put out his paw and smiled. "Pleased to meet you, Greg."

FIVE

The pounding on the door intensified. Osgood got up from the floor and walked to unlock the door. As he opened the door, a plan developed in his mind. He heard Yaunt's frantic voice.

He shook his head. "He is such a weakling."

Osgood turned the lock, opening the door only slightly. He peered out and spoke in a calm voice. "What is it, Yaunt? What are you doing here and why are you yelling?"

"Master Osgood, we couldn't locate you and were concerned that you might be in some kind of danger."

Osgood saw through Yaunt's false concern. He could read Yaunt like a cheap paperback novel. He barely held back the distain in his voice. "Yaunt, I am fine. Call off the alarm and get out of here. After you have calmed down, meet me in my study. I have something very important for you. Now, off with you!"

When the door slammed shut, Yaunt turned. The security team behind him shuffled their feet waiting for instructions. The staff, who he considered highly paid guard dogs, had again witnessed his humiliation.

He yelled at them. "Go on! Get out of here! Shut down the alarm and return to your stations!"

They made a quick retreat. Yaunt stood there, seized in anger. He wasn't sure which he hated the most, Osgood or his degrading treatment. He longed for the day he would have his revenge. He wondered if he would ever get the chance.

♦ ♦ ♦ ♦ ♦ ♦ ♦

Oliver gave Able Seaman Johnsen strict instructions about the information he was about to share. He spent the next hour telling Johnsen his story on the island. At first, Johnsen wavered between astonishment and wonder. As Oliver spoke, Snoop added occasional comments. Johnsen sat amazed at all that he was hearing. The only thing Oliver left out was the specific details about his future role.

When Oliver finished, Johnsen spoke. "Dr. Cohen . . ."

"Oliver will do."

"Mr. Oliver, sir, if it hadn't been for the little fellow there," pointing at Snoop, "I would think you were daft. But, I have to say, the longer I listened, the faster my heart beat. I almost wish I could see it for myself."

Oliver smiled. "You will someday. I think this is but a taste of our promised future."

"You really think so, sir?"

"Yes, I do, son. But we're not there yet. We both have our journeys to make before we arrive there. The Lord will direct you. And then, in due season, I'll meet you there."

A signal indicated to Johnsen that his duty time was nearing. He stroked Snoop's back, shook Oliver's hand, and then promptly left in a light step.

Oliver turned to Snoop, "Well, I guess we've learned something new. It seems that certain people can hear and understand you."

"Yes. At first I thought it strange how others did not understand what I was saying. But now I see how those who belong to the

Creator hear His voice. They are part of the Story and therefore can hear His telling. Is He not amazing?"

"He's more that that, Snoop. He's a genius. And that's putting it mildly."

Snoop closed his eyes and began to hum a familiar tune. Oliver recognized it and joined in.

Oh what beauty, Oh what wonder,
He has given me to see,
I will never become weary
Of the Maker's love for me.
Sing it daily, Sing it often,
With no end to say it all,
Boundless story for the ages
Is the Maker's love for all.

They sang it several times and then moved back into a slow humming. At the conclusion, they both looked at each other, "Truly."

Oliver stretched his arms. "I can really tell I'm not on the Island anymore. I had almost forgotten what it's like to be tired at the end of the day."

"Yes, I too have noticed that as well." Snoop scratched his nose.

"Well, Snoop, I think we should retire. We will make port sometime tomorrow. Things will begin happening in quick order and we'll need all the rest we can get."

"Oh, Oliver, this will surely be a great adventure."

"That it will be, my friend. That it will be."

Oliver picked up Snoop and headed to their cabin. When they arrived, Oliver found his backpack and pulled out a flat leather folder. He opened it. It consisted of a cover and only two blank leather pages. He stared at them for a moment.

Snoop looked over at it. Oliver had never opened it in his presence before.

"What is that, Oliver?"

He took a deep breath. "This, my friend, is our map."

Snoop hopped on Oliver's lap and leaned his head to one side. "But, Oliver, I do not see anything on the pages. How can this be a map?"

Oliver chuckled. "Yes, that does seem to present a problem, doesn't it. But, it was like this when it was given to me."

"Who gave it to you?" Snoop asked.

"The Maker."

"Ah," Snoop nodded his head and returned to lie down. Snoop could see the question on Oliver's face. "Not to worry, Oliver. What we need, will be there when we need it. Good night."

"Good night." Oliver smiled in admiration of the simple faith of his companion.

Before closing his eyes, Oliver whispered, "Truly."

◆ ◆ ◆ ◆ ◆ ◆ ◆

Yaunt sat on one of four chairs dispersed around the room. Each chair was equally spaced, yet no closer than ten feet from either the desk or the walls. Anyone who entered Osgood's study was made aware of the restrictions. No one was ever allowed to touch or go near the books filling the wall shelves of the study. Neither were they to sit in the chair facing the desk until they were summoned to do so.

And so, Yaunt waited. The wall shelves were at least twenty feet high and comprised three of the five walls. One wall contained gate-like double doors along with huge wall hangings on either side. The fifth wall consisted of a ceiling to floor viewing window overlooking the grounds below and the not-too-distant mountains.

The study conveyed power. Yaunt always felt dwarfed and subdued when he came here. He had never dared to walk close to the shelves to examine the books. Even when Osgood was away, Yaunt was certain that there were hidden cameras everywhere. He remembered the beating and disappearance of one servant who had violated the restrictions. As he waited, he tried to avoid being completely overwhelmed by his surroundings. Instead, he rehearsed in his mind the lessons his master had taught him of power and advantage. He patted the report sitting on his lap

♦ ♦ ♦ ♦ ♦ ♦ ♦

The lights were dim in the cabin. Both Brandon and Emma had extended their seats and were fast asleep. Not so for George. Sleeping on a plane was never easy for him. He looked over and could see sunlight peeking through a small slit on one of the shaded windows. He glanced at his watch. He reset it for Australian time. They would be landing in about three hours. His mind would not shut down. He kept evaluating the steps he had taken and any he would need to take. His main concern was for the care of his long lost friend. He tried to imagine scenarios of needs that Oliver would require. Even though the intellectual exercise was exhausting, he couldn't sleep. Finally, mental and physical fatigue won out. George slumped over and slept.

♦ ♦ ♦ ♦ ♦ ♦ ♦

Both doors of the study powered inward as Osgood made his entrance. Yaunt immediately got up and waited for his master to arrive at his desk and summon him over. Osgood first walked over to the window and stood looking out, silhouetted against the towering glass frame. Yaunt waited. After a few moments, Osgood turned and while walking to his desk, commanded Yaunt, "Come!"

Yaunt waited for Osgood to sit before he did. Osgood looked up to the ceiling before turning to look at Yaunt.

"Have you read any of the morning news?" Osgood's voice was firm but lacked the earlier anger.

"As always, sir, I have your morning brief." Yaunt rose slightly and passed it to Osgood.

Osgood didn't even look down at it. "Tell me, was there any news about a man coming back from the dead?"

Yaunt puzzled over the question. He knew better then to query his master. He thought over his brief and remembered. "As a matter of fact, sir, there was. It seems a doctor who was lost at sea fifteen years ago and presumed dead was found adrift and rescued."

"Excellent. Listen carefully. I want to know every detail about this man. I want to know all about his past, his family, and associates. Find out where is he now and what his plans are. And then I want him watched." Osgood paused as he took a deep breath. He looked directly into Yaunt's eyes. "Spare no expense or resource. This man is vital to my future."

"Sir?"

Practically screaming, Osgood rose to his feet. "Do not question me. Do it! Now get out of here. I expect reports daily or whenever new information arrives. Go!"

Yaunt bowed his head, turned, and left. His hate boiled but fear increased his pace. He was off to do his master's bidding.

After Yaunt left the study, Osgood fell back into his chair. He leaned back, lifted his arms into the air, and cackled a wicked laugh that echoed against the walls and ceiling. Even as light streamed into the room from the window, a coal black shadow hovered and seemed to paint the walls.

◆ ◆ ◆ ◆ ◆ ◆ ◆

The cabin lights came back on. A pinging sound preceded the steward instructing everyone to get ready for landing. George looked over at Emma and smiled as she awoke and stretched. He marveled how his little girl had grown so quickly.

Emma saw him smiling and had to ask. "What is it, Dad? Why are you smiling?"

"Oh, I was remembering you as a little girl."

"Dad, I'm not a little girl; that should be obvious."

"Honey, I know that. But, you'll always be my little girl."

Within ten minutes the plane thumped the ground and moved to their gate.

Brandon coughed toward George to get his attention. "George, what are your immediate plans?"

"Well, right after we get through Customs and Immigration, I plan to contact the U.S. consulate representative in Melbourne. A friend of mine helped me make some contacts in Washington. Hopefully some work has already been done to help get Oliver the documents that will allow him to travel back to the U.S."

Emma joined in. "Wow, I hadn't thought about all of the red tape involved, passports and all."

George nodded. "That's not even counting the fact that he's been missing and is technically dead."

Brandon had a questioning look on his face. "That is a lot of technicalities. Maybe the government will surprise us and efficiently handle it."

They all looked at each other and laughed.

After the plane stopped they retrieved their in-cabin items. Being in Business Class, they were the first ones off.

As they approached Immigration, George spotted a man in a suit holding up a sign with his name on it. He walked toward the man with Emma and Brandon right behind. The man spotted George and began walking toward him. When the man got close, he stretched out his hand to greet him.

"Dr. Franklin, how nice to meet you. My name is Jonathan Christian. I am from the U.S. Consulate in Melbourne. I arrived earlier today and am here to assist you and prepare for Dr. Cohen's arrival."

George turned to Emma and Brandon with a surprised grin. He turned back to Jonathan. "Mr. Christian, let me introduce you to my daughter, Emma Franklin, and our friend, Brandon Rivers."

Jonathan smiled and nodded to them all. "Very nice to meet you all. If you will all hand me your passports and follow me, I will get you through this quickly."

And without trouble or delay, they breezed through Immigration and Customs. Their bags were already inside a waiting black suburban. After a few short minutes, they were on their way.

As their vehicle sped off, Jonathan turned to the group, "This has all happened quickly, so I suppose you have some questions. Let me try to answer by filling in some details. Word of Dr. Cohen's rescue has become quite a news event."

George tried to ask. "OK, but . . ."

"Let me finish," Jonathan continued. "Dr. Franklin, after your call to the State Department, the news broke about Dr. Cohen being found. Secretary of State Emerson has taken a special interest in this matter. You see, Dr. Cohen's father was a personal friend of the Secretary. Not only that, but the Prime Minister of Australia has requested to meet Dr. Cohen."

Brandon grinned and nodded his head as he listened. He was privately congratulating himself for seizing the opportunity to be at the right place at the right time.

Jonathan continued, "Dr. Franklin, the State Department has confirmed with the Australian Navy that the person they have is indeed Dr. Cohen. I have issued a temporary passport for Dr. Cohen and a permanent one is being prepared once we get a current photo of him."

At the mention of a photo, Emma winced and lowered her head. George saw it and asked Jonathan, "How is Oliver? What I mean is, how is he physically and all?"

"The report from the Commander on the Melville, that's the name of the ship he is on, is that he is in good spirits and doing very well physically."

Emma squeezed her father's hand and gently smiled.

George responded, "That's good to hear. He's been through a lot. I can't even imagine what it's been like for him to be out there all of these years."

Jonathan smiled and responded. "Well, he's not alone."

All three looked at each other. Emma asked first. "What do you mean, 'he's not alone?'"

Jonathan looked at the report on his lap and answered. "It seems that he has a companion. He has a ferret with him, to which he seems quite attached."

The relief and release made both George and Emma laugh and almost cry. He held Emma's hand. "That's so funny. Ollie never took to animals at all. I remember us talking about it. His whole world was medicine and sailing until . . . Ma . . ." He almost choked on the word. Then he whispered it, "Mary."

Suddenly it gripped him. His chest pained as he held back the heaving flood of memories and emotions. Emma saw the distress and firmly gripped his hand.

She whispered into his ear. "Dad, remember. We're here for Uncle Ollie. He needs us. You can't fall back. Everything will be all right. You'll see."

George took a deep breath and swallowed back as best he could. He looked over to Jonathan. "I'm sorry. But as you may know, it was the loss of his wife that drove him out to sea. I was with her when she . . ."

"Yes, sir, I know. I read all about it. We'll be able to connect him with the best possible counseling care available. As I said, the Secretary is personally concerned."

George said nothing else. Emma continued holding her dad's hand. Jonathan smiled and discreetly turned and faced forward and remained quiet. The silence continued for several minutes.

Jonathan finally turned, "The ride to the port will take almost an hour. The Melville is docking at an Australian military base on an island off the coast called Garden Island. I was told that the base port for the HMAS Melville is actually in Queensland on the other side of Australia. But, because of Oliver, the Admiralty has ordered that they make port as quickly as possible."

George was impressed. "Wow, I guess Oliver's reappearance has caused quite a stir."

Jonathan grinned, "Yes, it has. I suspect that representatives from the press will be on hand as well. We'll try to lessen the impact, but I'm afraid a curious public wants to know."

"Inquiring minds." Emma whispered.

"Yes. Yes, I suppose that's right."

They each retreated to their own thoughts.

◆ ◆ ◆ ◆ ◆ ◆ ◆

Oliver stood on the most forward point of the ship. Snoop was sitting on his shoulder, his fur moving with the breeze. They could already see the port city.

"Well, Snoop, our new adventure begins very soon. This time it's my turn to be the guide. I will rely on the same One you rely on. We have places to go and things to accomplish. We will face obstacles and opposition."

Oliver stroked Snoop's head and back before continuing. "But what the Lord has declared, He will accomplish. So let's see how He writes this next chapter in the Story."

Snoop smiled and looked up. "It's sure to be surprising and wonderful."

Oliver smiled and nodded before whispering, "Truly."

SIX

Snoop sat on Oliver's shoulder watching as the Melville docked. Oliver spoke to the Commander, "Thank you, Commander, for everything. I'm sure you are ready to be back to your normal duties and such."

Just then, Able Seaman Everett walked up and handed the Commander a message. He reached out and shook Oliver's hand. The Commander read the message and then looked up at Oliver.

"Dr. Cohen, it seems your friends have arrived in Perth and are on their way here. A representative from your government is with them as well. The Naval Office has supplied a vehicle to carry you beyond the pier to an office area. Might I suggest that you wait here until we receive word that your friends have arrived? It seems the press is waiting a little way down the road." He pointed to a clearing beside some buildings not far from the end of the pier.

He continued, "They will provide you with a better transit through all of that. I will assign a couple of men to accompany you to the office."

Oliver thought for a second. "I guess that even after fifteen years, some things haven't changed."

The Commander nodded. "That's true, Dr. Cohen. But I must tell you; the world has changed a great deal since you went missing. We are in difficult times."

Oliver looked puzzled. "What do you mean, sir?"

"Well, Doctor, I'm a military man and in such things I'm not allowed an expressed opinion. I think you will find out soon enough. I wish you the best."

The Commander nodded before turning to walk away. He stopped beside Lt. Commander Agnew. "Number Two, see to it that the good doctor gets to where he needs to go."

"Aye Sir."

Agnew walked up to Oliver and smiled. "Sir, I have assigned Seamen Johnsen and Henderson to escort you to your friends. If you'll wait here, I'll let you know when we get word of their arrival."

♦ ♦ ♦ ♦ ♦ ♦ ♦

As they approached the dock at the base, they could see a crowd of news vehicles gathered.

Jonathan turned. "Dr. Franklin, we will be going passed all of this crowd and meeting with Dr. Cohen before you have to face the press. Do you wish me to address the press for you? They will want some sort of statement."

George turned to Brandon. "This is where your work begins. What would you suggest?"

"Jonathan is right. The press will hound you unless and until you give them something. I'd suggest a short statement and then announce a press conference either later today or tomorrow."

Jonathan nodded in agreement.

George decided. "Very well. Let's go meet Oliver. And, Jonathan, if you'll make a short statement about how glad Oliver is to be back and that we will have a press conference tomorrow morning. By the way, I haven't even taken the time to find us a place to stay."

Jonathan answered, "Don't worry about that, Dr. Franklin. All of that is already arranged."

"Okay then, let's go meet our long lost friend."

♦ ♦ ♦ ♦ ♦ ♦ ♦

Johnsen stood close to Oliver and Snoop. He whispered, "Sir, I will be praying for you both. I don't know what the Lord has in mind for you two. But as I've thought about it, it must be something special to provide such an interesting return and partner in the journey."

"Oh, He certainly has something in mind," Oliver whispered.

Snoop joined in. "Oh, Greg, the Maker has sent us on a great adventure and Oliver is to play an important part in it."

The comment stirred Johnsen's curiosity. "Sir, what is Snoop talking about?"

"Greg, I'm not at liberty to talk about it yet. But keep your eyes open. These are important times."

Greg nodded, "I've been hearing things to that affect and have wondered. So it seems we have entered perilous and wondrous days."

Oliver looked directly into Greg's eyes. "Brother, bare witness to the truth, knowing that the declaration of the Story will become a reality to all the world."

Snoop whispered, "Truly."

Just then Lt. Commander Agnew stepped up. "Dr. Cohen, your friends have arrived and are waiting for you. It was a pleasure meeting you. Good luck on your journey forward." He turned to Johnsen. "Johnsen, you and Henderson see to it that the good Doctor gets to where he needs to go."

"Aye Sir. Doctor, shall we go?"

♦ ♦ ♦ ♦ ♦ ♦ ♦

George and Emma were waiting in a conference room of the office. George was nervous and Emma was practically trembling. Brandon and Jonathan watched them and then smiled at each other.

Emma thought about the picture that Brandon had shown them of Oliver. Tears began to form. George debated about his first words for his friend. His palms were hot and tingling. Finally, he sat down and tried to calm himself as they waited.

♦ ♦ ♦ ♦ ♦ ♦ ♦

Henderson drove the vehicle up to the office area. Both he and Johnsen got out of the vehicle. Oliver retrieved his backpack while Snoop hopped up on his shoulder. Johnsen opened the door for Oliver. Oliver got out and for a second he and Greg simply looked at each other. Then they hugged. Snoop smiled and waved at Johnsen.

As Oliver turned to go, Snoop called out to Johnsen. "Be of good cheer, Greg. He is with you."

They walked into the office area and were gone.

Henderson looked at Johnsen puzzled. "What was that all about? You don't even know the chap."

Johnsen smiled looking at Henderson. He put his arm around his friend's shoulder as they walked back to the car. "Chad, I'd like to tell you a story."

♦ ♦ ♦ ♦ ♦ ♦ ♦

George heard a door close followed by footsteps. He and Emma looked at each other and got up. They stood next to each other waiting, holding their breath. They heard a voice in the hallway.

Oliver walked into the room with Snoop on his shoulder. George and Emma looked at Oliver and then at each other, their mouths wide open. No one said a word. No one moved.

Suddenly, Emma ran to Oliver and wrapped her arms around him. "Uncle Ollie, it's you! It really is you!"

Oliver embraced her and whispered, "Emmy, you're all grown up."

Snoop leaned over and put his head against Emma's head. He sniffed her and then moved over onto her shoulder.

Snoop's action startled her. Her voice trembled, "Ahhh!"

Snoop stood on Emma's shoulder and looked at Oliver. "Oliver, she is a very lovely girl. Is this what Mary looked like?"

Oliver chuckled. "Emmy, don't be afraid of Snoop. He likes you."

Oliver reached over and took Snoop and held him in his hands. "Emma, I would like to introduce you to Snoop."

Snoop reached up his paw and said, "Pleased to meet you, Emmy."

Emma looked at the extended paw and heard a soft ferret squeak. Not knowing what else to do, she shook his paw. "Nice to meet you, Snoop."

Emma was even more startled when Snoop tilted his head and appeared to smile.

As this was unfolding, George stood silently watching. He had not moved. He was unsure what to do or what to say.

Oliver looked over and saw George. Looking back to Emma, "Emmy, would you take Snoop for a moment?"

He handed Snoop over. Emma took him, now less startled and more intrigued by the creature. Snoop, for his part, snuggled up to Emma and purred.

Oliver walked over to his friend. George lowered his head as Oliver approached. Oliver stopped right in front of him. George was practically trembling.

Oliver broke the silence. "George, it's me O.B. It's Okay. Everything's fine."

Oliver wrapped his arms around George and whispered to him. "It's OK. I don't blame you. I'm sorry I was mad at you. I'm sorry for what I said. I love you."

The words slammed George in the deep places he had kept hidden. An uncontrollable flood poured over him. The strength in his legs left him and he leaned hard on Oliver who gripped him all the more. They both wept.

Snoop watched and sensed a breeze beneath his fur. He closed his eyes and began to hum and then sing.

Redeemed in love
That grace requires
Oh the new thing He has done.
What once was lost is now reborn,
Free to grow as new again.
Comes our hero to the rescue
Teaching us His way of love.
Comes our hero once again,
Who is like Him?
Who is like Him?
There is none.
Comes our hero once again
Teaching us His way of love.

As Snoop sang, Emma heard only the creature's rhythmic sounds. But there was something else. It was as if there was something behind the sounds. She sensed a distant memory of a forgotten song. And then it came to her. It was the tune that Mary used to sing to her. She couldn't recall the words, but the tune said it clear enough; *God loves you, Emmy.* She reached down and petted Snoop. The bond between them was set.

♦ ♦ ♦ ♦ ♦ ♦ ♦

Jonathan and Brandon stood watching the whole drama unfold. Some of the scene was understandable. Other things defied explanation. They looked at each other for a second, sharing courteous smiles. Jonathan stood silent, with his arms folded. He was used to waiting on others.

Brandon's thoughts were altogether mixed. Although he was somewhat touched by the witnessed reunion, something else had him thinking. He looked at Oliver and studied his appearance. The photo he had produced was obviously a wasted effort. The man he was looking at had definitely not suffered hardship. But, there was something else. He regretted that he had left all of his material in the car. As he stared at Oliver, he kept thinking that there was something else that wasn't right. It was hounding him like a forgotten name sitting on the tip of the tongue. He racked his mind trying to get to it.

After calmness settled over George and Oliver, they both sat down. Emma came and joined them with Snoop now confidently sitting on her shoulder. Jonathan and Brandon sat at the far end of the table.

George collected himself and looked over to Jonathan and Brandon. "Oliver, I want you to meet these two gentlemen. They will be helping us . . . you, in getting back to life, now that you have returned."

George looked at Brandon. "Oliver, this is Brandon Rivers. He is someone from the media. He has agreed to assist us in navigating through some of the barrage that will be coming at you. I'm not sure if you know, but you've become a big story in the news. Not far from here the media have gathered and are waiting. Jonathan has agreed to make a statement and then we thought it would be best if you held a news conference tomorrow."

Oliver looked confused.

"O.B., the media will not stop hounding you until you give them something. You are a big story and they have to fill in the blanks."

Oliver smiled, "The Commander told me as much. For the moment, I'll defer to you, gentlemen. We can talk more about it all as we go along."

George pointed to Jonathan. "This is Jonathan Christian. He is with the U.S. Consulate. He has made arrangements for us here and has a passport for you."

Jonathan rose and nodded. "Dr. Cohen, it is good to meet you. We are getting you a passport. I'll simply need a current picture and then we can make it so. If you'll stand against the wall please, this will only take a second."

Oliver obliged and Jonathan snapped a couple of quick photos with his phone.

"Thank you, sir. We have accommodations arranged for your group. Also, Prime Minister Owens is flying in this afternoon and would like to have dinner with you this evening. I will help you in any way I can to navigate your way until you depart for home."

The word "home" played funny in his ear. Oliver gulped and turned to George. "George, my Mom?"

George paused. He lowered his head before he spoke. "She's . . . she passed away almost ten years ago, O.B."

Oliver's eyes turned down.

"You know, O.B., she never gave up. I went to her about five years after you went missing. I had to have you declared dead in order to complete the probate of your estate. I wanted to tell her what I was doing. She looked straight at me and told me you weren't dead. I didn't argue with her, I just ... let her know."

"So she kept believing that I was alive?"

George reached back and retrieved an envelope.

"Oh, more than that. She insisted on it. But her health was failing and so she gave me this and made me promise to give it to you when I saw you."

George handed him a small beige envelope with her initials embossed on it. Oliver recognized it. She had often left notes on his pillow right before special occasions. He took it and held it gently. A flood of memories filled his mind. No one said a word as they watched him looking down at an unopened message.

After a few moments Oliver took in a deep stuttering breath and looked up.

"I think I'll read this . . . later," looking at the others in a soft smile.

They all looked at each other before Jonathan took the lead. He stood up, "I suppose we should be going now." He pointed toward the door.

◆ ◆ ◆ ◆ ◆ ◆ ◆

The phone rang only once. He picked it up with his right hand. It was the hand that bore his signature platinum skull ring. His stern voice answered with only one word. "Lanzig."

"Lanzig, this is Yaunt."

"Aye, Herr Yaunt, so good to hear from you. Are you well? And how is Herr Osgood?" His eyes narrowed. He grinned as he glanced at the report he had received earlier.

"He is fine. I'm sure you have already received a report from your security people here." Yaunt barely hid his fear and disdain of Lanzig.

"Yes. Most unfortunate. Perhaps there is some problem with the security sensors. I am having someone look into it. But that is not why you have called, yes?"

"Correct. I have sent you some new instructions."

"Yes, I was looking over them. Most interesting. And may I ask what Herr Osgood's interest is with this gentleman?"

"No, you may not. Carry out your instructions and find out all you can about this man."

"But of course Herr Yaunt. That is what we do best."

Yaunt took a deep breath. He did not trust this man whom he considered a Nazi throwback. But he was a necessary evil. He had worked for Osgood longer than Yaunt. If anything, he was thorough in all his dealings.

Yaunt continued, "Master Osgood expects daily briefs and immediate reports of any significant information."

"And how shall I know if something is significant?" Lanzig was toying with Yaunt.

"I trust you will know." Yaunt knew the power game Lanzig loved to play.

"Yes, of course."

"Just get on it right away." Yaunt wanted to sound authoritative.

Lanzig loved the game. "Actually, Herr Yaunt, I have already dispatched someone to Australia. He should be there in a few hours. My contact in the U.S. Consulate tells me that your gentleman will be staying at least one night in Perth. It seems the Prime Minister wishes to meet him. Whoever this man is, he has already attracted a good deal of attention."

Yaunt gritted his teeth. "Good, very good. Stay on it and contact me when you learn some more. Put together a full report on the man and get it to me as quickly as possible."

"Yes, of course, Herr Yaunt. I will have something as soon as I can. It was good speaking to you. Pass on my regards to Herr Osgood."

Lanzig loved dropping Osgood's name to Yaunt in conversation. Yaunt didn't understand the true connection between the two of them. Whatever it was, he both feared and envied it.

"Good day, Lanzig." He ended the conversation and set the phone down. He wondered how this entire situation with the man was important to Master Osgood. He was determined to find out and use it to his advantage.

♦ ♦ ♦ ♦ ♦ ♦ ♦

They were just beyond the mob of reporters and media types. Jonathan stepped out of front seat of the large Suburban and provided a brief word to them and announced the press conference for the next day. A few of the photographers attempted to get some pictures but the glass on the vehicle was tinted.

As they drove toward the hotel, Jonathan sorted through some of the documents Oliver had already signed. Oliver, for his part, continued to read and sign some remaining papers.

At one point he asked. "Jonathan, is all of this necessary?"

"I'm afraid so, sir. All of this will allow you to bypass the normal procedures of having yourself declared alive and to reinstate all of your rights and privileges as a U.S. citizen."

He chuckled and answered. "I guess it's complicated being dead and then alive again."

"Yes sir, it isn't something that happens very often."

"No, I guess it doesn't." Oliver thought for a second. He realized that coming back from the dead, was something he would experience more than once.

Brandon was sitting in the back row of seats behind Oliver and George. He was watching Emma and Snoop, who were seated next to him. Snoop was on her lap doing summersaults. After each one, he would face Emma and look directly into her eyes. At first Emma was taken back by it. But after two times of the same action, she found herself looking back at him. Something was being communicated between them that Emma didn't understand but she enjoyed it. After each time, Emma would take Snoop and hug him. Snoop would respond with a squeak and purr. Emma would then laugh.

George looked back and watched, then turned back smiling. He was so happy to see his girl enjoying herself. He had missed seeing her smile.

He looked at Oliver who was finishing with the papers Jonathan had given him. Something suddenly caught his attention. He thought for a second and then spoke.

"O.B., that shirt you're wearing, I remember that shirt. You bought it at the clubhouse years ago. But . . . it still looks practically new. Did you have it put away or something? And, another thing, you look like you haven't aged a day. You look just like I remember you. If anything, you look . . . younger."

George was even more stunned having said it. At the same time Emma, Brandon, and Jonathan looked up. The same question dawned on all of them.

Oliver knew that the hard questions were beginning.

SEVEN

George's words hung in the air. They lingered in a loud silence. Everyone waited for Oliver to say something, anything.

Oliver felt the tenseness. He looked directly at George. "Well actually, George, I have changed. I've changed in ways so profound that you will probably have trouble adjusting to them. As to my shirt, it is the same shirt. I've been saving it."

Jonathan went back to his paperwork. Brandon nodded but was not completely satisfied. He had questions building in his mind.

Oliver saw the questioning looks on their faces. He cleared his throat and continued.

"George, there's so much I want to tell you, but I'd like a little more private setting."

"Yeah, sure, O.B. This has all been unfolding pretty fast."

Emma was petting Snoop while she listened. A question came to her mind.

"Uncle Ollie, tell me about Snoop here. How did you meet? What's the story on the little fellow."

Snoop raised his head slightly to look at Oliver.

Oliver grinned. "Snoop has been my companion for most of my time on the Island."

"Island? What Island?" It was Brandon.

Oliver looked over to him. "I'll talk about that in a moment."

Back to Emma, "I met Snoop not long after I landed on the Island. He very quickly connected with me. He was with me through some pretty rough times and always remained true. I owe a lot to Snoop. I've rarely met anyone as faithful. And I'm glad he's with me now."

Oliver sensed Brandon's waiting. He turned to him.

"Brandon, before I answer your question, tell me about your story and how you find yourself in our group."

George jumped in. "O.B., I've asked Brandon to help us navigate through some of the media circus surrounding your return."

Oliver nodded at the answer but pressed on, "Yeah, George, I got that. What I want to know is, what's his story. What's in it for him?"

George smiled. He recognized Oliver's sharp mind for details. There was no getting anything passed O.B. He nodded in deference to his friend and let Brandon know with his eyes that the question was now his to answer.

Brandon cleared his throat. "Of course, Dr. Cohen."

"Oliver will do. Continue."

Jonathan's interest was peaked and he turned to listen.

"Well, my name is Brandon Rivers. I am an independent film producer. Most of my work is done with A&E and the History Channel. I typically do documentaries. When your story broke, I knew that I wanted to do something on you. You have to admit, someone coming back after fifteen years is amazing."

Oliver smiled, "You have no idea how truly amazing it is. Well, if George has some trust in you, we'll see how this goes. You just might prove useful."

George chuckled seeing his old friend in such good form. In fact, he could hardly believe everything he was seeing and hearing. It was almost as if no time had passed and everything was like it was. He wondered if such a thing was possible. He silently hoped.

Brandon spoke, "Dr. Cohen."

Oliver chuckled, "No, just Oliver."

"Thanks. Oliver, what about this island you mentioned. Where is it and how did you end up there?"

Oliver rubbed his chin. "Well, as to the island's location, we're probably talking somewhere west of Australia and south or southeast of India. But I can't quite say exactly."

Brandon asked again. "But how in the world did you get all the way over there?"

Oliver looked away and began his answer. "As everyone probably guessed, when I set out, I was basically going out with no intention of returning. I was angry and broken. I wanted to kill myself."

Oliver's words chilled both George and Emma. They each had differing memories of that time.

Oliver paused briefly. "A couple of days out, I encountered a storm. I drove into the heart of the tempest hoping to end my life. I was knocked out in the process. I awoke and found myself marooned on an island. My boat was eventually made seaworthy and Snoop and I left. We were then found by the Australian Navy and here we are."

Emma asked. "But Uncle Ollie, what did you do for all those fifteen years? How did you survive?"

Oliver thought before answering. "That, my dear, is a longer story that will require more time and another place to answer."

There was a tone of finality that Brandon and the others recognized. They each resigned their curiosity. Oliver needed to re-acclimate. The subject was closed for the time being. Oliver smiled, leaned back, and closed his eyes. They were all hoping the best for Oliver's recovery.

◆ ◆ ◆ ◆ ◆ ◆ ◆

Quan Li had received the call from Lanzig. On the trip from Hong Kong, Li read the full report on Dr. Cohen. He had obtained press credentials and was among the reporters who Jonathan had briefed. Not having any equipment to load, he left quickly and caught up with the vehicles transporting Oliver. His instructions were clear. He was to gather intelligence on Dr. Cohen and pass it on to Lanzig. He smiled, remembering his instructions, "Leave no stone unturned and spare no expense." His cruel mind could only imagine where such an assignment would take him. He kept the vehicles in sight all the way to the hotel.

◆ ◆ ◆ ◆ ◆ ◆ ◆

As they pulled up to the hotel, Jonathan turned to speak to the group. "Most likely some of the press will be present. Dr. Cohen, is there any short word you wish to give?"

Oliver thought a second. "I'm not prepared to make any statements yet, but I will be cordial. After all, I'm not a criminal . . . yet." He whispered that last word to himself.

Jonathan responded, "Yes, of course not. Very well, Brandon and I will lead the way. If the rest of you will follow the security team, they will show you to your suite. Don't worry about any of your luggage. That will be taken care of."

When they stopped, Emma scooped up Snoop and Oliver grabbed his backpack. As they were walking to the front door, the cameras started flashing and the air exploded with questions. Snoop leaped from Emma's hands onto Oliver. Oliver caught him and held him close. Oliver could feel Snoop's heart beating quickly. He stroked his head and whispered to him. "Don't be afraid, they mean us no harm."

Snoop pressed close to Oliver and whispered in his ear. "Oliver, someone is watching us."

Oliver smiled. "Yes, Snoop, that's obvious."

Snoop pressed the point by grabbing his neck. "No, Oliver, this is something different. Do you not sense it?"

Beyond the waving hands and shouts, Oliver suddenly sensed it as well. His eyes scanned the crowd not even sure what he was looking for. But it was there like a low tone and deep chill. He petted Snoop's head and nodded.

Jonathan and Brandon led the way. They were both yelling, "Dr. Cohen will not take any questions at this time."

Oliver looked over to Emma and George. He took a deep breath and signaled with his head that they should move on. Emma and George lowered their heads as they made their way through the group. Oliver pressed forward, his head up and eyes probing the faces. After they had pressed through, Oliver turned back and waved. Snoop watched him and started doing likewise. Some of the reporters watched curiously as the little creature imitated the man. A few of them chuckled in mild bewilderment.

Quan Li went unnoticed in all of the activity. While the media were pressing to get close to Oliver and his group, he took extensive photos and watched the front desk. Among his many skills was his ability to read lips. Keying in on the conversation of one of the security team and the attendant, he learned the suite number of Dr. Cohen's group. He sneered and considered his next move.

As Oliver and company entered the elevators, Li walked up to the front desk.

"Yes sir, may I help you?" asked the desk attendant.

Quan Li handed her his card. "Yes. I am with Osgood Ltd. Our chairman is possibly coming to Perth soon. I am here to inquire as to accommodations and security. He will require a large suite. Do you have what I need?"

"Yes sir, we do. Our top floor consists of two such suites."

"When the chairman comes, he will require both suites but for now, one will do. Is it available at the moment?

"Yes sir, right now one is still open," she answered as she checked the computer.

"Excellent, I will take it."

"How long will you be needing it? Are there others in your party?"

"I am alone and I will need it for at least tonight and perhaps one more."

"Very well, sir. I will need your passport and a credit card. And will you need help with your luggage?"

"Yes, thank you. I had the valet park my car. If you'll have someone bring up my bags to the suite."

"Most certainly, sir." She smiled as she looked over the information on Osgood Ltd. on the computer. "You should know that we have the most current Ultra-net communications here at our hotel."

"Outstanding. That certainly will sit well with my superiors."

"Here is your entry card."

Just then a security alert flashed on the screen. "I am sorry, sir, but I must inform you of an issue concerning your suite. It seems that a government security alert has been issued. You must vacate the suite for several hours this evening."

"What? Why is that necessary?"

"I cannot disclose that, sir. I do apologize and in consideration for the inconvenience, your stay for the evening will be free, compliments of the hotel."

He feigned displeasure.

"And, sir, we would also like to treat you to dinner while you are out of your room."

"I trust this will not occur when or if Mr. Osgood comes?"

"Oh, no, sir. This is an extremely rare occurrence."

"Very well."

"Thank you, sir. I hope you have a pleasant stay with us. If there is anything you need, please let us know."

"Thank you." He took the card and made his way to the elevator. Before he entered it, he examined the floor plan for the hotel on his handheld. A plan was forming in his mind.

♦ ♦ ♦ ♦ ♦ ♦ ♦

The suite occupied half of the top floor and had four bedrooms and a large living area as well as a patio balcony. George suggested

Oliver settle in and get some rest. Oliver did not resist.

George and Emma decided to use the time to go out and buy Oliver some clothing and other items he would need now and for his trip back. Emma wanted to take Snoop with her. Jonathan pointed out that it was best for him to remain with Oliver. He explained how the Australian government had made a limited exception to allow Snoop to remain with them. He then left them to go and make preparations for the evening's events.

What none of them realized was that Quan Li had already managed to extend a listening device into the ventilation within enough proximity to overhear all of their plans. He decided to follow the group going out. Information was his first priority.

Brandon decided to tag along. With Oliver's earlier inquiries, he knew he would need to continue to gain the support of George and Emma.

The hotel connected directly to a shopping area. After only an hour, they had bought more than enough to provide for Oliver's needs. The group decided to eat at the nearby sidewalk cafe. They were all glad to rest their feet. They each had unspoken questions running wild in their minds.

Emma wasted no time. She looked at Brandon and then her dad.

"If no one else wants to say it, I will. Can anyone explain to me how Uncle Ollie looks like he does? I mean I'm so glad that he's not wasted away like the picture you showed us. But it's more than that, isn't it?"

George nodded in agreement. "Well, obviously he did well. He's healthy and strong."

Emma interrupted. "But, Dad, he looks like he hasn't aged a day. How is that possible? It's been fifteen years."

Brandon wondered the same thing and wrestled for an explanation. He finally ventured a response, "Clean living, maybe."

Emma looked at him over the top of her sunglasses. "Really?"

She reached into her purse and pulled out a photo and handed it to Brandon.

"Look at that picture. See me there with my dad, Uncle Ollie, and Mary. I was a little girl. Now, look at his face. He looks exactly like he did in the photo. My dad doesn't. I certainly don't. Can either of you explain it to me?"

They looked at each other. No one even had a suggestion, much less an answer. They each ate their meals in silence.

Across the street Li sat on a bus stop bench. He looked like someone listening to some music through tiny ear buds. On his lap sat what looked like a mini laptop. From the back of it, a colorless laser was aimed on a water glass sitting next to Emma. Li was recording the conversation as he looked over the file he had on Dr. Cohen. The file photo confirmed the young woman's statements. "Curious," he thought. He knew the information he was gathering would please Lanzig.

Brandon changed the subject. "Is it just me or has Dr. Cohen, I mean Oliver, been less than forthcoming about what happened to him on this island of his?"

George nodded. "No, it's not just you. It's like he's hiding something. It's not like him. But who am I to say how someone acts after fifteen years of isolation."

"But, Dad, he seems so happy. He sails out in order to kill himself. Fifteen years later he suddenly appears and he acts like everything's great."

Brandon spoke. "Well, he did just get rescued after fifteen years. That's enough to make even the saddest person excited."

George thought about his own struggle over the past fifteen years. He jumped in, "There's no way to tell how Oliver's isolation has affected him. For all we know, he could be on the edge of breaking down. I think we need to give him some leeway. He's going to need some adjustment time and we should give it to him. Let's go easy on the questions."

Emma nodded.

They were back where they had started, with many questions and few answers.

Brandon looked at the other two, "Well, we ought to get back. I need to make some calls and do some work at the hotel business center. You two need to get back to Oliver."

They each wondered when and how they would start their inquiries with Oliver.

Li made personal notes on the conversations and began sending his report. The more he listened, the more curious he became. He wondered about what his employers were after and how he could use it to his advantage. He considered strategies and their outcomes.

◆ ◆ ◆ ◆ ◆ ◆ ◆

Back at the hotel Snoop and Oliver were relaxing. The suite was luxurious, to say the least. There were electronic devices in the room Oliver didn't recognize. He felt a little intimidated.

Oliver saw Snoop's concern. It was an unfamiliar look for Snoop.

"What's troubling you, Snoop?"

"Oliver, I am not sure how to explain it. Do you remember when I said that someone was watching us?"

Oliver nodded.

"I have never sensed anything like that before. It was like an unseen presence. It felt dark and not at all pleasant. Oliver, is this what you meant when you spoke to me about evil?"

"I'm afraid so. You probably sensed it before me because it's a totally new experience for you. What we are going to face is not merely the idea of evil. Snoop, we shouldn't doubt that we are to face evil itself. We were warned to expect as much."

"This is true, Oliver. But understand that I was not afraid. For we were also told that we are never alone."

Oliver chuckled. Once again his little companion was there to help him see things clearly.

♦ ♦ ♦ ♦ ♦ ♦ ♦

Lanzig read over Li's report with interest. He was pleased that Li was as thorough as always. He made a copy of the report. He began making alterations to the report going to Yaunt. He detested Yaunt and considered him a sniveling weasel. He had seen others like him come and go. He also wondered about Osgood. What were his intentions with this castaway doctor. But, he knew Osgood better than anyone else. What he knew was both powerful and dangerous. Although they had been together a long time, he knew that with Osgood there were no guarantees.

♦ ♦ ♦ ♦ ♦ ♦ ♦

Oliver heard the door opening. It was time for a frank conversation with his friend.

EIGHT

George and Emma walked into the suite. They hoped Oliver was resting and didn't want to disturb him. Brandon remained downstairs at the business center.

As they walked by the living room area, they saw Oliver standing by a window with Snoop in his arms. He slowly turned and smiled. Without saying a word, he signaled them to come to him. They were puzzled, but complied.

Oliver leaned over and whispered in Emma's ear. "Emmy, I'm not familiar with any of the electronic devices in the room. Would you please turn on some music? It doesn't matter what kind, just make it louder than a normal voice."

Emma looked at Oliver with a curious squint. Oliver quietly nodded. Emma shrugged her shoulders, picked up a remote and did it. She settled on some American country music station. Oliver gave her a thumbs-up when the volume was where he wanted.

Without a word, Oliver turned toward the balcony, signaling with his head for them to follow. When they joined him, Oliver slowly closed the sliding door.

Oliver pointed to some patio chairs. They looked at each other as they sat down.

Oliver softly chuckled. "You're probably wondering what this is all about?"

Their faces were a mixture of worry and curiosity.

♦ ♦ ♦ ♦ ♦ ♦ ♦

In the adjacent suite, Li listened with growing anger. He turned down the volume on his listening device. For one thing, he hated American music. He wondered if they suspected being monitored. He thought it through. There was no way they could know. He prided himself on his abilities of stealth and reading people. Nothing from the afternoon indicated that anyone suspected his surveillance. No. It was just the Americans and their love for loud and obnoxious music. He continued listening. Maybe even they would eventually weary of the noise.

♦ ♦ ♦ ♦ ♦ ♦ ♦

Oliver grinned before starting. "I don't know how else to say this, but I think we are being monitored."

"What?" George's responded with a slight edge in his voice.

Emma gave her dad a corrective look. "Dad, let him finish.

Oliver looked down at Snoop. He turned to his friends.

"I know that you both have a lot of questions. And I do want to answer them. But, I have to explain some things. I think it will provide some answers."

Oliver looked away for a second. He was trying to decide where to start. George and Emma waited.

"More than anyone else, I want you two to understand what has happened to me these last fifteen years."

Oliver took a deep breath before going on. "George, you mentioned that it appears to you that I haven't changed. And appearance wise, that's true. There's a reason for that and I'll get to that later. But, in every other way, I am completely changed."

Oliver rubbed his chin. "George, do you remember how I used to resist and even ridicule Mary for her faith?"

George nodded. Emma wondered where the conversation was going.

"Well, she was right. Everything she said is true and now I believe it."

"O.B., are you telling me that you got religion while you were out there? What, did you have 'a come to Jesus' moment stranded on that island of yours?"

"No, George, I didn't come to Him. He came to me."

"What do you mean He came to you? What, like in a vision or a dream?"

"George, what I mean is that I met Him, face to face."

George's volume increased slightly. "Wait a minute. Are you telling me that you believe that you met Jesus, the real Jesus? That He came to you while you were on this island."

Oliver swallowed as he recognized the look on his friend's face. "Yes, George, that's what I'm saying."

George tightened his lips. "Well, you don't mind if I tell you that I'm having a little trouble accepting what you're saying. After all that time isolated and alone, the mind can play all kinds of tricks on you. A person can come to believe all kinds of things."

Oliver rubbed his hands across his chin. "What you're saying makes perfect sense. I can hear myself saying the same thing if someone said what I just told you. But I didn't come to believe certain things and then see Him. I saw Him and then believed."

George sighed, "O.B. you've been through a lot."

Oliver responded immediately. "George, you have no idea what I've been through."

"Fair enough. But I advise you to keep this part of your story to yourself. What we need to do is get you back home and back to work at what you do best. We'll find out what it takes to get you certified to practice medicine again."

Oliver waited a few seconds. "George, I'm not going back to medicine."

"What!" Now George was irritated. "Oliver, you are a great doctor, prodigious in fact. Even with your absence, you are ahead of most in your field. You surpassed everyone in medical school and I'm sure re-qualifying will not be a problem for you. You don't have to fear getting back in."

Oliver looked down. Snoop was smiling at him. "George, you don't understand. It's not about being afraid. It's because my life is now going in a different direction. I have something I have to do."

"What?" George rubbed his forehead in frustration. "Look, buddy, I'm glad that you have a sense of…meaning and all. But you have to make a living. All of your previous assets are gone. They went to your mother and were used caring for her."

"That's okay, I'm glad." He paused for a second. "George, can you get me back to the U.S.?"

George's voice calmed a bit. "Yeah. Your passport should be ready by tomorrow. The State Department is fast-tracking everything. Seems you have friends in high places."

Oliver chuckled. "You might say that."

George smiled. "At least getting religion hasn't taken away your sense of humor."

Oliver's eyes pleaded. "George, I know this isn't easy to understand. But this is not about religion. It's not about a new moral standard or some visionary experience. It's about a person. That person is Jesus. I met Him…face to face. He is real. He rescued me and He changed me. And He has something for me to do."

Now Oliver's eyes were moist as his hands trembled slightly. Stillness surrounded them like some nostalgic memory drawing them inward. They both lowered their heads. Snoop moaned softly as he remembered the night of Oliver's rescue.

Ever so faintly Snoop broke the silence. "Truly."

Oliver smiled as the others only heard the creature purring.

85

George finally spoke. "O.B., you know I love you. But I'm having trouble accepting everything you said."

Emma interrupted her father. "Dad, don't."

She looked directly at Oliver. Her own eyes tearful. "Uncle Ollie, I don't know what all to think about what you said. But I know that the two men who mean the most to me threw themselves into medicine, a field that I am pursuing. And I know that they did not and have not found their fulfillment in it. I know I haven't. And then I look at you and I remember Aunt Mary. I remember all the things she used to tell me about God."

She paused as her voice trembled. "Uncle Ollie, I don't understand but I want to believe you. I want to believe…" Her voice cracked and she clasped her hands tightly. "I want to believe that such things are possible. This world, my world, is falling apart. I need to know that there's something more."

She lowered her head and wept. George covered his eyes. He felt helpless to answer his daughter.

Snoop began with a low hum and then added words to the tune.

Come softly to us now,

Tell us once again.

Reach into the place they hide,

Shine the light that heals the pain.

Come softly to us now,

Say it in our hearts.

You are, You truly are.

All that You proclaim.

Come softly to us now.

Come softly.

Snoop's song gripped Oliver. He wanted to say something, but the words wouldn't come. Slowly he looked at his hands. He reached over to touch Emma. When he touched her, they both felt it. It was like the light he had seen on the Island. It had substance and weight.

86

Even with her eyes closed, she saw and felt the weight of its brightness. She trembled even more as she whispered, "I want to believe. I want to believe."

Oliver leaned and whispered, "Then believe. Believe because it's true. It's really true."

In a single moment of clarity she gathered her heart and mind and looked up at Oliver. "I believe."

Snoop whispered. "Oh, Emma, the Maker is so happy for you. Is that not so, Oliver?"

Emma's eyes widened as she turned and listened to Snoop speak. She looked back at Oliver.

Oliver placed his index finger over his lips, smiled and nodded. And with only his lips, he said the words, "It's real."

Emma bit her lip and smiled as the tears continued.

♦ ♦ ♦ ♦ ♦ ♦ ♦

Brandon's first call was to Martin. A single question was bouncing in his mind.

Martin answered after two rings. "Yo, Brandon, you needing my brilliant assistance already?"

"Yeah, now look, here's what I need. Remember the aging process we ran for Dr. Cohen? I need you to run another one, except this time put in some different parameters. Instead of hardship, make them healthy years. And run it for five years, ten years and then fifteen."

"Sure, man, I can do it. It'll take about an hour. But what's the deal on the guy? Did we miss the projection by much?"

"You wouldn't believe it. In fact, I wouldn't have believed it if I hadn't seen him myself. This guy doesn't seem to have aged a day from his file photos. If anything, he looks a bit younger."

"No way."

"Yes way. When you get them finished, just email them to me."

"Sure. And send me a clear photo of the dude, would you?"

"Can do, thanks." Brandon hung up and made a few notes. He wrote in big letters on his note pad, THERE HAS TO BE AN EXPLANATION.

He closed up his laptop. He wondered how best to get an answer for his questions without undermining his contact.

♦ ♦ ♦ ♦ ♦ ♦ ♦

After thirty minutes of listening in vain for any conversation, Li took off his earphones. He would check the recording later but doubted it would provide anything useful. He thought about his next step. A question came to him. He grabbed his camera and reviewed the photos he had taken. From the groupings and the cafe recording, Li narrowed the cast of characters. There was of course Dr. Cohen, his friend, and his daughter. But who was the other guy in their group?

Li called a contact he had at the immigration office. A short search and he had a name, Brandon Rivers. Li applied his skills and extensive network to build profiles on all of the characters. He was looking for an angle. He had learned that most people had something in their lives that opened them up to exploitation. The key was to discover which person was most vulnerable and open to manipulation.

As he reviewed the profiles, it didn't take him long to decide that the person in this group was Brandon Rivers. He had no personal connection to Cohen, yet for some reason he was part of the inner circle. Rivers was most likely looking to benefit from the Cohen story and had found a way into their confidence. From his profile, Li determined that Brandon was ambitious. He leaned back in his chair and smiled. Li had met and used many like Brandon. The ambitious could always be bought. Ambition always had a price and few recognized they had been bought until it was too late. Li left to find Brandon. For now, he would concentrate on him.

Li whispered to himself, "Power belongs to the smart."

♦ ♦ ♦ ♦ ♦ ♦ ♦

George stared at his daughter. There was a different look in her eyes. The unspoken exchanges between her and Oliver told him something. Simultaneously he felt jealous and curious. Oliver spotted it.

"George, I realize that all of this is a bit much. But please, I need your help. Don't resist me. Trust me as best you can. In time, all of this will begin to come together. But for right now, I really do need your help."

George took a deep breath and nodded. "It's true, I don't understand. I'm haunted by the past and I can't seem to make the present work very well. And I certainly don't get what happened just now."

His daughter's pleading eyes were ripping at him. She reached out and took his hand. "Dad, I'm OK. I don't understand it fully, but I'm OK. No. I'm better than OK." She looked at Oliver and then Snoop. "I really am."

She looked back at her dad. "And we need to help Uncle Ollie."

George saw a hope in Emma's eyes that he had not seen since her childhood. It was like all of the anger was suddenly lifted off of her. He didn't understand, but one look at her melted him. He surrendered to the moment.

"OK, I'll ride along. What do you need?"

Oliver grabbed George's hand. "Thank you, George. First of all, I need to get back to the U.S. as soon as possible. Then there are other travel arrangements to be made. And you're right, we are all in for a ride."

George got up. "I'll go make some calls and talk to Brandon about getting us home."

He turned to Emma. Her eyes gleaned with love for him. It had been so long. He didn't know how to process it all. He bit his lip, turned and walked away to leave the room.

Emma turned toward Oliver. "Uncle Ollie, what happened to me? It's like all of the clogged up stuff inside of me is gone. I've been through years of therapy and anger management. None of it worked. And yet, in one unexplainable moment, it's all gone. And Snoop, how is that possible?"

Oliver smiled. "Emma, you're a smart girl. You wouldn't be in medical school if that weren't the case. And I'm a pretty smart guy, too. But sometimes our smartness defines and limits what is possible. What I've learned is that all of that changes with God."

Snoop looked up at Emma. "This is very true, Emma. You have been given a great gift. The Maker has done in you what only He can do. Do not seek to over analyze it. What He has done says more of Him than of you. You are now free to fulfill what He has planned for you."

Emma sat stunned. Not only was Snoop talking, but what he said made profound sense. All she could do was enjoy the moment. It almost seemed magical.

Oliver took her hand. "Emmy, it'll take you some time. It did for me. Let me tell you what happened to me."

For the next thirty minutes Oliver told Emma his story of what happened on the island. Periodically Snoop would inject his part. Emma sat and listened. She felt like a little girl again. It was like finding out that the wondrous was not only possible, but true.

♦ ♦ ♦ ♦ ♦ ♦ ♦

George found Brandon in the hotel business center making notes on his laptop. He sat down next to him. He paid no attention to the gentleman at the other end of the room working on his laptop. Neither did he notice the tiny dot on Brandon's back. At first glance it would look like a piece of lint. In fact, it was a micro transmitter that Li had attached to Brandon by bumping him when he passed by him.

Even though George spoke softly, the words were crystal clear to Li.

"Brandon, I spoke to Jonathan from the consulate. The Prime Minister arrives at 6:30 tonight. The PM desires a private dinner with

seem to have much of a future. But now, with what you've said, I can believe that the fantastic is real."

Oliver softly added, "And that the ultimate reality is fantastically true."

Snoop cuddled on Emma's lap. He looked up at her. "And, Emma, you too have been rescued so that the Maker can use you in His Story. You have a part to play, larger than you can now imagine."

Emma giggled at Snoop. "I still am amazed to hear you speak."

Snoop tilted his head to one side. "May you never cease in amazement at the many ways the Maker will speak to you."

"What do you mean?"

She turned to Oliver when he touched her hand. "What he's saying is that the Lord will constantly amaze you if you will take the time to hear the many things He has to say."

"But how do you hear God? How do you know it's Him?"

"That's a big question that I'm still working through. But what I do know is that He has spoken very clearly in what He has written."

"Written?"

Oliver had his hand on Mary's Bible which he had pulled out of his pack.

"Emma, you're a student of knowledge and information, like me. The very best available knowledge and information is in this book."

"But, Uncle Ollie, I'm not into religion and that kind of stuff."

Oliver smiled. "Emmy, you know where I've been these many years. It hasn't been in any institute of religion. It's been right here." His finger was on the Bible. "I know it seems a bit simple. Mary tried to explain it to me but I never listened. But, she was right."

The mention of Mary's name was enough. "Okay, I'll try."

Snoop added, "That is all you need do. He will do the rest."

Emma looked at Snoop and once again chuckled.

For the next twenty minutes Oliver shared with Emma how to read and understand the Bible.

♦ ♦ ♦ ♦ ♦ ♦ ♦

Virgil Yaunt read the report he had received from Lanzig. For most of the day he had suffered increasing verbal abuse from Osgood. He was demanding information concerning Dr. Cohen. It was more than the usual mistreatment he regularly dished out to everyone. No, there was a darkness hanging over Osgood. The presence and power of it both intrigued and frightened him. He wondered why this long lost doctor meant so much to Osgood. He was determined to find out.

Yaunt stood outside Osgood's study. Just before knocking he heard voices coming from inside. He could make out Osgood, but it was the other voice he didn't recognize. He was reluctant to disturb Osgood, but his instructions were specific. He wanted immediate notice.

He tapped lightly.

Osgood shouted, "Come in."

Yaunt entered timid as ever.

Osgood stood behind his desk. He looked worn and exhausted.

Osgood saw the papers in Yaunt's hand and shouted, "Don't just stand there, bring it to me and get out!"

As Yaunt crossed the room he looked around, but there was no one.

Osgood grabbed the papers from him and waved him away. There was little doubt that he wanted Yaunt out.

Yaunt walked toward the door, continuing to scan the room. There was no one. He knew that there was only way in or out of the room. Yet, he had no doubt that someone else had been there.

NINE

George and Brandon returned to the suite just as the phone rang. George answered it and listened before thanking the person on the line. He walked back into the living area of the suite where all of the others were sitting.

"That was Jonathan from the U.S. Consulate. He said that prior to the Prime Minister coming, they are sending a security team. They have to sweep the rooms and safeguard the area."

Brandon then asked, "When are they coming?"

George looked at his watch, "They'll be here in about an hour. The Prime Minister will arrive in about three hours. Also, when the security team is finished, one of the team members will stay here and everyone but Oliver will have to leave."

Oliver looked at the others and shrugged his shoulders. Brandon responded, "It's probably their way of making sure the room remains secure. He is the Prime Minister after all."

George added, "Oh, one more thing. Since we are being asked to leave, the rest of us will be guests of the government and taken to a very nice place to eat."

Brandon looked over and smiled at Oliver, "Thank you in advance for the lovely meal."

"It's the least I could do." He laughed.

Emma added, "Then I guess we should get ready. And, Uncle Ollie, all the things we bought you are in your room. You should have everything you need."

They each went to their rooms.

♦ ♦ ♦ ♦ ♦ ♦ ♦

Li received a call from the front desk informing him that he would have to vacate in an hour. He sat and listened to what had just been said in the adjoining suite. He knew what he had to do. The drone device was designed for a one-way trip. It didn't have enough power for extraction. He would simply disable it. The bug on Brandon was different. He would monitor it remotely and hope it would avoid detection.

♦ ♦ ♦ ♦ ♦ ♦ ♦

The security team arrived on schedule. The team consisted of three young men, carrying suitcases. They looked all business.

Everyone came out of their rooms and the team leader introduced himself. "Hello, my name is Giles, Peter Giles. Thank you for your understanding. My team and I will conduct a complete sweep of this room and the bedrooms. I don't expect to find anything but it is standard procedure whenever the PM makes such a visit. I'd ask that you all remain seated in this area while we work. Thank you."

With that said, the security team members went in different directions. Oliver and the others looked at each other, shrugged and went to sit down.

After about thirty minutes, Giles came to them grinning and holding something in his hand.

He looked directly at Oliver. "Dr. Cohen, have you noticed anyone or anything suspicious around you since your return?"

He stroked Snoop as he answered. "I did have the sense someone was watching me."

Brandon looked puzzled. George and Emma looked at each other.

Giles asked, "How do you mean?"

"It was just a feeling."

Giles grinned. "Well, Dr. Cohen, your instincts were correct."

He held open his palm. It contained two tiny objects. "These are each highly sophisticated transmitters."

He picked up one of them. It was about the size of a common housefly. "This is a drone transmitter. It was found in the air vent. It was flown here and landed in the vent. It could have come from anywhere in the hotel. It is passively activated by voice. The owner obviously knew we were coming because they signaled a self destruct."

Giles then picked up the other object. It was small and flat. It looked almost like a piece of paper from a hole-punch.

"This was found in Mr. River's room. It was on his shirt."

Brandon looked stunned.

"Don't worry, Mr. Rivers. This was placed on you without you knowing. Someone probably placed it on you by bumping into you. It's less sophisticated than the drone, but still pretty high grade. It has a shorter range than the drone."

Brandon broke in, "Then the listener is close by?"

"Not necessarily. They could have a relay nearby. Anyway, they knew we had found it and broke the connection. So we can't trace it."

Giles turned his attention back to Oliver. "The meeting with the PM was entirely undisclosed. So I have to assume that these are for you. I know that several news organizations are after your story. But, this is a little more sophisticated than they would use. For all practical purposes, this is military grade. Whoever this is, they are serious. I tell you this so that you can be aware and take care."

They all looked at Oliver. Even Snoop drew close and looked up at him. Oliver shrugged in an attempt to defuse the moment.

Looking at Giles, "I understand, thank you. We will take care."

Giles looked at the others, "We are finished. As you were told, you will be leaving now."

The matter-of-fact tone said it all. Within a few minutes everyone was gone and only Giles remained with Oliver.

Oliver watched Giles stand near the door after escorting the others out.

"Why don't you have a seat, Mr. Giles? There's no need in guarding the door. I'm sure your people are restricting access to the room."

Giles walked toward the couch. "As a matter of fact, they are, sir. But, how would you know that?"

"It's not that hard to figure out. After all, he is the Prime Minister."

Giles grinned as he sat down and looked at Snoop sitting on Oliver's lap.

"That's a nice pet you have there, sir. Seems awfully tame."

Oliver stroked Snoop. "Oh, he's not a pet. He's my companion and has been for some time."

Giles watched as Snoop looked up at Oliver when he spoke and then looked at him. Giles squinted. He was perplexed that the animal seemed to be smiling at him.

Giles asked Oliver while still watching Snoop, "So you found him out there where you were?"

"No, actually, he found me. And it was on an island. That's where I have been all these years."

Giles turned to Oliver. "Pardon me, sir, but surely you became lonely?"

"Oh, it was at first. But after meeting Snoop and . . ." Oliver paused. "Well, I discovered things about the Island and myself that made the difference."

The answer intrigued Giles. "If you don't mind my asking, sir, but how could he make such a difference to help you with that amount of isolation? You see, sir, I have studied the effects of isolation. Extended periods of it are devastating to almost everyone. It breaks most people, but leaves no one unaffected."

Oliver continued to stroke Snoop. "But I wasn't alone."

Giles began to assess if Oliver might possibly be unbalanced and a threat to the PM. "But, sir, didn't you desire someone to talk to? My understanding is that you sailed out not long after the loss of your wife."

"Very true on both counts. But I soon understood that I wasn't alone. I made peace with what had happened to my wife. It was hard at first, but then . . ." Oliver looked off, pausing a moment. He looked back at Giles. "The Island rescued me."

"How do you mean that, sir?"

"Mr. Giles, I understand that your job is to keep the Prime Minister safe. I didn't lose my mind on the Island. I found my purpose there. God rescued me from myself and gave me a reason to live. That's why I am safe and alive today."

"Sorry, sir, I didn't mean to pry into your personal beliefs. Thank you for understanding that I am simply doing my job."

"Not a problem. But, may I ask you, how are things between you and God?"

Giles noticed that Snoop had sat up and was looking directly at him. Both Snoop and the question unnerved him. "I'm sorry, sir, but I would rather not go there. My job here is singular and I don't see how answering your question is a part of that. With your permission, I will leave it at that. Now, if you will excuse me, I have some calls to make before the PM arrives."

Giles quickly got up and walked over to the window. He immediately used his phone.

Snoop looked at Oliver. "Oliver, why are people so

uncomfortable talking about the Maker?"

"Most people don't want to talk or think about such things. I know I didn't."

"But why is that?"

"I think part of it is about control. We have some measure of control over what we can see and understand. Even religions have ways of controlling God. But God is something bigger than anyone can control. And that frightens people. So, we either disbelieve or avoid."

Snoop lowered his head. "The Lie is truly strong in the world."

"Yes, Snoop, it is." The words faded as he answered.

♦ ♦ ♦ ♦ ♦ ♦ ♦

A waiter delivered the meal ahead of the prime minister's arrival. He set everything up and was then escorted out.

Prime Minister Owens arrived right on time. Giles received word that he was on his way up, so he stationed himself outside the door. When the door opened again, Oliver stood to greet the Prime Minister. His two bodyguards preceded the Prime Minister, scanning the room as they walked passed Oliver.

Oliver then saw Prime Minister Owens. He looked to be in his mid fifties. He was a little over six feet tall, light brown hair, blue eyes with a calm and assured appearance. Seeing Oliver he extended his hand. He was surprised to see Snoop perched on Oliver's shoulder.

"Oh my, so this must be your companion I have heard so much about."

He moved his attention back to Oliver.

"Dr. Cohen, I have so looked forward to finally meeting you. I must say you don't look much worn for the wear and tear of fifteen years being lost."

The bodyguards returned to the living area, having searched the entire suite. They nodded an OK to Giles who followed them to stand guard outside the door.

"Seems our meal is here. Shall we sit and enjoy?"

Oliver sat across from Owens with Snoop still on his shoulder. Snoop then hopped down and sat on the table next to Oliver.

Oliver didn't hesitate asking. "Prime Minister, would you mind, it is my custom to give thanks before a meal."

Owens tilted his head. "Not at all. I remember my grandmum doing the same."

Seeing Oliver bow his head, close his eyes, Owens lowered his head but kept his eyes opened.

Oliver prayed. "Lord, we give You thanks for this meal and for this time. Keep us ever safe in You. Truly."

Snoop softly added, "Truly."

Owens ventured a peek when he heard a squeak come from Snoop. But what really surprised him was that Snoop had his head bowed and had his paws together as if he were also praying.

"I must say, Dr. Cohen . . ."

"'Oliver' will do, Mr. Prime Minister."

"Yes, well Oliver, I must say that you have a well-trained animal there."

Oliver didn't answer. He merely smiled.

They both began to enjoy their meals. Oliver shared with Snoop from his plate. No one spoke. Owens took an occasional peek, watching the interaction between the two.

Owens put down his fork and broke the silence. "Dr. Cohen?"

"Please call me Oliver."

"Yes." The Prime Minister seemed almost nervous. "Oliver, you do know that it is almost miraculous how you survived all these years? And then to be discovered at sea by one of our vessels, you do see how amazing it all is?"

"Mr. Prime Minister. . ."

"Let us speak less formally. Call me 'Charles.'"

"Very well, Charles. What if I told you that it was miraculous?"

"I'm not sure I follow you."

Oliver looked away a second. "What if I told you that Snoop here can talk. Not only can he talk, but when he does, I can understand him but you can't. What would you think?"

"I would probably think that you had lost your mind."

"But what if it was actually true? What if you and I spoke to Snoop and he understood us and he spoke back? If it truly did happen, would that not be a miracle?"

Owens thought for a second. "I suppose, if such a thing occurred it would be somewhat miraculous. It would require . . . an explanation."

"Yes, it would." Oliver looked down at Snoop. "Snoop, go and greet Mr. Owens."

Snoop tilted his head and smiled before walking across the table. He stood on his hinds, reached out his paw and spoke.

"I am very pleased to meet you, sir."

Owens looked stunned. He watched Snoop come over and extend his paw. Even though he heard only squeaky sounds coming out of Snoop, it unnerved him.

He looked up at Oliver. "A very fine trick, sir. The animal is well trained."

"Charles, you are smart enough to know that trained animals only act in response to a master's voice. And they respond mostly to simple and not complex commands. Without looking at him, ask Snoop to do something complex which a simple animal would not understand."

"Sir, this is not a circus and I am not. . ."

Oliver interrupted. "Please, Charles. You said a miracle requires an explanation. I wish to give you one, but first you must experience what you and I would call the miraculous."

There was something in Oliver's eyes that tempted Owens to take up the challenge.

Owens looked directly at Oliver. He wanted to choose his words carefully. "Very well. I ask your comrade to . . . to reach into my left inside coat pocket. I have two pens in there. Have him get them both out, select the green one and place it in my hand." Owens smiled and leaned back.

Snoop looked back at Oliver who nodded. Snoop then went right up to Owens and looked at him. He then proceeded to unbutton one button on his coat and reach into his pocket. He took out the two pens and laid them on the table. He spotted the green one. He then grabbed Owens' arm and moved it on the table. He took his right hand and opened it up. Snoop turned around, grabbed the green pen and placed it gently in his palm.

Owens looked down at the pen and then at Snoop.

"Will there be anything else, sir?" Owens heard Snoop's squeaky sounds but only stared at the pen resting in his hand.

"I will admit that what the creature has done is amazing and begs an explanation. But, I am quite sure there is an explanation."

Oliver looked deep into his eyes. "Mr. Prime Minister, what is the real reason you wanted this meeting?"

The words caught him. "What ever do you mean?"

"What I mean is that such a meeting would normally be a great opportunity for a politician to gain public good will. And yet, the public is unaware of it. Why did you want to meet me?"

Owens looked down. The normal confidence was gone. He placed his right hand over a fisted left. With his elbows on the table he leaned on his hands and thought about how to answer. His eyes finally looked up.

"I have to admit that when I received word of your rescue, my people advised me on the benefits of meeting with you. Your story is a hopeful message in an otherwise desperate world. But, as you say, that wasn't the real reason."

Owens almost choked on the words as he continued.

"It was the dreams."

"Dreams?"

"Yes. They started the night before I got word that you had been found. I saw you. Not exactly, mind you. You know how dreams are? But I did know about you and even your friend. I saw that there were two of you. But that wasn't the most troubling part of the dreams. I say dreams because the dream repeated twice."

Owens rubbed his fingers over his palm.

"Anyway, the most troubling part of the dream was the voice."

"Voice?"

"Yes, there was a voice talking to me in the dream. The voice said that I needed to talk to you, that I needed to hear what you had to say. Now, I want you to understand that I don't take to such things. I am a very pragmatic and reasonable person. Mine is the real world of hard facts. But, I couldn't shake the dreams and the raw emotions they created."

Snoop then spoke. "Oliver, he does sound so much like you did when we first met. Why is it so hard for those in this world to believe?"

Owens was a bit frightened that the animal seemed to be talking to Oliver.

"Would you have me believe that this animal is talking to you and that you understand what he's saying?"

Oliver responded. "I was also an extremely pragmatic person. As a doctor, I dealt in knowable facts. My wife would always talk to me about the reality of God and His miraculous ways. I doubted her and even ridiculed her. But, I have learned that there is more in this world than meets the eye."

He paused for a second. "You want an explanation? You want me to tell you how Snoop can talk and respond? You want me to explain your dreams and the voice? Very well, it's God."

"Dr. Cohen," he had returned to the formal. "I am not a religious man."

"And neither am I. I certainly wasn't before I left. And there were no religious places or institutions on the Island. But this isn't about religion. It's about the reality of our divine Maker. I was rescued on and from the Island for a purpose. I can now see that you were given the dreams for a purpose as well."

Owens had skepticism written on his face.

"Charles, when you walked into this room you had all of the swagger of a man of power. But, that's not who I see now. Now I see a mere man frightened and uncertain."

"I don't know why I'm telling you this. Maybe it's the dreams, I don't know. But you're right. I am uncertain."

He paused before going on. "My world is one filled with leaders and people of power. Swaggering and posturing is the currency of the realm. But currently, I look into the eyes of my peers and I see the uncertainty. We've all run out of answers. The stage, the situations, and the problems have grown so massive we are losing any semblance of control. I fear what all of this might mean. People sense it as well, and hope for the future is dying. I don't know if I have strength or reason for any sense of optimism. I'm just . . ."

Owens had his head down and his voice trailed off. After a few moments he looked up.

"Oliver, what gave you hope when you found yourself out there all alone? How did you go on and push forward enough to survive?"

"You're right to speak of hope. It's a powerful thing. But, there is something even more powerful, … truth. Because hope built on a lie crumbles. But hope based on truth survives. It does more than survive, it triumphs."

"What truth? Whose truth? So many make claim to having the truth."

Oliver rubbed his chin. "Charles, you say you are frightened by what you see happening around you. And so you should be. But it is what you cannot see that should terrify you. Dangerous times are coming, more perilous than ever before. And men will lose hope. But, there is a reason to hope. It is a hope founded on the true reality above all things. You need to hear this. Your people will need you in the coming days. I believe that is why we have met this evening."

Owens sat silent. He wasn't accustomed to having anyone talk to him in that manner. He didn't know how to respond. He looked at his hands as they trembled. Finally, he managed a question.

"Who are you, Oliver?"

TEN

Owens' question hung in the silence shouting for an answer. Oliver stroked Snoop's back before looking up to answer. "I'm just a man. A man rescued for a purpose larger than my own life."

Owens stiffened a bit. "You're talking about God again, aren't you? I get it that you believe in God. I know that you think God rescued you. But, you must understand that in my world perception is reality. You were in a desperate situation. You've come to believe in God and now it's real and true for you. But it's not true for me."

Oliver raised his finger to stop him.

"No, you're wrong. It's just the opposite. I have seen Him. And I have accepted and now believe Him. And He has changed me."

Owens frowned. "What do you mean, you've seen?"

Oliver took a deep breath and with an intensity that even took Snoop back a bit, he answered.

"The time is coming very soon when great numbers will see. And when that time comes, it will be frightening to many. But to those who see and believe, there is a way and a reason for hope. And though you do not believe now, I pray that when the time comes that you will remember and understand. God has chosen to give you an opportunity and a warning. I will pray for you so that when that time comes you can help others."

Owens was stunned to silence. He was unable to shake his feeling of powerlessness.

After a minute of dead air, he reached in his pocket and touched a device signaling to his security staff that he was ready to leave. Within seconds the door opened and Giles walked in. Owens got up from the table and turned to leave. He waited as if he was about to say something but didn't. He took a few steps when he heard Oliver clear his throat.

Owens stopped and turned.

"Prime Minister, when you get to the point where you run out of answers, pay attention. Look for me. I won't be hard to find. But it's most important that you remember what I said. A lot depends on it."

Oliver looked down and went back to stroking Snoop.

Owens furrowed his brow and stared at Oliver. After a moment he turned.

He looked at Giles who stood waiting, "Let's go."

Oliver looked up when he heard the door close.

Snoop glanced at the door. "Oliver, do you think he accepted what you told him?"

"Not at the moment. I understand what he's experiencing right now. I remember going through the same process. He's trying to get it to all make sense. And it won't work without the most important part. But when the time comes, he'll remember. And I have no doubt that someone will make sure he does."

"You mean the Maker?"

"Yes. And when the time comes, he will be rescued."

"How do you know this, Oliver?"

Oliver chuckled. "I'm not sure. I just do. It's almost like I can already see it. I suppose it's part of this new work I've been given."

Oliver gently grabbed Snoop and got up. He leaned down and whispered. "What do you say we go out on the balcony and see the stars."

And so they did. They remained out there until George and the others returned.

♦ ♦ ♦ ♦ ♦ ♦ ♦

Yaunt's phone rang. It was Osgood, who wasted no words. "Yaunt, get up here right away." He immediately hung up.

Yaunt began making his way to Osgood's lair wondering what abuse awaited him when he arrived.

Reaching the room, he lightly knocked and entered.

Osgood was looking down at something on his desk.

Without looking up he growled across the room. "Come."

Yaunt stood right in front of the desk and Osgood never looked up. Osgood kept reading a few of the crumpled pages. Osgood looked away from the pages for a second and tapped his left index finger on the desk. After another few seconds he looked up.

"It seems Dr. Cohen and his party will soon be leaving for the U.S. I want you to make contact with Brandon Rivers before they leave Australia. We have made some contact with the company he most often works for . . ."

"We?"

Osgood narrowed his eyes. "Don't interrupt me. As I was saying, the company he works for has no record of funding any project with him. Select an appropriate company from our group. Tell Rivers we are very interested in financing his project on Dr. Cohen. Say whatever you have to, but secure his cooperation. Tell him you will meet him in the U.S. to finalize the details."

"I take it that I am traveling to the U.S.?"

Osgood rolled his eyes. "A brilliant deduction, Virgil. Spare no expense and obtain an agreement. Find out his plans and then get someone into their group. I want more direct information on what

Dr. Cohen's plans are."

Yaunt waited to see if there was anything else. Osgood cued in on his hesitant look.

"Virgil, do you understand what I'm saying?"

"Yes sir. I'm simply curious about what interest you have with this doctor. Why is he so important?"

Osgood stood straight up. His bloodshot eyes were practically bulging.

In loud staccato phrasing, he shouted, "That is none of your concern. Get Rivers under contract and get me eyes and ears on their team. Is that clear?"

Yaunt was completely humiliated. Over time he had learned to hide his anger and submit. He was about to turn and leave when something happened. It was as if some hidden force took hold of him. Yaunt's endurance of Osgood's abuse had reached its limit. A switch had flipped and something in his personality emerged. He looked directly into Osgood's eyes.

His voice deepened. "Brandon Rivers will be under contract and I will be your eyes and ears. I will take control of the situation myself. And I will find out all that needs to be known concerning the doctor."

The firmness in his voice and demeanor surprised Osgood. His eyes narrowed and he remained silent for a bit. Slowly, a grin formed.

"Very good, Virgil. I wondered how long it would take you or if you would ever get there. Finally, you begin to understand that my work, and now your work is one of power."

Osgood walked around his desk and placed his hands on Yaunt's shoulders.

"I need you to feel and know the delicious sensation of power. Money, fortune, or fame is nothing compared to power."

Yaunt did feel it. It was like electricity energizing the muscles of his body. He felt taller and stronger. Thoughts and images filled his mind.

Osgood's grin had a wicked twist. "Now go. If you do well, I will show you unimaginable things. Only do not fail me. For in this game we play, power destroys those who fail. But with success comes increased power."

Osgood's grip on his shoulders increased. Yaunt trembled as if a surge of fire coursed down his shoulders all the way to his feet. He almost collapsed when Osgood released him and fell back on his desk.

Without a word Osgood waved for him to leave. As Yaunt walked off, he looked at his hands. They vibrated. He loved the feeling. When he walked into the hallway he looked up with an evil grin and began to laugh uncontrollably.

♦ ♦ ♦ ♦ ♦ ♦ ♦

Oliver and Snoop came in from the balcony when George, Emma, and Brandon returned. Brandon was intensely curious about the meeting.

"So, did you and the Prime Minister have a good talk?"

Oliver smiled but didn't answer.

Brandon understood. "I know a *no comment* look when I see it."

George chuckled before adding, "I trust you didn't create an international incident?"

"Dad," Emma punched his arm. "If Uncle Ollie wanted to tell us something I'm sure he would. Wouldn't you, Uncle Ollie?"

"You guys don't hide your curiosity very well. The Prime Minister is a good man. We had a very interesting conversation that I think he would prefer to remain confidential. But, I do think I will see him again some day."

Brandon rubbed his chin. "Really? And why do you say that?"

Oliver didn't answer but looked at George. "Our plans are to leave tomorrow morning, right?"

"Yes, Jonathan has arranged a short press conference for you in the morning before we leave. The State Department has arranged a special charter flight for us. It helps to have friends in high places at the state department."

Brandon felt his phone vibrate in his pocket. He saw that it was from Andros. He excused himself and went to his room before picking it up.

"Andros, I didn't expect to hear from you. Is there a problem?"

"No, there's no problem. I just wanted to give you a heads up. I received a call from a Virgil Yaunt. He's with a company called Osgood Communications. They are part of Osgood Ltd. They are a worldwide multi-billion dollar corporation. He found out you were working for me and wanted to buy out your option."

"And you sold it?"

"Are you kidding? The offer was extraordinary. Plus, you know, a bird in the hand and all. Anyway, I gave him your number and told him I'd let you know to expect a call. So, good luck on the project. And remember, they have deep pockets, so enjoy yourself. Let me know how it all works out."

"Yeah sure, thanks."

He had no sooner hung up and his phone vibrated again.

"Hello."

"Ah, Mr. Rivers, I presume?"

"Yes, and you must be Mr. Yaunt."

"Excellent. Then Mr. Manning has already contacted you?"

"Yes, I just spoke with him."

"Very well. Then you know we have picked up the option for your project. But, so that you will not think us pirates, let me explain. I am special assistant to Mr. Malcolm Osgood. He is the majority owner of Osgood Ltd. He is involved in various enterprises around the world including communications in various forms. On hearing of Dr. Cohen's rescue, he was immediately touched. It is an extraordinary story, don't you agree?"

"Yes, that's what attracted me as well."

"Yes, of course. Anyway, Mr. Osgood has authorized me to finance your project and assist you in any way I can. Now, will you be returning to the U.S. soon?"

"We're leaving tomorrow morning. But it's a long flight and I'm not sure of all the details."

"Yes, of course. You have my number now. We can communicate during your long flight on some of those details. I will arrange to meet you when you arrive and finalize our agreement. It's been so good talking to you. Oh, and Mr. Rivers, Mr. Osgood is a generous man. As well as financing your project, he plans to compensate you generously. Thank you."

The call ended before Brandon could respond. A part of him was relieved from the burden that financing always presented. He had a guarded curiosity about what sort of people he was now working for. It wasn't his first time to maneuver this road. It was just the first time that substantial financial reward was a possibility.

He whispered to himself, "Well, here we go."

♦ ♦ ♦ ♦ ♦ ♦ ♦

When he returned, George asked, "Everything OK?"

Brandon delayed in his response. "Yeah, sure. It was a business call. Speaking of business," he looked over to Oliver, "don't forget you talk to the press tomorrow before we leave. Think carefully about what you want to say and what you don't want to say. I'll put down some ideas for you, if you like."

Oliver nodded. "Thanks, Brandon, you do that and I'll look at it."

Brandon looked around at the others. "Well, I think I'll retire for the night. I want to work on some ideas I have for the filming project and all."

Oliver nodded and continued to stroke Snoop who was sitting on his lap.

Brandon left.

George looked at Oliver. "Brandon looked a bit distracted."

"George, as we move along we will face many challenges. As you heard from the security team, someone is following us. I'm talking about someone with less than virtuous intentions. And, our friend Brandon, is connected to that somehow."

"You mean Brandon is a spy?"

"Yes, he just doesn't realize it."

"How do you know this?"

Oliver moved his head side to side. "That's a great question. I wish I had an answer you'd accept. But I know. I just don't know who these people are yet."

"So, do we want to lose Brandon? Nothing says he has to be with us."

"No. Somehow he's necessary and I think he will become important."

"But, what if these people are dangerous? You heard the security fellow. They are serious. Aren't you afraid of what they might do?"

"They may well be dangerous. But, I'm not afraid. They have no idea what and who they are dealing with."

"Now you're starting to sound scary."

Oliver chuckled. "I'm not talking about me, at least not directly. Anyway, we'll watch Brandon. He may not lead us to these people but he'll bring them to us."

Emma wondered where all of this was going.

Oliver got up with Snoop in his hands. "Guys, we've had a long day and another one coming. I think it's time to retire for the evening. If you'll excuse me, I'm heading to my room. Goodnight."

"Goodnight, O.B."

"Goodnight, Uncle Ollie and Snoop."

Snoop turned and perked up. "Goodnight, sweet Emma."

Emma giggled like a little girl.

George squinted a questioning look at Emma.

"What's going on with you, girl?"

"What do you mean, Daddy?"

"Well, take that for instance. You haven't called me Daddy in years. And you seem . . . different somehow."

Emma thought a second. "I feel different. No, I am different. I can't explain it. A lot of anger and hurt has been lifted off of me."

Tears were beginning to trickle down her cheeks. "I feel younger."

She wiped her face. "I love you, Daddy." She went over and pecked him on the cheek and left.

George sat alone. He felt envious of his friend and daughter. He wanted to know but was almost afraid to ask. The word that floated in his mind was "undeserving." His thoughts only made his loneliness more acute.

Rest. He wanted, and needed rest. He went to his room.

♦ ♦ ♦ ♦ ♦ ♦ ♦

Oliver sat on his bed. He held the envelope from his mom. Memories. He recalled the many times she would sing to him. Although his father had forbidden her to speak to him about God, now that he recalled, every song she sang whispered His name.

He took the letter out and read it.

Dear Ollie,

I'm so glad that you are finally getting to read this letter. George and others told me that it was foolish to think or believe that you are still alive. I suppose it does seem foolhardy, except I know what my heart tells me. Oh, I'm not talking about the heart of a mother where hope springs eternal. No, it's that part of my heart where I know what God has told me about you. When you were a little boy God let me know that He had something great in mind for you. I never knew what it was exactly, but I had the growing sense that it was extraordinary. I never told you, but the day before Mary died I shared this with her. She cried and embraced me. She told me that she had the same sense. She spoke about how much you resisted any such talk. I reminded her that God is faithful.

There is so much I would like to tell you about the Lord that Mary and I know. I have no doubt that some day you will know His reality. This sounds silly when everyone tells me you're dead. But maybe you had to become dead to find life. I don't know. But, I do know that you ran away to escape. But you really can't flee from His presence. He pursues His purpose with passion and you are destined to be a part of His purposed plan. I know this with the deepest fiber running through me. It's almost as if He is writing a story and you have a part to play in it, you just don't know it yet.

I feel myself getting weak these past few days. That's why I decided that I needed to write you. I have also had a deep sense of peace settle over me concerning your journey and your struggle.

Since you are reading this letter, I am no longer here to speak to you in person. But know that I am well and with my Lord. Mary and I will be waiting for you after you complete the work God has for you.

I am proud of you, son. I am proud that you never settled for less than the best. I am convinced that this passion will drive you until you find the absolute best, the One who is your Maker, God, and Savior. Fulfill well the task He has for you. I count it a privilege to be the mother of one who God will use so mightily.

To Him who is truly amazing, be all the glory.

Make Him proud of you, son.

Love, Mom

ELEVEN

Oliver and Snoop were up before anyone else. He had ordered breakfast and it would arrive soon. In the meantime, he and Snoop sat out on the patio enjoying the quiet.

"Oliver, the air here seems thicker and smells different."

"That's the smell of industry and progress. It certainly isn't like the Island."

"And everyone seems in a hurry. No one seems to know how to relax and enjoy the world around them. And there is another thing, there is so much fear."

"You're right, my friend. The world was bad when I left and it has only gotten worse. There is a lot of fear in people's eyes. They have no idea exactly how bad it will get."

They both turned around when they heard someone open the patio door. It was Emma.

"What are you guys doing out here?"

Snoop stood up on his hinds. "Good morning, Emma. Did you sleep well?"

Emma giggled. "I did sleep well, thanks. It still tickles me to hear you speak, Snoop."

Snoop looked back to Oliver. "Oliver was the same way at first. Most amusing, I must say."

Emma saw the look on Oliver's face.

"Uncle Ollie, what is it? You looked worried about something."

He looked at her and half smiled. "Oh, Emma, I'm so excited for you in the new discoveries you are making. But, the mission Snoop and I are setting out on is a dangerous one. And, I'm concerned for you in the days ahead."

Snoop rubbed his little chin before speaking. "Yes, Oliver, it is true that the days ahead are ones of dangerous possibilities. But you must not forget that the Maker knows these things. He will care for us and He will care for Emma."

Oliver chuckled softly. "You're right. Thank you for reminding me and don't stop."

"What dangers, Uncle Ollie?"

"At the moment I can't say specifically. But the task that God has for me will put me in opposition to powerful forces in this world. I can't say much about it right now, but it will become apparent as time passes."

Emma looked at Snoop and then at Oliver.

"Well, even from what little I've read and certainly from what I've seen, God is able to accomplish what He wants."

"That's very true and simply put, Emmy. Be sure and remind me of that as well."

Just then the patio door opened. It was George with Brandon standing right behind him.

George noticed the look on their faces.

"What's going on out here? And what's with the serious faces?"

Oliver answered. "Oh, just thinking about what's up ahead, you know, getting back home and all."

"Yeah, I'm not looking forward to the long trip back. I'm still on

California time. I talked with Jonathan last night. After your morning press conference, our chartered flight back leaves at 10:30 this morning. And even though it's nineteen hours of flying time, we'll get to LA by 4:30 pm the same day."

Oliver squinted. "What?"

George looked at his watch. "Yeah, right now it's 7:00 am here and 4:00 pm yesterday in LA."

Brandon spoke up. "No wonder I'm feeling so hollow. At least we haven't been here enough to get adjusted to this time. We'll soon be back on LA time."

They all laughed and then groaned.

Oliver pointed to the door. "Let's go inside. I want to talk some things over before we get going."

♦ ♦ ♦ ♦ ♦ ♦ ♦

Virgil Yaunt was three hours from arriving in Los Angeles. He had already sent some messages to Brandon and contacted some banks in California. He would be ready when the group arrived from Australia. He had contacted Hermann Lanzig, who was also on his way to California. Li would follow Oliver's group on their return. Yaunt had also sent a message to Osgood. Although he didn't understand Osgood's obsession with Dr. Cohen, he knew that whatever it was, it involved power. Having tasted real power for the first time, he knew he wanted it and more.

♦ ♦ ♦ ♦ ♦ ♦ ♦

As the group sat in the living room, everyone looked at Oliver.

"OK, I know that you have a lot of questions for me. But, for now they will have to wait. We'll have a long flight and I promise each of you some private conversation time to answer what I can."

Oliver looked at Brandon. "Brandon, you know your way around LA, don't you?"

"Yeah, pretty much. Why?"

"After we arrive, I want you to find me a local high end jeweler. I prefer that they be Jewish with connections to jewelers in Israel."

Brandon looked puzzled and George spoke up.

"O.B., what's this about?"

"George, I'll explain on the flight back." Looking back at Brandon, "Well, do you think you can find somebody for me?"

"Yeah, sure. I'll start on it this morning."

George again spoke. "O.B., are you going back to San Diego?"

Oliver thought for a second. "No. Since my Mom isn't there anymore I'm staying in LA until I leave. As soon as I can, I need to get to Israel and then to Jordan."

"What? O.B., you just got back and now you want to go to Israel. That's . . ." George shook his head in confusion. "I . . . I don't think you can. With all the unrest these days, I don't think commercial flights are going into the Middle East right now."

Oliver turned to Brandon and he understood the unspoken question.

Brandon remembered his conversation with Yaunt. "I might know someone who can get us in. Of course, they'll want to know something about what we're up to."

Oliver thought before answering. "Tell them I'm reconnecting with my Jewish roots. I'll tell you a bit more on the flight. You pull this off and you'll earn that story you desperately want. Oh, and one other thing. At the press conference, I'm going to refer to you as my liaison with the media. That OK?"

"Sure, great. Let me go and start making some phone calls on the jeweler and some travel possibilities to Israel."

Brandon left for his room. He couldn't believe how this was all working out.

George and Emma watched Brandon leave and then turned back to Oliver.

"Uncle Ollie, are you sure you can trust Brandon? I mean, we hardly know him."

Oliver smiled and looked down at Snoop before answering. "You're right, I don't know him and I don't entirely trust him. But I do believe in what I'm doing. And right now he's useful. I don't think it's an accident that he's here with us."

"So, Uncle Ollie, you're using him?"

"Actually, he's trying to use me. He has things he wants and I'm a part of that. He just doesn't have any idea what he's up against. So we will help each other and in the process I pray that he can be rescued from himself, because he is in danger, as are so many others."

"O.B., you're talking in riddles. What are you up to?"

"What I'm up to is something very important. There are dangerous and perilous times coming to this world."

"O.B., I think that anyone who watches the news already knows that."

The intensity in Oliver's eyes caught George by surprise.

"No, they don't, not really. What's going on today may be bad but it is nothing compared to what's coming. Time is running out and I have much to accomplish before . . ."

Oliver caught himself. "Look guys, where I'm going and what I have to do will be difficult and dangerous. Maybe you should remain in . . ."

Emma interrupted. "No, Uncle Ollie, we're coming with you."

George added. "Listen, O.B., I don't understand anything about what you just said. But I lost you for fifteen years and I'm not losing you again. Help us understand along the way, but we're sticking with you."

Emma reached over and took Oliver's hand.

Oliver's lowered his head. "Thanks, guys."

Snoop whispered to Oliver. "These are truly good friends, Oliver."

Oliver looked at each of them. "Good friends, truly."

♦ ♦ ♦ ♦ ♦ ♦ ♦

Everyone had eaten breakfast and packed by nine when Jonathan arrived. Everyone was waiting in the living room. There were two porters standing behind Jonathan.

"Well, the press is waiting in a conference room downstairs." He looked at Oliver. "Are you ready, Dr. Cohen?"

"Yes, I think so."

"Alright then." Looking at the luggage, he asked. "Is this all of your luggage?

Everyone nodded.

Jonathan pointed the porters to the bags. "Good, we will leave right after the press conference. So let's go."

Oliver spoke up, "George, go let Brandon know we've left. Tell him to join us when he can."

Oliver scooped up Snoop and Emma grabbed her purse.

George caught up to them by the time the elevator arrived. On the way down everyone seemed nervous except Oliver. He simply smiled and stroked Snoop who softly purred.

Within seconds of leaving the elevator, cameras flashed and voices yelled out questions. Jonathan took the lead and directed everyone to the press conference while Oliver smiled and waved.

When they reached the room they immediately went to the podium set up for the conference. Jonathan took to the microphone and addressed the crowd.

"Ladies and gentlemen, thank you for coming. My name is Jonathan Christian. I am with the United States State Department. As instructed earlier, you have pooled your inquiries into five questions, which Dr. Cohen will answer. He may answer more if he chooses, but as you can imagine, he is anxious to get back home. You already know the selected order of the questioners. So without any delay, Dr. Cohen."

Oliver walked up to the microphone with Snoop on his shoulder. He looked across the crowd and nodded.

A woman immediately stood. "Blanche Owens with Associated

Press, Dr. Cohen. Fifteen years ago, why did you sail off and where have you been?"

"That's good. You got two questions into one."

The reporters chuckled.

Oliver's smile left him as he reflected a moment.

"When I sailed off fifteen years ago, my intentions were to sail out and die out there somewhere. As you know, I had lost my wife. I was broken and angry. I didn't want to live anymore. As it happened, I sailed into a storm and became ship wrecked on an island. And it is on that island that I have been these fifteen years."

There was a brief silence and then another woman stood.

"Thank you, Dr. Cohen. We are so sorry about your loss. Susan Hardon with World News. Can you tell us about your animal companion?"

Oliver looked up at Snoop. "Yes, of course. This is Snoop. He came to me not long after I arrived on the Island. He has been friend, guide and companion these many years. I owe a lot to him. You might say that he helped rescue me. It would take too long to fully explain, but Brandon Rivers, who is not here at the moment, will be my liaison with the press. He is writing and will be producing a documentary on my journey. So you will hear more from him on that. Next question."

A tall gentleman on the left stood. "Yes, sir, Michael Freeman from the New York Times. You have been gone, presumed dead for fifteen years. You were forty at that time. And it has not escaped our attention that you do not look any older. If anything, you look even younger than when you vanished. How do you explain that?"

"As a medical doctor, I have no explanation. The island I lived on was pristine. It was thoroughly untainted by our world. Beyond that, I can only attribute it to God's good grace."

Freeman did not sit down but asked one more question.

"Were you always a religious person, sir?"

"No, not at all. If anything, I would say that I was completely and obnoxiously irreligious. It was my wife who persistently spoke of God and lived her faith before me."

Freeman continued to stand. "So you found God on the island?"

Oliver smiled. "No." He paused to swallow the emotion swelling up inside. "I didn't find God. He found me. And He rescued me."

The room fell silent. There were a few hushed voices and quick notes being scribbled. Freeman finally sat down.

Another gentleman from the opposite side of the room stood.

"Jeoff Hausman with EuroNews. Dr. Cohen, you were previously a doctor of some note. Do you plan to return to medicine or do you have other plans now?"

"Thank you, Jeoff. I will not be practicing medicine any longer. My life's direction has completely changed. I will be following the direction in which God leads me."

"And what might that be, sir?"

Oliver again smiled. "Well, Jeoff, I have found that God does not dispense the future as freely as we would like. So the full answer to that question remains to be seen."

Jeoff and others laughed as he sat down.

A woman on the front row stood.

"Elizabeth Weinstein with Haaretz in Israel. I am personally curious to hear more of your religious experience but that will have to wait. So let me get to my question. The world has changed greatly since you were gone. What has surprised you most about the world today?"

"Thank you, and Shalom, Elizabeth."

She nodded back.

"The thing that has caught my attention the most is the presence and overwhelming prevalence of despair in the world. I sense it everywhere. I see it in your eyes. I feel it in the air. And if I could say anything on the matter, it would have to be that... from a man seemingly back from the dead . . . hope remains. But you must take care where you look for it. Thank you very much."

Oliver stepped off the podium. Emma's eyes were moist. George stood looking at him with his mouth half open.

"Wow O.B., you've become quite the orator."

As more questions were shouted out, Jonathan grabbed Oliver's arm and moved him out into the hallway. They took a few steps when Oliver remembered something.

"Jonathan, I have to go back to the room. I just remembered that I forgot something in my room."

George looked at Jonathan. "Get Emma to the car. I'll go with Oliver and we'll be right there."

Jonathan nodded. He, Emma and Snoop left. Oliver and George made quick-step for the elevators.

♦ ♦ ♦ ♦ ♦ ♦ ♦

Upstairs in the suite Brandon finished locating a jeweler that matched Oliver's description. He had also left a message on Yaunt's phone. As he gathered up his small notebook, he thought he heard something.

♦ ♦ ♦ ♦ ♦ ♦ ♦

Quan Li had watched the porters and the rest of Cohen's party leave. He had waited a short time before deciding to go into the suite and see what information he might obtain. Gaining access to the room was relatively simple.

He scanned the large room but it didn't provide anything of interest. He moved into one of the bedrooms. He searched the dresser drawers followed by looking under the bed. It was here that he spotted and grabbed an old leather satchel. He then heard someone in the next room. He froze and waited. He then detected a door opening.

Brandon walked out just as Oliver and Brandon walked in.

"What are you guys doing back. Did you forget something?"

Oliver sounded a bit winded. "Yeah, I left something in my room."

Li listened at the door. He looked around the bedroom. There was no closet. He knew would have to run to make it to the restroom. He quickly decided on a course of action. Attack and run.

When Li jerked open the bedroom door, Oliver was several steps away from him. They were all startled when he raced out of the room. Oliver immediately saw the satchel in Li's hands and walked right into his path.

Out of pure instinct, Li launched into attack mode and took a swing at Oliver. As he did Oliver reached out his hand and caught his fist with his right hand.

The full force of Li's swing was immediately stopped. Oliver held the man's fist. Suddenly Li began to scream. He dropped the satchel and grabbed his fist. He held it with his other hand. Li let out a writhing cry. Li glanced at his fist and saw that it was badly burned and quickly blistering. He grimaced and ran for the door. He let go of his hand only long enough to open the door and run for the stairs.

George and Brandon stood stunned.

Oliver reached down to pick up his satchel as George muttered. "Wha... what just happened?"

TWELVE

The sound of Li's screams faded down the hallway as Oliver looked down at his hands. Brandon and George stared at Oliver. Everyone was trying to understand what had occurred.

Oliver looked at them. "We need to get out of here. Now!"

He turned and took a few steps. Brandon and George hadn't moved. "Come on guys, we need to go!"

"But . . ." It was all George could get out.

"Later. Come on."

Brandon grabbed George's arm and they both followed Oliver to the elevator.

♦ ♦ ♦ ♦ ♦ ♦ ♦

The herd of reporters noticed that Oliver was not with the group waiting in the car. They were starting to scatter when they heard what sounded like someone screaming in the distance. The elevator opened and Oliver and two other men came running towards the waiting car. A few of them managed to shout out some questions but the three men never even stopped to look. Oliver jumped in the front seat with Jonathan while the other two got in the back. The car quickly sped away.

Jonathan noted their entrance. "Well, you gentlemen certainly made your way through the gauntlet without incident."

Oliver nodded. "Yeah."

Emma noticed the look on her dad's face. "Dad, what's wrong?"

George looked at Brandon. He looked like a man trying to remember an answer to an important question. George placed his index finger over his lips and shook his head. He obviously didn't want to talk about it.

Snoop made his way to Oliver's shoulder and whispered. "Oliver, what has happened?"

Oliver whispered back. "I'm not quite sure."

He looked down at his hands. "I'm not quite sure."

♦ ♦ ♦ ♦ ♦ ♦ ♦

The car drove into the charter area and right onto the tarmac. They drove up to a fairly large and beautiful private jet. Across the side were the words United States of America.

Jonathan turned, "This beats flying commercial, doesn't it? This is the Ambassador's jet. He calls it his 8000. Being so far south, he requires a jet that can get him back on American soil in one trip. This jet has an effective range of 7900 nautical miles. Hawaii is 6777 miles. You will stop in Hawaii for refueling and to take on a new crew."

"How long will the trip be to Hawaii?" Emma asked.

"It's approximately fourteen hours to Honolulu. Also remember when you came you gained a day. On your return you will lose one. We always like to joke about going back in time."

Jonathan chuckled but the others were still trying to comprehend it.

"Anyway, you will be in Hawaii for a couple of hours and then move on. The trip to LA is only about five hours. Are there any questions?"

Oliver asked, "Jonathan, are you traveling back with us?"

"I'm afraid not. These are busy and challenging times. Tensions in the region are delicate at the moment. Not to worry, you will pick up an associate of mine in Hawaii who will help you with your re-entry. So, let's go and I'll introduce you to your crew."

Three people were waiting by the jet stairway.

Jonathan inspected the crewmembers and then turned for the introductions.

"All of the crew are employees of the State Department." He pointed to a pair dressed similarly. "This is Selena Dobson and Drew Sharpton. They are your stewards. They can assist you while you are traveling. Also this is Diana Fellows. She is one of two co-pilots. Captain Harold Church and Co-pilot Aaron Hansen are inside preparing for your departure. So that does it for introductions. If you need anything from your baggage you wish to take on board, get it. Otherwise, it will all be loaded. If there is nothing else, you may board."

Oliver reached over and shook his hand. "Jonathan, I don't know how to thank you."

"It's nothing, Dr. Cohen. You've been most enjoyable and a good diversion for me. I do hope your journey in the coming days provides you some resolution for the past years."

Oliver stepped back and lifted up his hand to say goodbye. Snoop did likewise.

Jonathan stepped back., and as he turned and walked away he shook his head side to side. Emma softly snickered.

Selena Dobson directed them toward the jet. "Shall we board?"

♦ ♦ ♦ ♦ ♦ ♦ ♦

At the same time they were preparing to leave, Li was receiving treatment in the emergency room of Mount Hospital. Having received some medication, the pain was receding somewhat. After the nurse left the room, he made a call to Lanzig.

Lanzig answered on the first ring. "Ah, Mr. Li. I take it that you are on your way to LA as instructed?"

"No, I am not."

"What is the problem?"

"The problem is, I am in a hospital."

"Li, I am not concerned with your personal problems. I pay you for results, not excuses. Now, when will you be on your way back?"

Li bit his lip as he forced his will over the remaining pain. "Herr Lanzig, what sort of man is this Dr. Cohen?"

"What do you mean?"

Even as he kept his voice down, he made no effort to hide his anger. "He is the reason I am here. I was caught searching his room and attacked him in order to escape. That's when he injured me."

Lanzig half chuckled. "You let the good doctor get the best of you?"

Li was not amused. "When I swung for him, he caught my fist with his hand and burned me."

"What do you mean he burned you?"

"I suffered second and third degree burns across the entire outer aspect of my fist. My skin even continued to burn afterwards."

Lanzig paused before asking. "How is that possible? Did he use acid of some kind?"

"I thought of that at first but ruled it out. I felt skin to skin in the attack. I can't see how he could have done it without injuring himself as well. I caught him totally off guard. I saw it on his face. He had no time to prepare such a defense. He seemed as surprised as me by what occurred."

"Then how do you explain it?"

Now he shouted, "That's just it! I have no explanation! This should not have happened!"

In all of his years working with Li, he had never seen him like this. Li almost seemed frightened. He knew he couldn't afford this kind of complication. Osgood had no tolerance for failure.

"Li, as soon as you are able, proceed to LA. If there is anything you need, contact the office. I'm on my way to LA and will check back with you after I arrive and meet with Yaunt. I have other assets, but I need you."

It surprised Li to hear Lanzig speak in such terms. The effects of the medication were taking effect. His temper had subsided.

"Thank you, Herr Lanzig. I will be on my way as soon as I am released."

"Very good, Li. We will get to the bottom of this doctor and his trickery. And when it is over, we shall both have our laugh over him. We have handled better than him over the years."

"Yes indeed, sir."

"Very well then."

Lanzig hung up. He repeated in his mind Li's question. What sort of person was Dr. Cohen? What was behind Osgood's obsession with him? What could explain Li's injuries? He took out a small note pad. He jotted down things he didn't want recorded in any electronic device. Information fingerprints were harder to erase than a simple piece of paper.

♦ ♦ ♦ ♦ ♦ ♦ ♦

Their flight was already two hours old. Everyone had settled into different areas of the plane. The Bombardier 8000 was an elegant plane. This one had also been modified for the needs of the U.S. Ambassador and staff in their travels. The front fourth held the crew area and galley. Next came an ample space with seating area for three and an office workspace. This spread out to a dining area seating four with a couch across from it. Then there was a stateroom with a large seat, couch, desk, and a large entertainment and communication screen. Lastly in the rear was a restroom with shower.

Snoop walked the length of the plane from front to back. Outside of the crew's amused glances, no one else paid him any mind. Snoop noticed everyone's quiet demeanor. George and

Brandon sat across from each other but neither had spoken a word. Emma sat in the seat with an adjoining desk. She had been reading the Bible Oliver had given her. She looked up and saw the confused look on her father's face.

Oliver sat alone in the stateroom. He sat rubbing his hands together and looking at them as if he were looking for something.

The attendants had offered refreshments but no one seemed interested. So they retreated to their own area.

Snoop made his way to Oliver and climbed onto his shoulder. Oliver didn't even notice until Snoop leaned in and whispered, "Why is everyone acting so strangely, Oliver?"

Snoop's voice startled him for a second.

"Sorry, Snoop." He had noticed the stupor hanging over everyone. He knew he had to say something.

Oliver stood up and walked into the main cabin area. He coughed loud and strong. Everyone got the message and looked up.

"Not to belabor the obvious, but we need to talk. First, I want to thank all of you for coming to get me and helping me get back. I promise I'll try to clear up some of the questions about my absence and return. You already know about me being stranded on an island, so I won't go over that again. It would be difficult for me to explain most of what happened to me on the Island. Suffice it to say it has changed my life in every way."

Oliver paused for a moment. He wondered how far to go with his comments.

"I don't expect you to understand what I'm about to tell you. In fact, I'd be surprised if you did. You've heard me say that I encountered God on the Island. When I say that, I'm not talking about some religious experience. I'm talking about a true, face-to-face meeting with God in the form of Jesus."

George and Brandon began to squirm.

"I saw Him. I spoke to Him on many occasions over the fifteen years on the Island. He told me that I would be leaving the Island

and He gave me an assignment."

Emma's eyes were fixed on Oliver but George and Brandon were looking to the ground.

A surge of boldness swelled up in Oliver. His voice took on a deep strength that almost seemed to vibrate on the walls.

"George, Brandon, look this way. Even if you don't believe my words, you are now both witnesses to something that you cannot explain. Know this, it is but the first of many things you will see, which will go searching for an explanation. I am giving you an explanation, which you may choose to accept or reject. I personally rejected it to the point of almost losing my life."

He took a deep breath. "You have witnessed the power of God. And that power is coming over me in order to validate the words and message I am given to declare. If you continue with me on my journey, you will see for yourself. But, with this comes danger. Before we reach LA you need to decide what you will do. That's all I have to say for now."

Oliver turned and walked back into the stateroom.

In the front galley, the two stewards had heard it all. They stared at each other with their mouths half open. Instead of serving the meal they waited for some kind of response from the main cabin.

George sat silent and nervous for his dear friend. Brandon shook his head, not sure if he wanted to laugh or cry at finding himself a party to a man who would say such things. Yet, a voice whispered in their minds one question. "How do you explain what happened at the hotel?" They both saw the flesh on the man's hand badly burned.

What if it was possible that what Oliver said was true?

A barrage of questions hammered them. Why was that man in the room? What was so important about Oliver's satchel? Why was someone spying on them? None of it made sense.

Emma's heart swelled with a fire that told her that everything Oliver said was true. It surprised her how so much in her mind and heart was changing. While she saw confusion on her father's face, she practically trembled in a sense of wonder that she was a party to these events.

Their minds wrestled to get a grip on the entire matter and reach a decision. The delayed response from all of them was out of exhaustion. So, one by one, they leaned the seats into beds and tried to sleep. Some were successful and others only rested their eyes.

The cabin stewards decided to turn down the lights and let everyone rest.

♦ ♦ ♦ ♦ ♦ ♦ ♦

Li sat in the terminal. His flight would board in a few minutes. He gingerly held his bandaged hand. The medication made the pain manageable. What increasingly gave him trouble was how to explain what had happened. He played the event over and over in his mind. There had to be a way to explain what had happened. He was determined to discover and obtain the ability that this man possessed. There were so many ways he could use such an ability. Perhaps this was what Osgood was after. Li plotted to make sure he would possess it first.

THIRTEEN

While everyone rested, Snoop cuddled up to Oliver. They carried on a whispered conversation.

"I must say, Oliver, I was surprised to hear you speak with such boldness. I know the Maker is proud of you and your willingness to speak on His behalf."

"Yeah, I kind of surprised myself. It just welled up inside of me and busted out. I couldn't hold it back." Oliver softly chuckled.

"What's so funny, Oliver?"

"I was remembering the look on everyone's faces. It's the same look I'm sure I had when the Keeper spoke to me in declarations of certainty. I also remember the thoughts I had. They must think I'm crazy."

"I think I can begin to see why you were so defiant back on the Island. Even when you saw the reality of God you resisted. But here, the Lie is so strong and the Story so long forgotten, you will be rejected and opposed."

"Yes. He told me to expect it."

"Oliver," Snoop paused before continuing, "what was it like up on the mountain and to be taught by the Maker?"

"Wow. You know, I've actually given long thought about how to answer that question, knowing it would come up. I've had trouble coming up with a point of reference to capture an answer. It was glorious...it was mind-blowing. It stretched me...it laid me low. I tasted light and began to understand nature and the danger of darkness. Sometimes I shouted in supreme joy while other times I wept hard at my failure. At times I would finish a day, completely exhausted yet invigorated, in a serene rest. He would answer so many of my questions, which often led to even more questions. He would pat me on the back and smile. He would say that when He didn't provide an answer it meant that I had to trust Him. And looking at Him at that moment, I knew He was right."

Oliver's last words drifted off.

"Oh my, Oliver, you have indeed been given a great gift not enjoyed by many."

Oliver looked directly at Snoop. "Yes, I know. I just don't want to fail Him. He has trusted me and I must trust Him. I must not fail."

With those last words, Oliver thought about the others. "Lord, help me help my friends to see and believe."

Snoop added, "Truly."

♦ ♦ ♦ ♦ ♦ ♦ ♦

It was 10:30 pm in Los Angeles. The streets were alive with the kinetic LA nightlife. In the top floor executive suite of the Four Seasons hotel, the mood was charged with a caustic ferocity of two warring egos. Yaunt and Lanzig sat across from each other. Having finished their meals they no longer had anything else to distract their mutual loathing. The only thing that brought them together was the power that held them both in their place. Neither of them could afford Osgood's wrath or even his displeasure. Both knew what happened to anyone, who once in Osgood's web, attempted resistance or freedom.

They each measured their approach like roosters preparing for a cockfight.

Lanzig saw Yaunt as a sniveling weakling who lived in the presence of power but never understood it and therefore would never be able to handle it. He also knew Osgood's tactic for his underlings. It was one Hitler had used. Give his subordinates a measure of power and let them fight among themselves. He would always remain on the top of the chaos controlling whoever might at the moment rise to prominence. No minon would ever rise to threaten the master.

Yaunt watched Lanzig's eyes and his twisted smirk. He knew the opinion Lanzig had of him. Lanzig's voice dripped with condescension every time they spoke. But Yaunt had his own secret. He had tasted from the elixir of Osgood's power and the exhilaration had not diminished. He was no longer the anemic lackey. He was now invigorated with the essence of the mighty and sensed the invincibility of a conqueror.

So they both sat silent for at least twenty minutes in a chess match of arrogance.

Finally, Lanzig made the first move.

"So, Herr Yaunt, what is the plan?"

"The plan is very simple. We need to know all we can about Dr. Cohen. As we relay this information, at some point you will be given directives."

"What exactly are we after? Who is this doctor and why is he so important?"

"Those questions are not your concern. You are merely to observe, collect, and report everything you can on the subject."

"Normally, Herr Yaunt, that would not be a problem. On the surface the good doctor seems harmless enough. Doctors are healers, not fighters. Except for their egos, they are for the most part innocuous to someone in my field. But, there seems to be more to this doctor than meets the eye."

"What do you mean?"

"My man, Quan Li, who as you know, is a man of unique skills and a deadly asset, had an encounter with the doctor. In order to extricate himself from a situation Li used a degree of force on the doctor. But, he encountered a problem. When I last spoke to Li he was in the hospital seeking treatment from injuries sustained in the altercation."

"Are you telling me that the doctor bested your man?"

"I don't think that is the best description of the incident."

"Then what are you saying?" Yaunt didn't hide his distaste for Lanzig's trickling revelation.

"When Li swung to strike the doctor, Cohen caught his fist in his hand and badly burned him."

"What do you mean?"

"Li suffered second and third degree burns on his fist."

"How? What did the doctor do?"

"That's what I asked Li. He had no answer. He only asked what I am asking. Who is this doctor? What aren't we being told? Who and what are we dealing with?"

Yaunt leaned forward placing his elbows on the table. He scratched his chin as he felt some of his confidence slipping away. Redirect.

"Do you or Li have any theories?"

"If we did I wouldn't be asking but acting. Li said he caught the doctor totally by surprise. And yet . . . well, you know the results."

"I don't know what to tell you. There's nothing in the doctor's past to indicate he possesses any special skills of this kind."

Lanzig did not like the unfamiliar territory of unanswered questions.

"Look, Herr Yaunt, we both know our individual and mutual relationship with Herr Osgood. It does neither of us any good to fail at our assignments. The power of information is in possessing and using it. But what we don't know can also hurt us. Now, perhaps if you could tell me why Herr Osgood is interested in the doctor, we can, to our mutual benefit, successfully complete our task."

Yaunt waited, pondered, and then surrendered. "I don't know. I've wondered the same thing myself."

Lanzig questioned out loud. "Perhaps it's money or some possession of the doctor's?"

Yaunt smirked, "Lanzig, you know Osgood. For him fortune is only a tool to something greater. For him it's about power. Maybe that's it. Maybe this event is a clue. Maybe the doctor possesses some sort of unusual power."

Lanzig's incredulous look spurred Yaunt on.

"No, wait. You know as well as I do that Osgood has a fascination with things . . . beyond the natural. He has that chamber where he goes and does who knows what. I was in there recently after one of his lengthy sessions. There was something almost tangible in the air. Maybe that has something to do with the doctor and Osgood's interest in him."

"Well, I certainly don't subscribe to any such realities. I understand bullets and bodies, not spirits and unseen forces. We will collect our data on the doctor. But until I know more, I cannot proceed with action until I understand what I'm dealing with. Information precedes action. And yet, Osgood does not tolerate inaction."

"You seem to know him very well."

"You have no idea." Lanzig looked away.

Yaunt was intrigued. "We both find ourselves in a mutual dilemma. Osgood is obsessed with this doctor. Failure is unacceptable. As you said, information precedes action. This also holds true in respect to Osgood. You know something, I can tell."

His eyes responded before his words. "What I know is destructively dangerous. It is like trying to hold fire."

"But what if two people hold it?"

Lanzig looked deep into Yaunt's eyes. He recognized the hunger. He knew he couldn't fully trust him. And yet, perhaps…yes, of course. He would somehow make sure that it was Yaunt who was burned and not himself. It must be played skillfully.

"Perhaps you are right, Herr Yaunt. I have held this fire to myself for too long."

Lanzig paused for added affect.

"How much do you know about how Osgood gained his fortune?"

"I know that much of it came from his father."

"Yes, Herrman, but originally it was Heindrich. But where did Heindrich gain his fortune?"

Yaunt nodded. "I never asked Osgood."

"And a good thing you didn't, or you wouldn't be here. Heindrich's name was not always Osgood. Originally it was Oswalt. Heindrich and his father, Fritz, were industrialists working with the Nazi's. They gained their fortune from the blood bath of millions who were tortured and slaughtered. They were ruthless and cruel even to fellow Germans. They practiced the dark arts along with Hitler and many of his closest leaders."

"Why is there no record of this in the history books?"

"Exactly. When the war turned bad, evil turned in on itself. Fritz saw it coming. He consolidated much of their fortune in diamonds and planned their escape. But even blood relation was not enough to ward off betrayal. Heindrich made it, but Fritz didn't."

Lanzig paused to catch his breath. "Heindrich crossed over into Switzerland. He murdered and stole the name Osgood and took the name Hermann. He lived in the quiet of a small village until after the war. He slowly and carefully made his way into banking and from there into the multitude of industries of Osgood Ltd."

"But what of Herr Malcolm Osgood?"

"His mother was a young Swiss girl bought to provide legitimacy. She lasted only long enough to bear a son. And the son is a shadowed reflection of his ancestors."

Yaunt was unsure how to react at first. Finally, he slowly

responded. "If this information ever became public . . ."

"It would all be stripped away. But trust me, I have discovered the names of hundreds of people who came upon this information and suddenly met with a tragic end. As we both know, his fortune can purchase many things, including death."

Lanzig's eyes grew large. "Now you see the danger of this fire."

Yaunt's eyes stared at nothing in particular. "Do you have documents for all of this?"

Lanzig slowly nodded.

"Where are they?"

"In a very safe place."

"How and when would you use such information?"

"Very carefully and only as a last resort. You see, Herr Yaunt, the trick to using a nuclear weapon is to not to be anywhere close to it when it goes off."

"Yes, of course. Seems we are partners in a deadly game."

Lanzig grinned. "Power is always a deadly game, Herr Yaunt."

Neither of them said anything for some time.

Yaunt finally told him of his work to infiltrate Cohen's group and the confederate he had recruited. He also told him of Cohen's desire to travel to Israel and Jordan. From there they made plans on how to best control the situation until they discovered the real jewel of Osgood's quest.

When they were finished they actually ended up shaking hands and laughing together.

It was strange that what had started as a dual had ended in an anomalous treaty of sorts. Stranger still would be their individual encounters with the thing they thought they wanted to possess.

♦ ♦ ♦ ♦ ♦ ♦ ♦

Oliver managed to drift off and get some sleep along with the others. Everyone now slept hard.

A full nine hours into the flight Emma was the first to stir.

George and Brandon were soon stretching out of the fog of a much needed rest. Snoop sensed the activity in the other cabin and began to gently wake up Oliver. His fur rubbing under his chin did the trick.

He opened his eyes to see his smiling friend with his nose and whiskers twitching side to side greeting him.

"Hello, Oliver. Did you rest well?"

"Yes, I think so." He moved his seat up and stretched out his arms.

"The others are waking. It may be a good thing to go and be with them."

"Yeah, I think you're right. This stateroom is nice but it isolates me. After my declaration, I know they have questions."

Oliver got up and walked into the main cabin area. The stewards were already preparing the dining area for a meal.

Oliver smiled big and clapped his hands.

"I think I'm ready for something to eat. How about the rest of you?"

His demeanor put everyone else at ease. Soon they had a very fine meal in front of them. Before anyone could begin, Oliver spoke.

"This is actually our first meal all together. While this may seem strange to you, it has become my custom to ask a blessing before I eat. So, if you will allow me. . ."

They didn't know what to do but took their cue from Snoop and Oliver as they bowed their heads.

"Maker of heaven and earth, I thank You for this meal. I thank You for these friends. I thank You for Your rescuing hands. Guard us in Your mercy. Strengthen us for Your purpose, always and only for Your glory. Truly."

Both Emma and Snoop softly repeated the words, "Truly."

George and Brandon reluctantly nodded.

As they all finished their meal, Snoop was on the last bites of some fruit when the stewards came to pick up their plates.

Oliver coughed and got everyone's attention.

"After my last declaration, I'm sure each of you has some questions. Since each of you will have to make your own decision, I'd like it if each one you would sit down with me so we can talk."

Oliver could see the stalemate of indecision in the group.

"If you can hear me, nod your head."

Oliver's attempt at humor broke the moment's tension.

"I'll tell you what. Let's do this in alphabetical order by first names. Brandon, Emma, and then George. OK?"

They nodded.

"Brandon, give me a couple of minutes to wash my hands and such and then just come on in."

Oliver clapped his hands once and then turned and left for the stateroom.

♦ ♦ ♦ ♦ ♦ ♦ ♦

Osgood sat in a den adjoining his bedroom. The den led out to a garden area where he would often go for midday meditations. He finished reading the latest report from Yaunt. He set down the report and gave a verbal command to secure the area. All entrances locked and all monitors turned off.

He walked back to a small stand that sat in the rear of an enclosed garden. The foliage was arranged in such a way that this specific spot stayed hot and humid.

Osgood peeled off his shirt and sat on the ground before the stand. On the stand sat a single item measuring eight inches in height. It had the head of a bull with folded wings. With long talons it grasped a collection of skulls. And in its arms was a coiled serpent.

Osgood rocked back and forth as he entered his meditative state. The ambient light around him began to darken. For twenty minutes he rocked while repetitively mumbling the name of the deity before him. The rocking became faster and. It reached a crescendo when a blast of cold air knocked him over. He remained on the ground shaking uncontrollably. Steam from his breath rose in the freezing air. A shadow hovered above him like a wave of dark miasmic swamp water. Slowly the shadow sank into him. When it did, the shaking stopped and his clinched fists pounded the ground. His eyes opened wide and wild. They darted side to side as if looking for something. The color in his eyes, fully dilated were barely visible. Suddenly he sat up. He raised both fists into the air and let out a high-pitched scream. He then collapsed back to the ground.

The cold air vanished, replaced by the humid hothouse air. Osgood remained silent for a full hour. He shook his head a few times, then got up from the ground. He picked up his shirt. Before walking out, he turned to face the image. He bowed low, coming up slowly. He suddenly turned and broke out into wicked laughter. The laughter increased like an angry river. By the time he reached the den he was spinning with his arms in the air laughing in a wild madness.

As if by a switch, he stopped. He closed his eyes, took a breath. As he slowly exhaled he looked down at his closed hands. In slow motion he unfolded his fingers whispering one word, "Power."

FOURTEEN

Brandon had a notepad in his hand when he walked into the stateroom to speak to Oliver. He sat down on the couch opposite Oliver's seat.

Brandon looked at the obviously expensive accommodations.

"Pretty nice."

Oliver chuckled, "Yeah, your tax dollars at work. Before we get started, let me say thank you for the help you have provided. I know you have unique interests in all of this, but you have been a help and I wanted to thank you."

Oliver smiled when Brandon returned an appreciative nod.

"Well, Brandon, I promised you exclusivity. So fire away. I know you have questions."

"Thank you, Dr. Cohen."

"Oliver."

"Right. Oliver." Brandon looked down at his notes.

"You've told us some things about the Island. A while ago you told us something about what happened to you there. But as you can imagine, I'm having difficulty understanding it in practical terms. I guess what I'm saying is, did you have some sort of vision? Have you considered your isolation as a factor for what you say you saw?"

Oliver nodded and rubbed his chin.

"I fully understand your skepticism. I remember hearing my wife talk about her faith and thinking she was delusional. Not long after arriving on the Island I began to encounter things that I had no way to explain."

"What sort of things?"

"I don't want to get into that right now. But suffice it to say, for this highly educated cynic it rocked my socks. On this island the natural and supernatural peacefully and blissfully co-existed. I tried denying what was everywhere around me. And when I could no longer deny it, I willfully resisted it. It was like falling off a building while denying gravity."

Brandon was listening without taking any notes. Oliver closed his eyes and rubbed his forehead. The memories were vivid and painful.

Tears were now forming in his eyes.

"I witnessed true and pure goodness. I also experienced undiluted evil. I saw it in myself. I also saw its manifestation coming against me. Despite continued warning, I allowed myself to be seduced by this evil. When I finally saw it for what it was, it almost killed me. When I cried out for help, I was rescued from its grip."

Oliver's hands were trembling. "It was then that I met my Maker. I was given an unvarnished look at my own evil heart and life. It was horrible."

Oliver was now weeping.

"But you know what? As He looked at my evil, He didn't reject me. He took it away from me. He forgave me. He . . . He rescued me."

Brandon felt nervous and a bit embarrassed. The man who had earlier displayed such boldness now sat broken and humbled. And

146

yet, Oliver somehow stood taller in his estimation. Brandon was not convinced about what Oliver had shared. And yet, he had to admit a sudden admiration for the good doctor. There was mystery here that begged for an explanation. Without all his questions answered, Brandon decided to not continue in his present course.

As Oliver wiped away the tears, Brandon spoke.

"Oliver, I don't know what to make of what you have told me. If it were in a book I would want to read it. I am not religious or even remotely spiritual in any way. But I am moved with an uncomfortable curiosity to continue with the group if you will allow me. So I'll hold my remaining questions and doubts in check and see where this all goes."

Oliver looked at Brandon and smiled. "I have to say, Brandon, your response is better than mine when I encountered what seemed totally preposterous to me. I don't believe it's an accident that you are a part of our band. I look forward to seeing how the Story comes out and your part in it."

When Brandon got up to leave, Oliver reached out and shook his hand and patted him on the shoulder.

Brandon walked back in the main cabin with calmness written on his steps. He looked at Emma and tipped his head towards the stateroom. It was obviously her turn. She picked up Snoop and practically ran back. George stared at Brandon, curious at what had quieted his fellow passenger.

Emma wasted no time sitting down and beginning.

"Wow, Uncle Ollie, what did you do to Brandon? Before he walked in here he looked like a bull about to charge a matador. He walked out of here like a man who had taken a tranquilizer."

Oliver smiled as he watched her new found wonder. He could see the high regard she had for him. He repeated the story he had just shared with Brandon.

The re-telling was no less painful or penetrating. The impact on Emma was deep and punishing. It brought her to her knees. She wept hard. She saw in her heart her own darkness and the gift given to her.

Snoop sat humming slowly and softly an ancient tune. After a bit he added the words.

Never let my heart grow weary.
Never let the tune grow old.
Ever do I want to sing it,
Ever let me tell it new.

You alone can rescue.
You alone make me whole.
No one else is like You.
Champion of my soul.

Start again old weary heart
To beat anew for Him.
You alone can rescue.
You alone make me whole.

He repeated it twice. On the third time both Emma and Oliver joined in. When they finished, Emma looked up at Oliver.

"Oh, Uncle Ollie, Daddy has to know this. He has to find his way to Him."

Oliver swallowed a stuttering breath. "All in the Lord's time. All in the Lord's time."

♦ ♦ ♦ ♦ ♦ ♦ ♦

Yaunt's phone rang. He saw that it was from Osgood. He looked over to the clock beside his bed. It was three in the morning. He let it ring twice before connecting.

"Yes sir, how can I help?" He was trying to pry his eyes open.

"You sound as if you were sleeping."

"It is three in the morning here, sir."

"Ah, yes, I forgot. It is noon here. Nevertheless, I finished reading your last report. When do you expect Cohen and his group?"

He shook his head to clear his thoughts. "Somewhere between 4:00 and 6:00 pm, depending on how long they stop over in Hawaii."

"You reported that his intention is to travel to Israel and Jordan. I believe that he will want to proceed as soon as possible. Clear all obstacles and make it so. Is Lanzig there?"

"Yes, I met with him last night."

"Send him on ahead. I'm sure the doctor doesn't know his way around in that part of the world. Have Lanzig secure a guide for them. Make sure they belong to us in every way. I want this covered from every angle. The doctor has a plan and I want to know it."

"Do you know what the doctor is after?"

"That is exactly what you are tasked with discovering. And when you find out, that information comes to me directly. Do you understand?"

"Yes sir. I will make all the arrangements and have Lanzig on his way."

"You have much to do, so get busy. Let me know when the doctor arrives."

Osgood hung up.

Yaunt rubbed his eyes and looked at the clock again. He took a moment to calculate that it was 1:00 pm in Tel Aviv. He needed to make calls and make preparations for Lanzig and his group. Between transportation and payouts to some officials, the cost would be considerable. But Osgood made it clear to spare no expense. He would make sure not to spare any expense on his own behalf.

◆ ◆ ◆ ◆ ◆ ◆ ◆

Emma was all smiles when she came out into the main cabin. She stepped up to George and pecked him on the cheek.

"Your turn, Daddy. Uncle Ollie's waiting for you."

First it was Brandon and now his daughter. He couldn't imagine what Oliver was doing to them. Oliver had gone from a returning castaway to the de facto leader of a group going who knows where. This was not the friend he remembered.

He looked over at Brandon. He was busy on his computer. His daughter was playing with Oliver's animal companion. He got up, resolved to get to the bottom of what was going on.

He walked in and Oliver was grinning while leaning back in his large comfortable passenger chair.

"Have a seat, George. Take a load off."

George sat on the couch trying to decide where to start. Oliver beat him to it.

"That's one sweet girl you have. I know you're proud of her. She looks a lot like her mom."

"Yeah, thanks. Look … I don't know what it is you've done to Emma. She's changed over the last few days. When we left to come for you, things were not good. We had our own war going on. We agreed to an armistice of sorts in order to come for you. But something's changed. It's like my little girl's back."

George held his forehead down in his hands. "Truth is, O.B., I've been in a funk. After you vanished, I panicked. I did the 'be strong' routine for a while. Then the guilt began eating me up. First it was Mary. Then it was you. I felt like I had killed both of you. Medicine wasn't fun anymore. It was an economic bondage. Home life came next. A black cloud hovered over me and my family had to suffer it with me. I couldn't shake it. I felt like a man in a basement, digging holes. The only way out was down."

Oliver lowered his head. "George, I'm so sorry."

George looked up. "It's not your fault. I didn't blame you. How could I blame a dead man with a dead wife?"

George's hands were shaking and his eyes tearing up.

"But, you weren't dead. You didn't die."

He rubbed his fingers across his forehead. "Where were you, O.B? I needed you and you weren't here."

"But, I'm back, George. I'm here now."

George looked at his friend, his face squinting and almost angry.

"But you're not the same. You're different. I don't know what to think of this new you. And now with Emma and this thing you say about yourself . . . I, I . . . I just don't know."

"When you used to get all knotted up with Mary, I laughed. I thought it was funny to see you so frustrated at her and yet so much in love. But now . . . now it's not funny anymore. Now, it's me on the outside, alone."

"George, you're not alone. I've learned that you can start over. The past doesn't have to dictate the present or the future. Mary was right. I was a fool. And you're right. Emma is different. She doesn't fully understand it, but she knows it's real. She's discovered what real love is about. She forgives you, George. That's why she's not mad at you anymore. That's what love does to you."

The words baffled George as he looked at his friend.

Oliver was rubbing his hands together as he continued.

"Look, you remember how I was when I ran away. You remember the raging anger that had hold of me. I was angry with everyone. Most of all I hated God, Mary's God. I hated Him for the hold He had on her. Even though I didn't believe He existed, I hated Him. I was a ball of bitterness."

It troubled Oliver to revisit his former self.

"But you know what, George, it galled me just as much that I had lost control of myself. I prided myself in my ability to govern my mind and emotions. I was smart and in command of my life and destiny. I actually believed the whole story was about me. Even though I denied there was a God, I was acting like one. I was such a fool."

This was so unlike his old friend. George sat stunned.

"Wow, O.B. As a friend and a peer, I've always looked up to you. I always passed off your bravado as part of someone who was smarter and better than others. So, what happened on this island to change you?"

"I met someone who was much smarter, much better, much more in control. Me, the pretend god, met the True and Living God."

Oliver's eyes moistened on the edge of tears.

"And you know what? He's exactly like Mary described Him. And when it was all said and done, I felt like I was home. The home of my mother's heart, the home Mary had tried desperately to make me see."

"Do you still miss her, O.B?"

"Desperately. But you know, I . . . ah, the very best part of her is not gone. That beauty that captured me, that magnetic sparkle that energized her love, it still lives. She told me a hundred times always pointing me to Him. I always thought it was nonsense or false modesty. But it was God that was modest. He didn't force Himself on me until I was desperate enough to call out to Him. And when I did, He came running to me. He rescued me. He rescued me from myself. He brought me right into the love I've been talking about. It's like the song says, "I was blind, but now I see.""

He spoke the last words in a staccato whimper.

"Wow, O.B., that's a lot of heavy duty stuff to take in. I've never looked at life or myself from the perspective you've described. I'm not saying I'm hostile to it. I'm simply not ready to jump off into it with all my heart. I have to say one thing, it has changed you and my sweet Emmy. And when you touch my girl, you touch me. Thank you."

Oliver got up and embraced his friend. George responded likewise.

After a moment, Oliver released him and asked.

"So friend, are you in? Will you go with me on my journey?"

"Like I said before, I lost you once and I won't lose you again. You said there might be danger. Well, at least I'll be with people I love. I'm in."

"Great, because in the coming days you're going to have to

remember that decision. More than anything else, you are going to have to trust me."

♦ ♦ ♦ ♦ ♦ ♦ ♦

Yaunt secured clearance for everyone's entrance into Israel. He made initial contacts for Lanzig to secure entrance into Jordan when the time came. He was always amazed what money could accomplish that even governments were inept to manage. He waited until 7:00 am before contacting Lanzig.

"Good morning, Herr Lanzig. Have you heard from your man, Li?"

"Yes, he is on his way. He will arrive around 10:30 this evening."

"Very good. I have spoken to Osgood. As you know, Dr. Cohen wants to travel to Israel and Jordan. I have spoken to Brandon Rivers and informed him that we are financing his endeavor. He has asked me to help them get into Israel and Jordan. I have arranged everything for the group and for you and Li. I'm not sure when Dr. Cohen wishes to travel to Israel but it should be soon. Osgood wants you and Li to go ahead of us. You are to secure a guide for the doctor and his quest."

"And what is that?"

"That is what I will find out. As for the guide, pay him well. Buy his soul. We need to know the doctor's plan and prepare accordingly. You and Li should remain close and ready."

"So you still don't know what we are looking for?"

"No, but neither does Osgood. Judging from the amount of money he's throwing at this, it's big. Oh, one other thing, Osgood wants the information gained by the guide to come to him directly."

"I will secure him an encrypting transmitter."

Yaunt smiled. "Yes, of course. But make sure you and I receive untraceable copies as well. Do you understand?"

"Herr Yaunt, I have underestimated you. I'm beginning to like this side of you. Send me our travel information. I will secure a guide.

We will shadow them and make ready to strike at your command."

"Excellent. Stay in contact."

When he hung up, Lanzig opened up his contact list on his phone. He knew exactly who to call. He had never met him in person. He only had a name: Nasr. He called him.

Three rings and he answered.

"Ah, my German friend, how can I be of service?"

"I am coming to Israel soon. I need a guide. But, not simply a guide."

"Of course, or why else would you call?"

"We will be traveling in Israel and Jordan. His English must be excellent. I pay very well but expect complete devotion and discretion."

"I understand completely. Consider it done. I will send you the cost plus my fee. I know of your generosity."

"You mean that you are aware of my funding habits?"

"As you have said, you receive what you pay for. You will receive my best. Contact me when you arrive. Good day."

Lanzig grinned. "No wonder he is called Nasr – Vulture."

FIFTEEN

The plane arrived in Honolulu very close to 8:00 am, a day earlier than they had left. State Department workers took care of the paperwork for Immigration and Customs. The group enjoyed a nice breakfast while a new flight crew arrived and readied for the remainder of the trip.

Brandon was handed a note. He coughed to get their attention.

"Hey guys, listen to this. I hope you have had a comfortable trip so far. Your breakfast comes compliments of the State of Hawaii. State officials wish they could meet you, but I informed them of your desire to get home. Mr. Rivers told me that he has made arrangements for you once you arrive in Los Angeles. The Secretary of State has told me that if there is anything he can do to help in your transition to let us know. Best wishes to Dr. Cohen and to all of you."

Emma was sitting next to Oliver. Snoop was on his lap eating some peeled oranges. She turned to Oliver.

"Wow, Uncle Ollie, the Secretary of State. Pretty impressive."

"God has given us favor. We will need all of it for what's ahead."

Brandon asked. "And just what is it that's up ahead, Oliver?"

Oliver nodded. "I'm glad you asked. What sort of progress have you had with the jeweler?"

"Well, I found someone in LA who meets your requirements. By my calculations, we will arrive in LA around 4:30 pm. I have a service picking us up at the airport. It should take us about thirty to forty minutes to get to the place. He closes at 6:00, but agreed to wait if he needed to. I explained that you were the guy in the news, Mr. Lost and Found. He's excited to meet you."

George chuckled. "Seems celebrity status has its advantages."

Oliver shook his head. "Before this is over the advantages will fade, trust me. We will all desire anonymity. But, for right now it's helpful."

Brandon scratched his chin. "Oliver, where is this going?"

"Well, it's taking us to Israel and then to Jordan."

"Yes, I know that. And all the arrangements are made. What I mean is, what's this about?"

George wondered how much Oliver would reveal to Brandon.

"Think of this as a search for treasure. Yeah, that's it, a Treasure Hunt."

Brandon's sarcasm was evident before he said a word.

"So I suppose you have a treasure map?"

Oliver grinned as he picked up his leather satchel. He wrapped his arms around it and gently patted it. "As a matter of fact, I do."

Brandon's eyes widened. "You wouldn't care to let us see it, would you?"

"Not just yet. Later, when the time is right."

Snoop jumped on Oliver's shoulder and whispered in his ear. "Well done, Oliver."

George and Emma looked at each other, both curious but for different reasons.

They all finished their breakfast with little more than small talk.

Heading back to the plane, Oliver walked alongside Brandon.

"Brandon, I'd like to talk a little about the arrangements you've made for us. When we get settled in, can we do that?"

"Sure, is there a problem?"

"Not at all. I simply wanted some details and to ask some questions."

"Will do."

♦ ♦ ♦ ♦ ♦ ♦ ♦

The group settled in on the plane. The intercom came on.

"Good day, everyone. My name is Eric Stockton. I am your captain for this portion of your flight. We will be in the air approximately five hours. We will arrive in Los Angeles around 4:30 pm. You have all had a long day of travel already. I suggest using some of the flight time to get some rest. Thank you very much and enjoy your flight. Crew, prepare for take-off."

About thirty minutes into the flight, Brandon made his way to the state room.

He walked in and found Oliver on the floor with Snoop running and jumping from the seat into Oliver's arms. Brandon held back a smile while he watched them.

Brandon coughed.

Oliver and Snoop both looked up.

"That's right, we need to talk. Snoop, why don't you go to Emma for right now."

Snoop made quickstep and exited the room.

Brandon watched Snoop scurry by. "It's amazing how he does what you say. If I didn't know better, I'd think he understood you."

Oliver answered with a smile and nothing else.

"So, Oliver, you wanted to know about our arrangements?"

Oliver got up and sat on his large seat. "Have a seat. Again, thank you for what you've done. I wanted to ask about some of the arrangements."

"Yeah, sure."

"About our flight into Israel, George said that getting into the area isn't easy to do these days."

"That's right. Commercial flights are almost non-existent. And even then, they are highly restricted."

"So, how are we getting in?"

"Private charter aircraft."

"That's not cheap. Where's the money coming from?"

"I have received financing for my project. They are very interested in your story. I expressed your desire to travel to the Middle East and they made it happen."

"Who exactly is backing your project?"

"It's a corporation called Osgood Communications. They are part of Osgood Ltd., which is an international business enterprise. They have offices all over the world. They obviously have deep pockets."

"But why are they interested enough to go to such trouble and expense?"

Brandon looked at some notes on his phone. "Seems the enterprise is mostly owned by a Mr. Malcolm Osgood. I was told that he became immediately interested when he heard about your story."

"Will I be meeting this Mr. Osgood?"

"I have no idea. I've only spoken to his representative, a Mr. Yaunt. He has plans to meet us after we arrive in LA."

Oliver looked off before responding. "I look forward to meeting him."

He turned back to Brandon. "Brandon, I need you to know that my plans are not nor will they be restricted or dictated to by any outside interest. I have something important to accomplish. I want to avoid any hindrances."

"I know I've asked you before, but what exactly are you going to do?"

"And like I said before, all in due time. But know this, stick around and you'll have the biggest story you've ever had."

"That's quite a boast."

Oliver looked incisively at Brandon. "It's no boast."

He looked off and out the window. He softly repeated it. "It's no boast."

Brandon took the cue when Oliver didn't turn back. He quietly got up and left.

As he was about to exit the room he heard Oliver.

"Have Emma send Snoop back in."

◆ ◆ ◆ ◆ ◆ ◆ ◆

Oliver heard him scurrying toward him before he ever saw him. In typical Snoop fashion, once near enough, he leaped up on Oliver's lap and then up to his shoulder.

"Oh, Oliver, it is such fun to have Emma with us. She and I

have been playing a game. She whispers to me and then I talk out loud to her. Some of the others look but none can understand. It makes us both laugh."

"Yeah, I'm glad Emma is here and that she has come to know the Maker."

Oliver's tone communicated to Snoop that something was wrong.

"Oliver, you seem troubled. What is it?"

"I suppose I'm beginning to realize what's coming. And also, I want to apologize to you."

Snoop tilted his head, clearly not understanding.

"What I mean is that I'm sorry that I haven't spent much time with you lately."

Snoop nodded. "This most certainly is not like the Island."

"That's very true. In fact, that's part of what's troubling me."

Oliver paused to collect his thoughts.

"When I prepared to become a doctor, even after all of the training, none of it was as real as when you start to practice medicine. There's so much you can only learn in the real setting."

Snoop listened intently putting his paw under his chin.

Oliver continued. "On the Island, everything was an amazing reminder of the absolute reality of truth. There, the truth and the reality of God filled the air. It was like when words and music come together to form the perfect song. And that song always declares the Story. But here, the noise of this world screams something different. You have to work hard to drown it out. Mary used to tell me about it, the music and the voice of God. I thought she was a dreamer. Truth was, I couldn't hear it. Sometimes the Island seems distant, almost like a dream."

"But, it was not a dream, Oliver. I am not a dream."

"I know. That's why I need you to remind me."

Memories of the Island were filling his mind.

"Snoop, when I hear your voice, it takes me back. Right now, I can close my eyes and see it again. I can hear the songs in the breeze. I can even hear His voice singing."

Snoop's fur seemed to move in rhythm and he hummed a soft tune.

"Oh, Oliver, I was a very young one when I heard the Maker sing. I can barely remember. Tell me, what was it like?"

"His is an ancient voice tuned to perfection. I ...I . . ." Oliver's voice suddenly trembled. "His voice reached deep within me. I felt young and old all at once. It touched places I didn't know existed. I wanted to laugh and cry, to sing and dance. And every song was better than the one before."

"What was it like when He taught you?"

"Challenging. Exhilarating. At the beginning, it was baby steps. I learned basics. He would have me read from Mary's Bible and then ask him questions. Many times He would answer me directly. Other times He would respond by asking me a question and then directing me back to the Bible. He was patient and never condescending. He was . . ."

Oliver choked up a bit. "He was like a father and big brother wrapped up together. No question was too small. He always made me feel like I was making progress, like learning to ride a bike for the first time over and over. He'd celebrate every step I took. But, He never let me settle as if I had arrived. There was always more. But, that didn't frustrate me. I sensed and then discovered that every bit I learned was like a surprise. He constantly amazed me. I began to realize how Mary lived in that world of amazement and wonder. I had belittled it but now I know. There is truth in wonder. And more importantly, there is a wonder to truth."

"Oh, Oliver, to hear you tell it makes me remember. This must be why the Maker gave us the songs. It is to help us remember when other noises harsh and cruel proclaim the Lie. They seek to drown out the songs and the Story. The songs are for our hearts to remember and not be afraid."

"Ah, Snoop. Thank you so much for reminding me. Keep doing it. It is so easy to slip back into this world. I need His Word renewed in me daily. Give me this day my daily bread."

"Truly." Snoop whispered.

"Yes, friend, indeed. Truly."

The two of them spent the rest of the flight together. For a while they sang and played. They recounted times on the Island. And in all of it, they expressed the grateful memories that they knew they would need for the remainder of the journey.

♦ ♦ ♦ ♦ ♦ ♦ ♦

Brandon spent some time researching Osgood and his holdings. He eventually succumbed to travel weariness and drifted off. Emma and George spent a few hours actually having a father-daughter conversation. George relished every moment. She finally drifted off to sleep leaning on her father. He fell asleep, smiling at the amazing change in Emma. In the stateroom, Oliver leaned back in his seat and went fast asleep. Snoop did what he did best. He moved about the cabin snooping. He even wandered into the pilot's area. They welcomed and were intrigued by his curiosity. They each laughed when Snoop would jump on their laps and look at them directly and make noises. There was one thing that caught them all by surprise. It was when he would look at them and appear to smile. But of course, ferrets don't smile, do they?

♦ ♦ ♦ ♦ ♦ ♦ ♦

The plane arrived in LA at 4:25 local time. Lanzig had arranged a travel service for them. The vehicle was one of stylish luxury, and of course, ample monitoring devices. With little to no baggage, they were on their way in no time. Brandon handed the driver the address of the jeweler.

Emma asked Brandon, "Mr. Rivers, where are we going and how did you find this place?"

Everyone listened as Brandon smiled, excited to provide an answer.

"Oliver gave me some very specific perimeters about who he wanted to see. It took me a little bit of looking to find a place. It's a store called Yacov's Fine Jewelry. It's a family owned and operated business. When I contacted them they gave all the right answers. The owner told me that he had family connections in the business in Jerusalem."

Oliver gave a thumbs up. "Great work, Brandon. What's the owner's name?"

"Yacov Levinstein."

"Well, I do hope Yacov can help me. If he can, he stands to do very well for himself."

They wondered what Oliver meant and how many more surprises their friend had. When they arrived, Oliver immediately opened the door.

"Emma, watch over Snoop while I go in. Brandon, you and George find us a good place to eat supper. I'd really like some Mexican food. Come back for me in thirty minutes."

Brandon said, "Wait. Why aren't any of us going in with you?"

"I have some important business to discuss with Mr. Yacov that is better handled by me alone."

"O.B., what are you up to?" George was concerned.

Oliver smiled. "Don't worry, George, it's just business."

"What kind of business?"

"Jewelry business, George. Now, find us a place with some good Mexican food. I haven't had it in a long time and can't wait. Oh, and Brandon, I trust you have some place for us to stay tonight. Make it nice, I'm treating."

With that he stepped out and shut the door. With his satchel in hand, Oliver walked into the store and out of sight. They looked at each other stunned.

Snoop snuggled up to Emma's ear and whispered to her.

"Surprises are such fun, are they not?"

Emma giggled and nodded her head. She couldn't help but think out loud.

"Uncle Ollie is sure full of surprises, isn't he?"

Brandon looked at George. "What is your friend up to?"

"I'm not at all sure. He's different in a lot of ways from before. But one thing that O.B. doesn't do is random. He's got something in mind and a reason he's not telling us yet. I trust him. I don't understand him, but I trust him."

He looked over to Emma who was smiling and petting Snoop. "I guess we have thirty minutes to find a good Mexican restaurant and a nice place to stay tonight."

He turned to Brandon and then to the driver. "Anyone have some suggestions?"

The driver chimed in, "Sirs, I can't park here. May I suggest we go somewhere to discuss this?"

And they did.

◆ ◆ ◆ ◆ ◆ ◆ ◆

The shop seemed empty when Oliver walked in. Behind the counter was a gentleman in his early sixties. His hair was short and black and graying gracefully. He had a dark brown kappah perched on his head and a light tan sweater, obviously hand knitted. When he spotted Oliver, he smiled contagiously and immediately lifted his hands in greeting.

"Ah, Dr. Cohen, what a privilege to meet you. When I received the call from your friend I was speechless. To think that such a famous person as yourself would come to my shop. You look in fine health for someone lost for so long and considered dead." He laughed at his own joke.

"Now, how can I help you?"

"As I'm sure Mr. Rivers mentioned, you do have business connections in Israel?"

"Yes, yes of course. It is a cousin from my wife's side. We often trade good buys and designs. Fine people, even in such troubling times they still seem to be doing well. But, what do you have in mind?"

Oliver placed his satchel on the counter. He reached in and pulled out a small exquisite dark blue velvet pouch. The edges were trimmed in gold twine. Oliver held the pouch by its dark red pull string. He looked and spotted the black display pad. He opened the pouch and carefully poured out the contents on the pad.

Yacov's eyes widened as he looked down. Seven different but elegant gems glistened before him on the pad. They varied in size and color, but Yacov's eyes were glued on the gems. He reached into his pocket and pulled out a short glass rod. He used it to move each of the gems on the pad, taking his time with each one. He then reached into his sweater pocket and pulled out a lighted loupe and tweezers. One by one he carefully lifted each gem to inspect them. He never said a word but with each gem he gasped and his hand slightly trembled.

When he had completed his inspection he pushed the pad back in Oliver's direction and let out a soft sigh.

163

"I must first ask you, where did you get these?"

"On my journey. On the island I was on these last fifteen years. You might say they were a gift from the Island."

"Do you know what you have here?"

"Not really. That's why I am here. And why I need your help."

Yacov rubbed his hands together. He looked out through his shop window.

"Excuse me a moment."

Yacov quickly walked to the door and locked it and returned behind the counter.

"First of all, Dr. Cohen, let me suggest you get these somewhere safe. Never in all of my years in this business have I seen such a collection. It is not an exaggeration to say that the value of these seven gems represents millions of dollars."

"Really?"

"Yes, really!" There was excitement in his voice. "For instance, see this elegant green oval stone?"

Oliver nodded.

"This is called jadeite. It is among the rarest of gems. The intensity of the color and the high degree of transparency tells me that this could easily sell for one to three million dollars."

His forehead had beads of sweat and his eyes almost glared at Oliver. "And you say that these come from the island you were on?"

Oliver nodded.

"But it is already marvelously prepared. Who did the work on these jewels? It's masterful."

The question in Yacov's eyes demanded an answer.

"Well, don't look at me. I didn't do it."

Yacov looked hard into Oliver's eyes. "No, of course not. But it is a mystery, is it not?"

Oliver smiled, hoping Yacov would press no further. Yacov saw that Oliver had nothing else to say.

Pointing down to the gems, he continued his comments.

"This is a red diamond. Again, beautifully cut and with amazing clarity. Easily worth a million, maybe more. This small black stone is called serendibite. Exquisite and also worth from point five to one point five million. You also have a blue garnet. What a marvelous stone it is. It changes color under different lights. Most magnificent. Its size and quality should easily fetch two million. This beautiful blue stone here is called grandidierite. While not as rare as the others, the delicate cut and brilliance make it rare and valuable. One hundred thousand. Ah, among my favorite of stones, the sapphire. The color of your stone is unlike any I have ever seen. There is absolutely no indication of flaw or heating. Cast with the right diamonds it would be fit for a queen. And last, but not least, is this diamond. Like the others, the quality is unlike anything I have ever seen. Its size and shape would bring a large sum."

Yacov glanced up, looking exhausted. "Now my question for you is, how can I help you?"

Oliver slyly smiled. "Perhaps we can help each other. You are right when you say that I don't need to travel with such a treasure trove. I am traveling to Israel. I wish to sell these and I need your assistance."

Yacov rubbed his forehead. "Dr. Cohen, you seem like a fine man. No prejudice intended but your name as well as your story made me interested to see you. But I am in no position nor do I have the resources to carry out a transaction of this magnitude."

Oliver chuckled. "Yacov, I realize that. I don't want you to be the buyer. Instead, I need you to be my steward in the matter. And for your help I will offer you twenty percent commission. If your friend in Israel sells an item you may add another ten percent and divide the full commission with him."

Yacov looked at Oliver with his mouth slightly gapping. It was obvious that Yacov was doing calculations in his mind.

"Why Israel?"

"It is because I am going there. And in time, I will need funds."

Yacov looked down at the gems. "So explain this to me. How will this work?"

"I am leaving the stones with you. You and your relatives seek buyers for the stones. Extract your commissions and have the remaining funds available to me in Israel. In the mean time, I need some funds now and the gems are security."

"You leave the gems with me?" He stuttered slightly as he said it.

"Yes."

"You would trust me?"

Again Oliver chuckled and put his hands on Yacov's shoulders.

"Yacov, you seem to be a good man. Your word is enough. Trust me when I tell you that you do not want to betray this trust I give you."

Yacov backed off. "Sir, are you threatening me?"

Oliver smiled and shook his head. "No, Yacov, I am not threatening you. It is a warning. Before God, you must believe that I trust you. And before God, you must not betray that trust. You stand to make a good deal of money. But, the money will do you no good if you betray your word."

Oliver looked directly into Yacov's eyes. "Yacov, God has chosen to give you a gift. Don't allow greed to harm you. If you do well, there is much more in store for you; things even more valuable than these precious stones."

The gentleness in Oliver's voice and touch unnerved Yacov. He almost trembled as he looked into Oliver's eyes.

"Who are you?"

Every feature on Oliver's face communicated his pleasure. "A friend bearing gifts and a hope for better things."

The words quieted Yacov. He rubbed his chin and then his forehead.

"I can't exactly say why, but I trust you. And it is obvious you trust me. So, how do we proceed from here?"

"I leave the gems with you now. I need thirty thousand dollars now. Put it in three envelopes of ten thousand each. Later when I am in Israel I'll need another fifty thousand. We'll work out arrangements for future funds as the jewels are sold."

Yacov nodded while looking down at the gems. He still couldn't believe what was happening.

"Very well. Let me put these in the safe and get you some money."

Yacov carefully picked up the gems and placed them back in the velvet pouch. He retreated to the back and returned shortly. Yacov handed Oliver three envelopes with the money. They exchanged the information each would need to keep in contact.

Oliver reached over the counter and they shook hands. Yacov

was still a bit stunned by what was occurring.

Oliver then reached over and placed his hands on top of Yacov's head.

"May the blessing and protection of God be upon you. May He give you the eyes to see the wondrous gifts He has for you. And may His light touch your heart in dark days. Truly."

SIXTEEN

A little over thirty minutes later, the group was back to pick up Oliver. He had his arm around Yacov's shoulder when they pulled up. Yacov nodded and wiped tears away from his eyes as Oliver finished speaking to him. They embraced and Oliver walked up to the car and got in.

George couldn't restrain his curiosity. "What was that all about? Had you known this gentleman before?"

Oliver nonchalantly answered, "No."

"Well it seems otherwise. And really, Oliver, what did you come here for?"

"Like I said, business."

George squinted and shook his head.

"Business? What kind of business? You've been gone, assumed dead for fifteen years. What business could you possibly have? And speaking of business, I need to call my office. If I'm going to go to the other end of the world with you, I need to let someone know."

Oliver snickered at his friend. "George, don't worry so much."

Emma began thinking out loud. "I suppose I need to let the school know that I'm dropping out for a semester."

George jumped in. "Wait a minute. Oliver, before Emma drops

out and I call my office, you need to let us know something. I know you told me about this important mission you're on, a treasure hunt and all. But what are we getting ourselves into?"

Oliver ceded the question. "Fair enough. Deciding whether you wish to join requires a little more than blind faith. How can I say this?"

They were all ears.

"I know some of you may view this with some skepticism, but remember I told you that on the Island I encountered the Lord. He told me that He had things for me to do. He told me that on my return I was to go and find... no recover something, something which I would need."

"Do you know what it is that you are after?"

"Not really."

"What do you mean?"

"Well, it means that I don't know what it is but I know that it's something I will need in order to continue the mission He has for me."

Brandon finally spoke. "Do you know what that mission is?"

Oliver slowly nodded his head. "My mission involves the declaration of His Story."

George asked, "You mean like a preacher or something?"

"Not exactly."

Oliver paused, rubbing his chin a few times.

"Look, I understand your confusion. The whole world is in a state of chaos and fear. But it is going to get worse. God wants His Story communicated in a very clear and powerful way before it's too late."

"Too late for what?" It was Brandon and his voice had an edge to it. "Are you talking end of the world, apocalyptic stuff? Is that what you mean by 'too late?'"

Oliver's voice deepened. The intensity in his eyes surprised everyone. "When someone dies, it's too late to respond to God's message. Many have died and many more will soon die. The end is coming. People need to hear and know."

Brandon wondered for a moment if he had attached himself to a delusional prophet of doom.

"Oliver, is this some type of end-times cult you're trying to create? Did you have a vision of some kind and we're all supposed to believe and follow you?"

Oliver realized Brandon's train of thought.

"Guys, I'm not looking for any followers. You asked about what I'm doing and I told you. None of you have to go with me. But with or without you, I am going."

No one responded. Then Emma softly spoke.

"I don't know about anyone else, Uncle Ollie, but I believe you. I trust you. Or better said, I trust in the God who is sending you. I don't yet know how to explain it, but He is moving me to go with you."

George looked at his daughter. He hardly recognized her. In her eyes was a softness he had not seen since she was a little girl. That look was enough for George. "I'm not saying I believe what you're saying. But I'm inclined to go with you because the two people I love most in this world are determined. So I'm still in."

Brandon looked away and rubbed his chin. "In for a penny, in for a pound."

Suddenly there was a cough from the driver in the front seat. "Don't mean to interrupt. I can't stay parked here. Can someone tell me where you want to go in the immediate future?"

The comments broke the tension. Even Brandon laughed and handed him the address of the restaurant. He turned to Oliver.

"You said you wanted Mexican, so Mexican it is."

"Great. And remember, it's my treat."

"How do you have any money?"

"Don't you remember? I just completed some business with Yacov. I have money."

Emma giggled. "Uncle Ollie."

He smiled. "Oh girl, you haven't seen anything yet."

George responded with a deep breath.

Snoop cuddled up to Emma's ear and whispered, "What is Mexican?"

Emma snickered softly. She cuffed a hand over her mouth and whispered back. "Don't worry, you'll love it."

The five of them had a wonderful time at the restaurant. To start off, the greeter questioned if he could allow Snoop to enter. Then someone recognized Oliver. They were all quickly escorted in and word spread throughout the restaurant. Much of the evening people came up and asked for autographs or wanted to take a photo with them.

The restaurant featured a Mariachi band. When the band came to their table things became very lively. Those around them watched as Snoop danced first on the table and then on the floor. Before long, some tables were moved aside as customers joined Snoop on the newly created dance floor. Snoop was an instant star as he danced and seemed to be singing to the music. Emma laughed so hard she practically fell out of her chair.

Snoop's new celebrity status prompted the kitchen staff to prepare a special plate just for him. Snoop discovered that he liked avocados and cheese very much.

In all of the excitement no one noticed Brandon sending and receiving messages. Yaunt let him know that rooms and transportation were arranged for the group.

The owner would not allow Oliver to pay for their meal. All he wanted was a photo with all of them. Oliver did leave a very large tip, which did not go unnoticed by George and Brandon.

◆ ◆ ◆ ◆ ◆ ◆ ◆

Emma cradled Snoop in her arms as they walked out. She looked around.

"Where's our car?"

Brandon answered, pointing to an even larger black Mercedes parked in front of them. "It's right here. It will take us to the hotel. Don't worry. Everything is arranged. Our bags are already delivered to our rooms."

George was impressed. "Wow, Brandon, you've been busy tonight. Anything else you want to tell us?"

"Only that we need to get in and get some rest. We'll meet Mr. Yaunt after breakfast tomorrow in his suite. So, let's go."

Oliver smiled as he held his satchel closely strapped around his shoulder. He whispered a short prayer as he wondered about what part Mr. Yaunt would play in the upcoming events.

♦ ♦ ♦ ♦ ♦ ♦ ♦

In the morning a message was delivered to each of their rooms. They were to meet in a certain suite where breakfast was waiting for them. As they arrived, the look on their faces betrayed the weariness each of them felt. The only exception was Snoop. He was on Oliver's shoulder. He immediately leaped off and scurried around the room sniffing, adding an occasional flip for good measure.

The suite had a large dining area where an ample breakfast waited. It seemed no expense had been spared on their behalf. Personal impressions were muted by their shared experience of jet lag. They ate silently with only an occasional sigh. All but Snoop, who seemed immune to jet lag and only expressed excitement with having new experiences and foods. Finally, after eating his fill, he cuddled on Emma's lap who had made her way to a large billowy chair. Brandon and George found couches for their naps.

As the others were drifting off, Oliver went to a corner and sat on the floor. He closed his eyes, but not in sleep. He prayed.

♦ ♦ ♦ ♦ ♦ ♦ ♦

Yaunt and Lanzig sat in an adjoining suite watching the group on a monitor.

Yaunt looked over to Lanzig. "I think I'll give them about an hour to rest before I go see them. A little rest, but not too much. I can use the fatigue of jet lag to my advantage, especially with the good doctor. Don't you think?"

"You always want an advantage whether with an adversary or prey. Now, the doctor remains a bit of an enigma."

"How so?"

"In my briefings with Li and recordings he has sent, there are many questions. For instance, why does Oliver appear so young and vigorous after fifteen years?"

"Some people retain a youthful appearance. Good genes."

"No, that's not it. I researched his family and neither his father, mother, nor extended families exhibited such characteristics. Even photos of him before his disappearance revealed a normally aging man. In fact, he appears even younger than when he left. Maybe something on this island provided such effects. If that is the case, then the location of this island is valuable. There must be an explanation."

Yaunt listened and pondered Lanzig's comments.

Lanzig continued. "Also, we had hoped Brandon would provide more direction to our long lost doctor. But it is the doctor who has assumed command of this band of travelers. And look, even now."

He pointed to the monitor.

"See how he sits separate from the group. What is he doing?"

"He's sleeping."

"No, he's not sleeping. Look closely. His lips are moving. It's like he's talking."

"Maybe he's meditating."

"No, you've heard him. He's praying. That's what he's doing. This man has certainty. He truly believes what he has told the others. He thinks that he can talk to God."

"So? He's delusional."

"Perhaps, but I have dealt with such people before. They are not easily swayed. They are unpredictable."

"Yes, I see what you mean. But the world is full of such religious dreamers. What does it get them? They are perpetual victims of those with true power. There is nothing they have that cannot be taken from them."

"This is true. But, I don't want to underestimate an opponent. Li was caught off guard and I don't intend for it to happen to me. That's why I have my questions."

"All of those are interesting but let's not lose sight of what we are after. You remember what we heard him say in the car last night? He is looking for something. This must be what Osgood is after as well. It is what you and Li need to concentrate on."

"Yes, of course. The doctor is the goose that leads us to the golden egg."

"Speaking of Li, how is his injury?"

"He is fine. I think his ego suffered the greater wound; all the more motivation. We leave this afternoon to complete arrangements in Israel."

Lanzig looked at the monitor as the group rested.

"This band of treasure hunters has no idea of the resources and powers they are up against."

Yaunt smiled. "Nor will they until it's too late."

They looked at each other and then turned their attention back to the monitor quietly releasing low, nefarious snickers.

♦ ♦ ♦ ♦ ♦ ♦ ♦

Oliver slowly opened his eyes. He looked up at a corner of the room at what appeared to be a typical smoke alarm. Somehow he knew otherwise. An all too familiar presence was about. He recognized it like the shadow of a coming change in seasons. A part of him wondered if he was ready. He closed his eyes and softly whispered the name. Immediately, he remembered.

♦ ♦ ♦ ♦ ♦ ♦ ♦

He had spent the night in a troubled sleep. It was a rare occurrence on the Island. But the troubles melted as he softly whispered the name.

The night before by a pond in the Lord's garden, the conversation had centered around Oliver's future mission. Though the Lord was short on specifics, it was clear that the coming task would test him.

In His deep soft ageless voice, the Lord asked. "Are you frightened? I will be with you. You will never be alone."

He looked up into those eyes; eyes that were always a perpetual mystery and provision. Questions melted in his heart as he gazed into windows that never ceased to amaze and lay him low.

"Forgive me. I don't doubt You. It is me. This task is so large. It is my failure that I fear.

He smiled. "And so you should. Such fear will allow you to rely on My resource rather than your own. That is always better than overconfidence. Self-reliance has caused countless failures."

"But I want to be brave in the task."

"And you will be. For I will provide you with all the courage and boldness you need. It will be beyond what you can imagine. I am your provision. Never forget this. Whenever you sense trouble or the sense of being overwhelmed, remember Me. I am as close as the mention of My name."

"Is it that simple?"

"Simple? Yes. But you may not always find it easy. You are gifted in many ways. But these gifts can often complicate the simple."

Oliver nodded. "And when I complicate the simple?"

"Call out to Me and I will make it simple again."

Oliver pondered as the Lord got up to leave.

As the Lord walked, away Oliver whispered to himself. "Close as the mention of Your name."

The Lord stopped and turned.

Oliver looked up. Those eyes once again captured him. His heart swelled as if he could hear the cheers of a roaring crowd. The words were clear as he watched the Lord's lips move to form the words. "Well done, truly."

The Lord slowly clapped His hands as He turned and walked away.

SEVENTEEN

Brandon could see that Yaunt wanted to meet the group on his terms. He had received a message about the meeting. He led the group to Yaunt's suite. When they walked in, it was everything Brandon had expected, extravagance to impress. It occupied half of the hotel's top floor. There were fresh flower arrangements appropriately scattered. Yaunt sat in the main room on a ten foot long leather couch. The windows behind him provided a panoramic view of the city. With his arms stretched out, he sat as if he were in command of everything behind him.

They all scanned the vastness of the suite. The whole scene had its desired effect on all of them, all except Oliver. With Snoop perched on his shoulder, Oliver quietly sighed. He had witnessed true power. In Yaunt he saw the pretention of power.

Brandon immediately made his way to his benefactor. He knew how the game was played.

"Mr. Yaunt, what a pleasure to finally meet you. I want to thank you and, of course, Mr. Osgood, for your support of my project."

Yaunt slowly got to his feet. He gave Brandon a smile of controlled condescension. He shook Brandon's hand while his eyes scanned over his shoulder toward Oliver.

"So this is the famous Dr. Oliver Cohen?"

Yaunt stepped around Brandon and approached Oliver, who remained standing where he had entered. Yaunt smiled at the others as he made his way to Oliver.

Snoop leaned down and whispered to Oliver. "I sense it in him, Oliver."

"Yes." He whispered.

Yaunt reached out his hand. "Dr. Cohen, what an honor it is to meet you."

Oliver only gave a small nod.

Yaunt stepped back. "My, you certainly look fit for someone lost at sea for fifteen years."

"Actually, I wasn't at sea."

"Yes, of course, an island. I heard your interview from Australia. How fortunate to be rescued after all these years."

"It most certainly was an amazing rescue."

"Yes. Well, let's come and sit together and discuss this journey you wish to make and Brandon's project, shall we?"

Yaunt led them out onto a patio. There was a small fountain flowing into a twelve-foot long lap pool. Chairs were arranged around a serving table with assorted beverages, fruit, and snacks. Snoop immediately leaped from Oliver's shoulder. He scurried over to the table and grabbed an apple and began to enjoy it by the fountain.

Emma chuckled and walked over to keep him company.

"Well, Dr. Cohen, your companion certainly knows what he wants."

"He's no stranger to adventure. Everything about our world is new to him."

"Yes, of course. Well, let's all sit down. If anyone desires some refreshment, please help yourself."

They all declined and began finding a place to sit. Yaunt made sure to place himself between Brandon and Oliver. George sat on the other side of Oliver closest to where Emma and Snoop were. Emma whispered to Snoop who was busy with the apple. She got up, picked up Snoop, and walked over to sit next to her father.

Before anyone said a word there was a knock on the door. Yaunt wondered who it might be. After another series of knocks, Brandon immediately recognized the pattern.

"Excuse me. That's my cameraman. I asked him to join us so you could all meet him. I'll be right back."

Before Brandon could reach the door, another series of even louder knocks began. He quickly opened the door to stop the pounding.

There stood Freddy. Most times Freddy was impressive at first glance. He stood six feet three, had light brown hair with hints of sun-lightened blonde and light blue eyes. Instead, Freddy resembled the pair of wrinkled pants he was wearing. His hair was barely managed and his eyes were somewhat glazed.

He reached over and put his right hand on Brandon's cheek, smiling a bit too broadly. In a slow and slightly slurred voice, "Hellloo, Brandy."

"You're drunk."

"Just a couple. You know, a little to celebrate our working together again. Lighten up. Don't worry; I'll be ready for the work. I'm always ready for the work."

"Yeah, I know that. If you weren't so good you wouldn't be here. Now get yourself together. The guy financing us is here and I need you to behave yourself."

Freddy forced himself straight and saluted. "You betcha." Freddy finger-combed his hair and hand pressed his shirt. It was the best he could do.

Brandon closed his eyes and shook his head. "Let's go."

When they walked onto the patio everyone turned toward them. Yaunt gave a dismissive glance before looking off. George and Emma looked at each other. Brandon measured everyone's expressions and forced himself two steps forward. Freddy squinted in the bright light and didn't move.

Brandon stopped before speaking. "Hey, everyone, I want you all to meet Freddy Collins. He is our cameraman.

Oliver looked steadily at Freddy who was rubbing his eyes, trying to stand up straight.

Oliver suddenly got up from his chair and walked right up to Freddy. Freddy continued to squint as he tried to focus on the man approaching him.

Freddy recognized Oliver. He reached out to shake his hand. "Ah, so you're the man back from the dead?"

Oliver looked directly into Freddy's eyes. He reached up and took hold of Freddy's face. He shook it only slightly. "Freddy. Wake up, Freddy."

Immediately Freddy was sober and alert.

Freddy blinked in stunned disbelief. Instant sobriety was a new experience for him. It was like someone had slapped him awake. He took in a deep breath and shook his head.

His focus was clear. He looked at Oliver in astonished perplexity. He wondered if the man in front of him had pulled off some form of hypnosis on him.

Oliver smiled as he stood before Freddy. "Good to meet you, Freddy." He turned and walked back to his chair.

Brandon continued with his fake smile. He looked over at Oliver and then back to Freddy. "Well, let's all have a seat, shall we?"

Freddy sat next to Brandon and provided a courtesy smile to everyone. Snoop quickly moved from Emma's lap and onto Freddy's. He got on his hinds and looked directly at Freddy.

Freddy's eyes rounded wide as Snoop smiled and tilted his head to one side.

Freddy looked up at Emma and chuckled. "Nice little pet you have here."

Emma, "Oh, he's no pet."

Oliver added. "No, he's my friend."

Freddy looked at Oliver. He was still trying to coalesce the last few moments. He searched for an explanation for what had occurred but none came. With an awkward smile pasted on his face, Freddy sat silent. He didn't know what to do with his hands as Snoop cuddled on his lap.

Emma chuckled. "Well, Freddy, it seems Snoop likes you."

Oliver added. "He doesn't do that with everyone. He must see something in you he likes."

Freddy shrugged his shoulders and smiled.

"Well." It was Yaunt. His voice was louder than normal. "Dr. Cohen, about your trip."

"There's no need for the Doctor title. Oliver will do."

"Very well. Oliver. As you probably know, arrangements are in place for the trip. Our guide will meet us when we arrive in Tel Aviv."

Oliver did not miss the "we" and neither did Brandon.

"You said, 'we'? Are you joining us?"

"Yes, Brandon. As I mentioned, Mr. Osgood is very interested in the Doctor's, I mean Oliver's, life and story. He instructed me to make sure that you all have everything you need for your project. He was very specific on that point."

Snoop noticed Freddy moving so he jumped off his lap and went to Emma.

Freddy pulled out a small camera from his pocket. He got up and began filming. His instinct told him that his job had started.

Brandon noticed Yaunt's frown at the sight of a camera.

"Mr. Yaunt, pay no attention to Freddy. Think of him as background. He's simply capturing moments he thinks might be useful. It doesn't include audio, does it Freddy?"

"Naw, filler for the narration. You tell the story. I just provide the pictures. Can't have too much footage. Like he said, just ignore me."

For the first time Emma wondered what sort of person Freddy was behind his carefully crafted facade. She was determined to find out.

Yaunt continued. "Very well. I suppose you can think of me like Freddy. I'm not here to be in the way. I simply want to make sure you have everything you need. With that cleared up, when would you like to leave?"

Oliver answered. "As soon as possible; today if we can."

Freddy lowered his camera. "I need to know the terrain and it will take a few hours to gather the equipment I need."

"Oliver, what about three this afternoon? We will reach the east coast by evening, refuel and fly overnight. We refuel in France and then continue on to Israel."

Oliver looked to Freddy who gave an affirmative shrug. "Sounds like a plan."

"One other thing before you leave." Yaunt leaned toward Oliver. "What exactly are we going to Israel and Jordan for?"

"Oh, let's not spoil the surprise. Think of it as an adventure that will answer everyone's curiosities." He coyly smiled.

Emma overheard Snoop whisper. "Very clever, Oliver. Curiosity is always a good invitation to an adventure."

The others exchanged glances. Freddy sensed that he was out of the loop of an inside joke. He whispered to himself, "Whatever."

The group agreed to meet at the airport well before their 3:00 pm departure time. Brandon and Freddy remained at the hotel to work on their plans. Oliver, Snoop, George and Emma took off for some area shops to gather clothing and supplies they would need. This included a sports store to secure some desert gear. Even in mid-September, the climate in Israel and Jordan would tend to be on the warm side. Brandon had offered to provide funds for their needed items but Oliver rejected the offer. Both George and Emma smiled in surprise as Oliver freely purchased all they needed in cash. Within two hours they were stocked up with bags in tow and heading to the airport.

Even with the LA traffic, they arrived one and a half hours before their departure. Once again they were at the private charter area of the airport. After clearing a modified security they were driven to their plane. They spotted Freddy inventorying his equipment while Brandon was having an animated conversation with Yaunt.

♦ ♦ ♦ ♦ ♦ ♦ ♦

The whole effect of the jet's design and logo created the impression that this was an elite class of travel.

Yaunt broke off his conversation with Brandon. He walked over to the group as they were unloading.

Yaunt scanned their luggage. "Ah, excellent. I trust you were able to find what you needed?"

"Yes, I think so." Oliver answered. Emma had Snoop on her shoulder while George helped a man taking their luggage.

Yaunt noticed how Oliver was looking over the jet. Although not much smaller than a large commercial airliner it was altogether unique in its design. The beautiful pearl white body of the jet glistened in the afternoon light with a large logo emblazoned on the tail. The logo appeared to be a stylized O. With closer inspection another uncertain letter or symbol was blended into the logo. Oliver tried to decipher it but couldn't make up his mind. Even squinting at it, he couldn't decide if it looked like the letters OG, the number six, or a face.

Yaunt smiled as he commented. "Quite a beauty, isn't it? Mr. Osgood was kind enough to allow us to use one of his personal jets for our journey."

"Mr. Osgood must be a wealthy man."

"Yes he is. He is extremely wealthy … and powerful." The last two words faded off into a whisper.

"Will we have a chance to meet Mr. Osgood?"

Yaunt looked at Oliver. He paused a moment before answering. "Perhaps." Then he smiled.

Yaunt stretched out his arms and spoke loud enough for everyone to hear. "Let's all get aboard."

Everyone made their way onto the plane. Freddy was giving the loaders a few choice instructions about his equipment before he boarded.

Yaunt led them into the center section of the plane. The first section consisted of six large seats not unlike a business class section of a commercial plane. The center section was a large lounge area. It took up as much as half of the plane. It had some seating areas, an eating area, and a general lounge and entertainment area. The last section was closed off. It contained private living quarters. Yaunt pointed to various seats.

"Please find a seat. I wanted to go over our travel itinerary with everyone and then allow you to relax for what will prove to be a long journey." He looked at his watch.

"We should leave here on time at 3:00 pm. We arrive in New York around 11:15 pm. We will be there about an hour for refueling and crew exchange. The trip to Paris is scheduled to leave around 12:30 am and arrive in Paris around 2:00 pm tomorrow. Again, we will refuel and change crews and hopefully depart for Tel Aviv by 3:00 pm. That should put us in Tel Aviv by around 7:30 pm local time tomorrow."

Yaunt looked up from the paper he was reading. "Altogether our trip involves nineteen to twenty hours of travel. I know you are still recovering from your earlier trip, so I suggest you take every opportunity to rest. As you can see, there is ample space and facility to do just that. A meal will be served about an hour into this first flight. If you desire anything at anytime, please don't hesitate to ask. The cabin attendants will be coming by and are at your disposal. Are there any questions?"

No one said anything. They all simply looked at Yaunt. They were also taking in the opulence of their surroundings. Yaunt was pleased that his guests were thoroughly impressed.

"Very well. I have some business to attend to and I will see you all later in the flight. Relax and enjoy yourselves."

He turned to leave when Freddy spoke up. "Pardon me, but do we have communication access on this flight?"

"Oh yes. You will notice net connection ports throughout. There is also a wireless net connection if you choose to use it."

"Excellent, thanks."

Yaunt nodded before walking to the back cabin area. Once there he went to a desk that was surrounded by three monitors. Each of the monitors displayed views from at least twelve cameras strategically placed throughout the plane. There were also listening devices planted into every seat and lounge area. Yaunt checked to make sure everything was being recorded. Looking at his watch, he knew it was time to report to Osgood. He could never predict his master's disposition. He wasn't sure if it was madness or manipulation. Either way, it kept him off balance.

They were in the air when he queued up the connection. He realized that it was around midnight in Switzerland. But Osgood's instructions were clear.

"I'm sorry to be calling so late, Herr Osgood, but you said call when we left…"

Without any acknowledgment, "Report."

"Yes, we are now leaving LA and should arrive in Tel Aviv tomorrow evening."

"Have you gained any information on Cohen's intentions?"

"Not yet. He is very clever. As far as I know he has not even revealed that information to the others in the group."

"What about Lanzig?"

"He should arrive in Israel very shortly. He is making the

necessary preparations for our arrival."

Osgood's voice slowed and intensified. "Listen to me very carefully Yaunt. The matters we are working on are extremely important to me. The sooner we discover his intentions, the better prepared we can be. I am leaving here for Israel shortly myself."

"You, sir?"

"Do not interrupt me."

"Sorry, sir."

"Contact me when you arrive. I will not meet with any of you unless and until I deem it necessary. You must find out what he is up to. Do you understand?"

"Yes, of course, sir."

Yaunt could hear Osgood's low sinister laugh. "I want this completed in such a way that when we have what we want, there is no connection to me in any way. I leave it to you and Lanzig in the disposition of anyone and anything that could make such a connection. Am I clear?"

"Absolutely, Master."

"Very good. Remember what I've told you. 'Power at any cost'."

Osgood ended the communication.

EIGHTEEN

Not long after takeoff Oliver called for Snoop to come to him. Snoop scurried over and made his way onto Oliver's shoulder. Oliver cuffed his hand over his mouth and very softly whispered. "Snoop, come close."

Snoop cuddled up while Oliver softly reached across as if to pet him. In a very low voice he continued to whisper. "Snoop, speak very softly. I want you to make your way to Emma and tell her something. Tell her that I think the plane is bugged and to be careful."

Snoop looked up at Oliver curiously and whispered, "Oliver, the area all around seems very clean. I have not seen or smelled any bugs on the plane."

Oliver chuckled and stroked his friend's back. "A bug refers to a very small listening device. I think that we are being monitored."

"Ah yes, I have sensed the presence with Mr. Yaunt. Truly sad."

"Well, the good thing about when you talk, no one but me and Emma understands."

Snoop snickered as he crawled down off of Oliver and made his way to Emma.

She welcomed Snoop as he jumped on her lap. Emma giggled as he positioned himself practically nose to nose. She always loved Snoop's playful ways.

Snoop whispered. "Emma, we must be careful to speak only in whispers. Oliver has said that he believes that bugs are among us."

Emma squinted a bit and looked up at Oliver. Without looking up, he was tapping on of his right ear with his finger. She understood. Emma cupped her hands over Snoop's face as if she were petting him. "Thank you." She then put Snoop on her shoulder. She got up and walked over to her father.

George looked up.

Emma yawned before speaking. "Dad, I think I'm going to take a nap before the meal. OK?"

"Sure." He was curious at Emma's announcement.

When she bent down to kiss him on the cheek, she whispered. "Uncle Ollie said there are bugs on the plane." She pecked him on the cheek. Then in a normal voice, "Please wake me up when the meal comes. Ok, Dad?"

He looked up at her and then to Oliver who was tapping his right ear. "You bet, honey, thanks."

He looked back down at a magazine he was reading. His mind immediately trailed off. He wondered what kind of intrigue or danger he and his daughter were involved in. A sense of calm came over him as he looked over at Oliver. His friend sat serene and smiling as he slowly nodded. He was suddenly very tired and decided to join his daughter in a pre-meal nap.

Oliver looked across the cabin. Brandon and Freddy were working at a desk, obviously planning. George quickly drifted off. Emma was fast asleep with Snoop on her lap purring. Oliver closed his eyes and began to pray. As he prayed, he again remembered the Island.

◆ ◆ ◆ ◆ ◆ ◆ ◆

Oliver had spent the morning playing with a few of the animals in the garden. He never heard a sound, but by the animal's reaction, he knew. The Lord was approaching. They all scurried up to Him. He took time to stroke each one and say a word to them before they delightfully ran off. He then came over to Oliver.

"Good morning, Oliver."

"Good morning, Sir." Oliver never tired of looking into those eyes. They never ceased to both humble and excite his heart.

"Today I want to talk to you about leadership. When you return, many people will look to you and your fellow witness for guidance. Some will even begin to look at both of you in ways that can harm their perspective. Admiration is one thing, but adoration is not something you should accept."

Oliver nodded.

"I will guide you, and you in turn will guide them. Accept that pattern and many problems are avoided. It is very important that whenever you sense a lack of direction, you waste no time in looking to Me."

"Master, I have little skill in leading people. I tend more toward hesitancy than overconfidence."

The Lord put His hand on Oliver's shoulder. "I am going to change everything about your life. I am not only calling you for this task, I am gifting you for it. You will begin to exhibit these gifts in ways that will surprise you at first. These gifts will embolden you. The danger always lies in becoming confident in the gift over the Giver. It is very easy to begin to rely on the gifts and forget the call. For in the calling, you are reminded of the nature of the call and Who called you."

"Master, I... I don't want to fail You."

He gently smiled. "And you shall not fail. Walk humbly before Me and all of these things will remain clear."

Oliver was amazed at the calm confidence that always filled him as he listened to the Master's voice.

◆ ◆ ◆ ◆ ◆ ◆ ◆

Oliver opened his eyes. He scanned the cabin. He suddenly looked directly at a certain spot.

In the back cabin, Yaunt was monitoring the lounge area. He watched as Brandon and Freddy worked on scripting ideas. He had seen and recorded everything from the time he had retreated to the back. No one seemed aware of being monitored. As he checked the screens, something caught his attention. Oliver was looking directly at the camera. With a sly smile he appeared as if he were posing for a picture. He then closed his eyes as if he were going to sleep.

This action unnerved Yaunt. He remembered the incident at the hotel. Was he imagining it or had Oliver found a way to detect what he was doing? He wanted an answer.

After a muted chuckle, Oliver decided that a short nap before the meal was a good idea. He quickly drifted off.

◆ ◆ ◆ ◆ ◆ ◆ ◆

Brandon, Freddy, and Yaunt remained awake while the others slept. The stewards moving around the cabin in preparation to serve the meal stirred the group. The meal was not the usual airplane variety. Both the taste and presentation were more akin to a fine restaurant. Snoop got excited when a large bowl of various fruit was placed as a centerpiece in the lounge area. Yaunt came out and mingled among the group. He attempted to stir up conversations trying to harvest information. But between enjoying the meal and the weariness of the group, his attempt only yielded small talk.

After the meal, the group went to the forward cabin and laid down to rest. Freddy, though not sleeping, reclined and watched a movie. Yaunt retreated back to his cabin and decided to rest. On occasion Snoop would slip away from Emma and wander about. He snacked on a small apple and then proceeded to sniff about wondering if he could find any of the bugs Oliver had spoken about. After a full hour of no success, he made his way back to the front and curled up on a pillow Emma had set on the floor next to her.

♦ ♦ ♦ ♦ ♦ ♦ ♦

A similar jet departed from Bern. Osgood sat on the floor of the back cabin. Swaying back and forth in a trance, he whispered a low guttural chant. The air filled with the smoke of bitter incense. The air thickened as his repetitive chanting intensified. The lights in the cabin were dim but a growing darkness was accumulating in one corner. Within the darkness, a darker shadow began to form.

From within the shadow a deep and dark voice spoke. "Osswaltt... Ossswaalltt."

Osgood's unfocused eyes slowly opened. "Yes, Master."

The shadow moved toward him and finally engulfed him. Within the envelope of darkness, the voice continued. "You have found the man. Now you must obtain the prize. Let nothing stop you."

Osgood closed his eyes while swaying back and forth. "Yes, Master."

The darkness pressed in on him. He could feel a cold touch grasp his left forearm. "Remember what you seek ... Power."

He was jolted by a surge that jerked his body practically off the floor. He collapsed on his side. The darkness was gone.

He rolled onto his back and lay there as if in a drug induced stupor. He opened his mouth to quietly laugh. A small puff of black smoke drifted up off of his tongue and into the air.

♦ ♦ ♦ ♦ ♦ ♦ ♦

Oliver's eyes suddenly opened. He knew what he had to do. He slipped out of his seat and onto his knees. He looked at his hands as they softly trembled. He felt a familiar and oppressive heaviness. He pressed his face into his hands and whispered the Name. Gone in an instant, the oppression replaced by a calm inner breeze. A tear ran down his cheek as he remembered.

♦ ♦ ♦ ♦ ♦ ♦ ♦

It was late afternoon. From the highlands, he could see the landscape of the entire island. The sun was low and not long from setting. He leaned against a rock as he took in the fading golden light.

He smiled as he sensed His presence behind him.

"Beautiful, isn't it?"

Without turning he answered. "Yes Sir."

He trembled as he watched the scene and realized that its Author was standing behind him.

"You've created it to always be different, yet always consistent."

"Very good, Oliver. You are learning quickly."

Oliver turned. "In some ways it's like a refresher course. Often times Mary would talk to me about You. I pretended to dismiss what she said. It would make her sad. But part of my heart knew. I would argue with myself, but I could never really shut it off and lay it to rest."

The Lord continued looking into the distance. "I was pursuing you, Oliver. I was laying the seeds. I also knew that it would require you coming here to complete your rescue."

Oliver took a deep breath. "Part of me would prefer to let this go on forever."

"And it will once you have completed your part of the Story."

"My part of the Story ..." The words faded as he slowly spoke them.

"I know you are wondering and somewhat frightened. That's not all bad. The reality and capacity of failure on your part is something you should comprehend. But understand this, I will not fail you. The Story will be written. Remember always where your true strength lies and you will know My victory."

Oliver looked down and remembered. "Yes ... always close."

Then they said it together. "Close as the mention of Your name."

◆ ◆ ◆ ◆ ◆ ◆ ◆

Oliver got up from his knees ready to rest. Before he closed his eyes he whispered a short prayer of thanks. He fell asleep quickly.

♦ ♦ ♦ ♦ ♦ ♦ ♦

No one stirred until the cabin lights came on and the pilot announced the beginning approach to Charles de Gaulle Airport. One by one, the seats came up and faces emerged. Snoop got up, stretched and jumped up onto Emma's lap.

A steward's voice came on. "If I can have your attention. We will be landing shortly. We will be in Paris for approximately one hour. During that time, government representatives will come on board. Please have your passports available. Now, if you would all prepare for landing. Thank you."

Freddy snickered. "Even flying fancy class, some things don't change."

♦ ♦ ♦ ♦ ♦ ♦ ♦

The late afternoon sun created more shadows than light as Li and Lanzig entered the walled Old City of Jerusalem through the Damascus Gate. They made their way down El Wad Road, in the Arab section of the city. Li checked his notes. The small alleys and paths coming off of the main road made it easy to miss what they were looking for. Before reaching Sheikh Rihan, Li spotted it. They stepped into the shop and made their way to the back. It was here that they found Amir Hasim.

Amir had a small table set up with some freshly brewed mint tea waiting for them. Though he was a young man in his early thirties, many years beyond that were written on his face. Lanzig recognized the look in his eyes.

"Come, sit my friends." Amir pointed to the two chairs.

Lanzig began to sit as Li quickly scanned the room.

Amir watched and smiled. "You need not worry, friend. We are alone and will not be disturbed. Sit please."

As Li took a seat, Lanzig extended a greeting. "As-salamu alaykum."

"Wa alaykumu as-salam. And thank you for the kind

consideration. Now I hear you are in need of a special guide both here and in Jordan?"

"Yes. There is a group arriving later today. The guide is for them. The group has a leader but that is not who you are truly working for. He will think that he is in charge, but you answer to me."

"Ah, I see, a little deception. That always makes it a bit more interesting."

"And the group must not know that such an arrangement exists."

"Yes, of course. And what does the group wish to see?"

"The leader of the group will let you know. Perhaps you have heard of him. He was recently found at sea after being lost for fifteen years."

Amir took a sip of tea. He put the cup down, nodding his head. "Yes, I remember seeing something about that. And you say that this man is the group leader?"

Lanzig nodded as he took a sip of his tea. He enjoyed both the taste and aroma.

"And what does such a man want to see in Jordan?"

"That is what we want you to find out."

Amir saw the desire in Lanzig's eyes. "This information is very important, is it not?"

Lanzig understood the game. He reached into his pocket and pulled out a bulging envelope. The flap was open and the money was visible. He slid it across the table.

Amir smiled as he bowed his head. Lifting his teacup with one hand, he took the envelope with the other. He slid it unto to his lap. "Most generous."

"You will receive two more similar envelopes at the completion of your work. Mr. Li will provide you with the means to contact us regularly. This is especially important when you find out what the leader is searching for. Remember, you work for me."

Amir bowed his head slightly and looked at the envelope on his lap. He placed his right hand over his heart.

"You have my undivided loyalty."

"We will make certain of it. We will be watching you at all times."

They both lifted their cups and took a sip. They understood each other very clearly. Mutual greed and distrust irrevocably bound them.

NINETEEN

It was the final leg and most everyone was either resting or drifting off to sleep. Earlier they had agreed they all needed a day to recoup. Oliver had suggested it and no one argued. The exhaustion of the last few days was catching up with them. Even Snoop's ever-cheerful eyes were droopy.

The first day after they arrived, they would have no set schedule. They could see some sights or simply do nothing. Oliver knew that they all needed it.

The lights in the cabin were dim. The only sound was the constant soft hiss of the jet gliding through the air. Oliver sat at one of the small worktables. A single beam lit up a small area in front of him. He looked out over the rest of the team. Yaunt was in his cabin. No one had seen him for hours. As Oliver's eyes moved from one person to another, he whispered a short prayer for each of them. He knew that all of them would face challenges in the days ahead.

After he finished the prayers, he reached down and picked up the satchel. He placed it on the desk. He put his hands over it and took a deep breath. He loosened the small leather string that kept it closed. He remembered the instructions he had received.

♦ ♦ ♦ ♦ ♦ ♦ ♦

Oliver sat beside a pond in the garden. As had become his habit, he had spent the morning reading and praying. In his peripheral vision he noticed some animals running. He knew the Lord was approaching.

He tossed a pebble into the pond and turned toward the Lord. He was stopping to pet the animals that had run to Him. Oliver also noticed something tucked under His arm.

Oliver waited. He knew the Lord had His own pace.

The Lord made His way to Oliver. Coming closer, Oliver saw that the Lord had a leather book in His hands. Something about His smile excited Oliver.

He suddenly felt like a little boy and the word that popped into his head was "Surprise!"

"Good morning, Oliver."

"Good morning, Sir."

"I have something for you."

Oliver jumped up as the Lord began to hand it over to him. The book-like satchel was about the size of a large coffee table book. The outside was made of dark and smoothly polished leather. It was held closed by a long leather string that wrapped around a button knob. As he rubbed his hands across the surface, it had the feel and smell of old.

Oliver wrapped his arms around the satchel as he looked at the Lord.

"Open it, Oliver."

He slowly unwrapped the string. He lifted the flap and opened it. One single blank leather page stretched across the width of the satchel book. It was stitched down the center of the page attaching it to the cover of the satchel. He stared down at the blank page, not knowing what to think. When he looked up, his perplexed look said it all.

The Lord smiled as He placed His arm around Oliver's shoulder. He pointed down at the book.

"This book will provide you with directions in part of your future journey."

"But there's nothing on it."

"Well, Oliver, that's because right now it's not necessary. But at the time when you need them, they will come."

The Lord then reached down and closed the book.

"Now seal up the book and keep it with you. Now, let's talk about faith."

◆ ◆ ◆ ◆ ◆ ◆ ◆

Oliver rubbed his hands across the cover. He slowly laid it open. A single blank leather page spread out across the entire inner surface of the satchel. He knew it was time. He took another deep breath, closed his eyes and whispered a prayer.

When he finished and opened his eyes, it began to appear. Almost like a developing photo coming into focus, lines emerged. The image darkened and then stopped.

Oliver smiled as he looked at a map of Israel and the surrounding countries. He turned the book from landscape to portrait orientation. The cartography was exquisite. The geographic landmarks were intricately drawn. There were no roads or highways on the map and only one city was marked and labeled.

Oliver looked at the map in amazement. He placed his hand over his mouth to muffle his excitement. When he finally lowered his hand, he whispered the name of the marked city. "Tel Aviv."

◆ ◆ ◆ ◆ ◆ ◆ ◆

Yaunt watched Oliver the entire time. He was irritated that the camera angle prevented him from seeing what was on the page of the open satchel-book. He saw that Oliver had said something. He ran the tape back and repeatedly played back the audio. He was unable to decipher what Oliver had whispered. Yaunt pounded the table in frustration.

Oliver took another deep breath and closed the satchel.

Yaunt looked at the live feed monitor.

Oliver had his hands over the closed satchel. He then looked straight at the hidden camera and smiled.

Startled, Yaunt jerked back in his seat. His eyes narrowed as he clinched his fists to the point that they shook. "How are you doing that?"

Oliver slowly moved his head back and forth, closed his eyes and reached over to turn off the overhead light.

♦ ♦ ♦ ♦ ♦ ♦ ♦

The plane landed in Tel Aviv at 7:35 pm local time. As everyone was gathering their things, Oliver pulled George, Emma, and Snoop together in a small huddle. He reached into his backpack and pulled out two envelopes. He handed one to George and one to Emma. They curiously looked at him and then at the envelopes.

George whispered. "O.B., what is this?"

"Money."

Oliver saw the questions on both their faces.

"Each envelope contains nine thousand dollars. I want you to carry them for me. You can return them to me after we get through customs."

They still had questioning looks.

"On your customs forms you are asked if you are carrying over fifteen thousand dollars. I didn't want to make liars or criminals out of you. At least not yet."

"What's that supposed to mean?" It was Emma this time.

"Relax. If you want to take some out to buy yourself something, feel free."

Emma saw the sly look in Oliver's eyes and snickered. She put the envelope in her purse.

Snoop whispered up to Emma. "Oliver is very clever, is he not?" She looked down and nodded.

♦ ♦ ♦ ♦ ♦ ♦ ♦

The limousine service Yaunt promised took them all to a beautiful hotel by the sea. Not long after getting to their rooms, they all collapsed and slept through most of the night.

The following morning George and Emma rested in their room and by the pool. Emma's new demeanor allowed for some much needed father and daughter time.

Snoop remained with Oliver the whole day. His presence attracted attention like that of a newborn. Many people walked up to him and asked about Snoop. A few even recognized them and wanted to take photos with them. By afternoon they made their way to the beach. The sounds and smell of the waves ignited memories for both of them. They ran and played and talked about the days on the Island. They sat singing together as they watched the sun sink into the waters.

"We may never do this again, my friend."

"That is perhaps true, Oliver. But even so, we can always remember it in the songs of the Story."

"You're so right. Mary tried to tell me. The music can be heard everywhere. Even though in this world, it is almost gone."

"But that is part of why you are sent, to sing them again to those who have forgotten. I begin to understand what the Keeper said about the sadness in this world. It is surrounded by the beauty of the Maker's work and has lost the songs."

Oliver added, "It's like having words that can't seem to come together for a complete song. You know something's missing and don't even know that it's the song."

"Truly sad, Oliver. Truly sad."

"Yes … and I remember that sadness. I also remember trying so hard to fill or cover up the sadness with anything. It would work for a while but then it always came back."

"Such memories are a great gift, Oliver. I know you will use them wisely."

"I certainly will try. But for now, I think it's time to get back. George and Emma are going to be looking for us soon."

Snoop tilted his head. "How do you know this, Oliver?"

Oliver chuckled. "I don't know. I just know."

"A great gift indeed."

Snoop popped up on Oliver's shoulder and hummed a familiar tune all the way back.

♦ ♦ ♦ ♦ ♦ ♦ ♦

Only a few minutes after getting back to the room, there was a knock on the door. Snoop smiled while Oliver tilted his head to one side and grinned.

"Come on in, the door's open."

As they came in, Emma had her arm wrapped inside her father's arm. Oliver could tell that they had enjoyed the day together. George looked like a man totally on holiday.

A tray with three fruit drinks, assorted fruit, along with the leather book sat on the coffee table.

Oliver waved them over. "Come on guys, have a seat."

George looked down at the drinks as he sat down.

"Were you expecting someone tonight?"

"Yeah, you two."

"But, … we just now decided to come over."

When Oliver smiled and shrugged, Emma giggled, not quite as surprised as her dad.

George grabbed one of the drinks and joined Emma, who had reached over for Snoop before sitting down.

"O.B., I want to thank you for the day. It's what we needed."

"Yeah, Uncle Ollie, we went to the beach and went shopping."

George grinned. "We used some of the money you gave us."

"Good, glad to hear it. I needed you to get some R & R. Our pace will pick up starting tomorrow."

"Where are we going, Uncle Ollie?"

"Jordan."

George chuckled. "Just like that? We're going into Jordan. You know, O.B., the Middle East was a hot bed when you left. Well, it's on fire now. I mean…"

"George," Oliver raised his hand. "this may be a little hard for you to understand, but current conditions don't interest me. We are going to Jordan."

George didn't want to argue with his friend, so he surrendered the point.

"OK, so we're going to Jordan. Exactly where in Jordan?"

"Let's see."

Oliver picked up the leather book. He untied the sting. Before opening it he signaled the two of them to move in close.

He whispered to them. "I have little doubt that someone is watching and listening. I need you to whisper and not over-react to what you see."

George and Emma traded looks and nodded.

Oliver slowly opened the book. A single blank leather page spread out across the book. George looked down and then up to Oliver with a question on his face. Oliver's eyes directed George to look back down. Once again, like a developing photograph, an image emerged.

George's eyes widened as a map slowly formed. The geographic marking left no doubt that it was the northern half of Israel. Along with the Sea of Galilee, Jordan River, and Dead Sea, three city names appeared from west to east; Tel Aviv, Jerusalem, and Ma'daba in Jordan.

Oliver put his finger on Ma'daba. "This is where we are going."

Oliver looked up at his friends. Emma was cuddling Snoop and smiling large. George could only rub his forehead as he looked at the image and then back at Oliver.

Oliver saw his stunned expression. He placed his index finger over his lips before reaching down to close the book.

"Why don't we go out on the patio, the evening lights are beautiful."

Oliver got up. He took a few steps and turned. He pointed his head to the patio and walked toward it. Emma nodded to her dad. Holding Snoop with one hand, she reached over, took her dad's arm and they followed Oliver.

♦ ♦ ♦ ♦ ♦ ♦ ♦

Yaunt, Lanzig and Li all watched the monitor. They had seen the whole thing.

Yaunt's eyes narrowed in anger. Li stared hard at the screen as he held his injured hand and rubbed the bandages.

Lanzig scratched his chin. "It's almost as if he knows we're watching and listening. Did Brandon tip him off?"

Li answered. "They haven't been in contact. I was on both him and Freddy. They were together all day and neither of them even used their phones."

Yaunt's voice was muted but firm. "He knows. Don't ask me how, but he knows."

Lanzig shook his head. "How? What's in that room is so

sophisticated that without the right equipment, you'd never find it. And anyway, I've studied this man. He is an amateur."

Yaunt looked over to Lanzig. "You're right, he is an amateur. But that doesn't change the fact that he knows. Even on the plane, it was like he knew not only that I was watching him, but when. It was unnatural."

Yaunt's phone buzzed. It was a message. He saw that it was from Osgood. "Send me a status report right away. When does the doctor plan to leave for Jordan? Reply immediately!"

Osgood's condescension irritated him to no end. But until he had the upper hand on the situation, he was stuck.

Yaunt saw Li still staring at the monitor.

"What do you think, Li?"

Li didn't turn away from the screen. He stared and continued to rub his hand. "I don't know how that man does what he does."

He turned to Yaunt. "But rest assured, I will find out. That I promise."

TWENTY

Oliver looked out at the lights of the beachfront hotels. He listened to the surf and spotted a few boats out on the water. The scene calmed him. George and Emma were behind him, waiting. When he turned, he saw the anxiety in George's eyes.

Oliver took a deep breath.

"Tomorrow is going to be a busy day. I have some things I need you to do for me."

He pulled a piece of paper out of his pants pocket and handed it to George.

"That's a list of some supplies we'll need for tomorrow. Get with the concierge and find out when and where you can get these by early tomorrow morning. Use the money I gave you."

George read through it. "Looks like someone's going camping or something."

Oliver chuckled. "You know me. I want to be prepared."

George affirmed with less than an enthusiastic nod.

"Guys, I know that I have been a bit vague at times. Some of that comes from the fact that I don't know everything that's going on. In the coming days, I may give you an instruction or command. It is very important that you do not doubt me. Your safety may very well depend on your following my instructions."

"Uncle Ollie, you sound like there's danger ahead."

Oliver paused a second. "Actually there is. But if you pay attention to what I say, you'll be fine. There are ... sinister forces at work. I don't know all the details, but I know they are there."

"O.B., what's all this about? What danger? What sinister forces?"

Oliver rubbed his chin. "What I am sent to do is very important. There are some who know this and want to stop me. I am at the beginning of a battle that will eventually take my life. But not until I have completed the task I have been given."

George and Emma looked at Oliver and then at each other in disbelief.

Snoop cuddled up to Emma's ear and whispered. "It is true. But do not be afraid. Listen to Oliver and do as he says. The One who protects him will protect you as well."

Emma trembled at what she had just heard. A tear rolled down her cheek as she stroked Snoop across the back. She slowly walked back inside.

George stood stunned as Oliver placed his arm around his shoulder.

"Don't be frightened, my friend. For some time now I have been preparing for this. I am not afraid. It's important that you listen carefully to the things I say. Rescue is available, but you must pay attention."

For George, the pieces of the puzzle were not fitting together. And yet, he saw in Oliver's eyes the confident strength he needed to trust.

He softly whispered, "Ok."

Oliver patted him on the back as George followed Emma back inside. Oliver turned back to look out into the darkness. As he hummed a tune, he didn't hear the tiny footsteps. Snoop crawled up on the patio chair next to him and joined in the song. Soon the words came and filled in the melody.

> *There is a road You bid me go,*
> *Beyond where I can see,*
> *Where love requires all I have,*
> *For steps You made for me.*

Once again Your voice says come
And do not be afraid.
Inviting me to walk with You,
Beyond where I can see.

♦ ♦ ♦ ♦ ♦ ♦ ♦

Almost everyone was in the dining area by 10:00 am. Freddy was hovering about, shooting footage of the group while Brandon and Yaunt conferred with Amir. George was sitting next to Emma. She was watching Snoop scurry about and entertaining them with several forms of flips. Everyone looked up when Oliver walked in. He immediately noticed the new member of the group, Amir, and walked to him.

Oliver reached out his hand. "You must be our guide?"

Amir rose and took his hand. "Yes, and Shalom, Dr. Cohen. Amir Hasim at your service." He bowed slightly.

"A pleasure to meet you, Amir, As-salamu alaykum."

Amir lower his head, "Wa alaykumu as-salam. You are so kind."

Oliver turned to the whole group. "I hope everyone is ready?"

Brandon responded. "Yes, Oliver. I have two vehicles waiting for us. What's our destination?"

Oliver looked at Amir. "We are going to Ma'daba."

Time seemed to stand still. It sounded like approaching thunder. Then the glasses on the tables began to vibrate. All of a sudden a rumble moved across the entire room and the ground vibrated underneath them. It lasted about ten seconds and then stopped.

Amir slowly nodded. "We've been having more of those lately. But do not be afraid, they have remained small and pose no danger."

Snoop jumped up to Emma and moved to her shoulder.

He whispered to her. "Oh my, what was that Emma?"

She smiled and replied out the side of her mouth, "Earthquake."

Snoop scanned the room. "He is speaking."

Emma and Oliver smiled. The others were humored by the curious actions of the creature.

Oliver then addressed everyone. "I'd like to leave in the next thirty minutes. I want to talk to Amir about our route. Everyone else can make sure that they're ready."

Yaunt nodded. "Oliver, I was just telling Brandon I will not be going on this portion of the journey. I have some business matters that need my attention. I have full confidence in Amir and his ability to get you there and back. Brandon will let me know if there is anything else needed. I'll make some calls to assure safe passage into Jordan. Amir, that would be the Allenby crossing, correct?"

Amir nodded and Yaunt left.

♦ ♦ ♦ ♦ ♦ ♦ ♦

Yaunt was out on the street when he called.

"They leave for Ma'daba in thirty minutes."

"Very good." The line went dead.

Yaunt exhaled his anger at Osgood. His conversation with Lanzig last night let him know that their agreement was still in place. Their treachery and its inherent danger made his fingers tingle.

♦ ♦ ♦ ♦ ♦ ♦ ♦

Osgood put away his phone and turned to Lanzig. They were in Jerusalem and had completed a late breakfast.

"They travel to Ma'daba. Yaunt will fly by helicopter to Jericho and we will cross over ahead of the group. Make the arrangements we spoke of earlier. Where is it that we meet up with our mercenaries?"

It's called Shunat Nimrim. It's just past the border crossing in Jordan."

"Are these men reliable? Can they be trusted?"

Lanzig smirked. "Trusted? No one can be truly trusted, Herr Osgood. But they can be bought. Desperation and fear keeps them in line. They understand that powerful hands will crush them if they fail. As for reliability, most of the group are highly trained and seasoned. I am also relying on numbers to make up for what some lack in skill."

"How many have you acquired?"

"Sixty as well as Li and myself."

"Very good, old friend. Very good."

Both men exchanged sinister grins. They both understood that their long relationship was built on their mutual distrust as well as their respect of the other's power. Only time would tell where their dangerous dance would end.

♦ ♦ ♦ ♦ ♦ ♦ ♦

Emma sat in the back seat of the second vehicle. She looked at the passing scenery as Snoop rested on her lap. Next to her, Freddy surfed some news stories on his phone. He finally put the phone down with an irritated puff. He looked over at Emma and Snoop.

"That's quite a pet you have there. How long have you had him?"

"Oh Snoop isn't my pet."

"Then who does he belong to?"

Snoop purred softly as Emma rubbed his neck and back.

"Snoop doesn't belong to anyone. He came with Uncle Ollie from the Island. He's Uncle Ollie's friend and now he's my friend."

Snoop turned his head and looked up to Emma. "Thank you, Emma, so kind of you to speak of us as friends. But why does everyone think I belong to Oliver? I belong only to the Maker."

Emma smiled and again stroked Snoop's head and back.

Freddy watched as the ferret directed squeaks toward Emma. He chuckled.

"It's almost like the little fella's talking to you."

Emma's smile expanded into her eyes while barely holding in laughter.

"What's so funny? All I'm saying is that you seem to be able to communicate with it."

"First of all, Snoop is not an 'it'. And yes, we communicate."

Now it was Freddy's turn to snicker. "Right. I used to have a pet. It's all trained response. Animals don't really understand."

"Really? Then why don't you try?"

"Try what?"

"Try talking to Snoop. Communicate with him. You haven't had any opportunity to train any response from him."

She looked down at Snoop. "You wouldn't mind talking to Mr.

Freddy, would you, Snoop?"

Snoop smiled and shook his head no. He stood up on his hinds. He faced Freddy, tilted his head and smiled.

Freddy backed up against the door behind him. "Ok, that's weird."

"Go ahead, talk to him. He's waiting."

Snoop looked to Emma and then turned and looked directly at Freddy.

Caught off guard, Freddy nervously wondered what to do next. "Well?"

"Well what?"

"Talk to him. Ask him to do something while looking at me."

Freddy thought for a second. He looked at Emma, "Ok Snoop, come sit on my lap and place your right paw on my chest."

Freddy felt proud of the puzzle he had presented.

Without hesitation, Snoop stepped off of Emma's lap and onto Freddy's lap. He then placed his right paw on Freddy and looked up at him smiling.

Freddy took a deep breath. He looked at Emma. "How do you do that?"

Emma smiled. "I didn't do anything. You asked Snoop to do exactly what he is doing."

"How is that possible?"

Emma laughed. "I think after hanging around us for a while you are going to expand your understanding of what's possible."

Snoop turned to Emma. "Oh, Emma, I do hope I have not frightened Mr. Freddy."

Emma knew that she was having fun at Freddy's expense. "Ok, Snoop, you can come back and sit with me. I don't think we have frightened Freddy too badly."

Emma watched Freddy attempting to figure out what had happened. She decided to help him out and change the subject.

"So Freddy, how did you get involved in video photography?"

Freddy was relieved to move on. "Well, at first it was sort of a rebellion thing against my parents. You know, what are you going to make of your life? They had high expectations for me. But then I began liking it. And now, it's basically a way to make a living in this crazy upside down world."

"Where are your parents now?"

Freddy looked slightly away. "They're dead."

"I'm so sorry."

"Thanks. They died in what they are calling one of the numerous world disasters. Like I said, these times are crazy."

"Yeah, they're pretty bizarre."

"Keeping busy with video work helps me cope. Looking at the world through a camera lens helps me not have to look at what's going on in the bigger and scarier real world."

They both paused as they thought about some of the things presently happening on the world stage.

Freddy broke the silence. "So how do you cope? Developing animal tricks?"

Emma chuckled. "Funny. My diversion is school and my studies. I bury myself in them and away from the madness. I thought it would simply come back together by the time I graduated."

"I don't see how that's possible, unless you plan to be in school a very long time."

Emma smiled and looked away.

Freddy wondered how she could smile after discussing present world conditions.

"Well, you're not at school now. We're right now in the most dangerous region on the planet. We're also driving into an area that's anything but peaceful. And yet, you don't seem anxious. Can you explain that to me?"

Emma giggled. "It does seem strange after saying what I did. I'm not sure how to fully explain it other than to say it involves God and Uncle Ollie."

"Is he really your uncle?"

"Technically, no. But he might as well be. I've always referred to him that way."

"He does seem confident about what he's up to. I know Brandon is a little nervous about where we're heading. But he's hungry for the story and trusts that the rich guy can provide us the safety we'll need.

Emma's expression got serious. "I'm sure that before this is all over, it's going to take more than money."

Freddy smiled politely and wondered what Emma meant. She rubbed Snoop's back and Freddy turned to stare out the window.

♦ ♦ ♦ ♦ ♦ ♦ ♦

After having picked up Yaunt in Jericho, Osgood's group passed through the border crossing on the Israeli side with little delay. Lanzig had made prior arrangements to insure that their crossings on both sides of the border would go smoothly.

They pulled into a coffee shop near the center of the small village of Shunat Nimrim where they were to meet the leader of the mercenaries. His name was Nidal Hasuri. Nidal sat alone. He was a large man, seasoned by many miles and a dangerous life. Four others, bound to him by loyalty and fear, sat at a table next to him.

Lanzig and the others walked into the dimly lit and smoke filled shop. Lanzig wasted no time walking toward Nidal's table. Nidal got up and they embraced like two seasoned thugs. Even at six feet, Lanzig was four inches shorter than Nidal. Lanzig whispered to Nidal. Nidal listened and nodded. Yaunt then turned toward Osgood, Li, and Yaunt.

Then Nidal threw his arms wide. "Welcome. Come let us have tea together."

Lanzig motioned the others to come and sit. He had explained to them earlier that in the Middle East, the keeping of customs was important. No business could supersede it. So after tea and other formalities, the plans were set in place. Nods from Lanzig and Nidal assured Osgood that everything would go according to his wishes. The loyalties and distrust were written in their eyes. Greed and power were the cheap glue that bound them together. Only time would tell the tale of which of them would survive.

TWENTY ONE

Most who come to Israel find a way to spend some time in Jerusalem. As per Yaunt's instructions, Amir arranged a lunch stop for the group in Jerusalem. Oliver preferred to press on, but Emma was excited at the chance to see even a little of the great city. Brandon and Freddy were glad for the chance to get some footage that could prove useful to the project. So Oliver deferred, but insisted that their time there be limited. He knew that this would not be the last time he would visit the city or the part it would play in his life.

The group's mood was festive as they enjoyed the tastes and sights around them. Amir chose a place just outside the Old City with ample varieties for the palate and a nearby shop for a few souvenirs. Oliver took pleasure watching Emma and Snoop as they browsed. Snoop squealed at all of the colors and curios.

Within three hours they were on their way to Jericho. Emma had a new cashmere scarf and Snoop was snacking on some olives and figs. Freddy continued filming. He spent extensive time capturing footage of Emma. This did not escape the attention of either George or Oliver.

Emma enjoyed herself and Oliver did not want to rob her of it. The time would come when the laughter would cease.

Not long after leaving Jericho they reached the Israeli

checkpoint. As they pulled up another earthquake hit. This one was a bit more intense and lasted almost twenty seconds. People came running out of the checkpoint building. It was a full hour before soldiers continued processing people through the border.

At first the process proceeded smoothly. Some questions arose concerning Amir and the whole group was detained. Brandon called Yaunt but wasn't getting an answer. As they were waiting in a holding room, a lead officer passed by and noticed Oliver holding Snoop. He stopped and looked in. He recognized them and walked into the room.

"Pardon me, but are you Dr. Cohen, the man who was lost at sea?"

"Yes I am. How did you know?"

"Well, Dr. Cohen, you have been in the news. And, of course, your name drove the curious in the media to discover that your heritage is Jewish. Welcome to Israel. But why are you traveling to Jordan?"

"Our guide is taking us to Ma' daba."

"Ah, you go to see Mount Nebo?"

"But of course."

"And how long do you intend to be in Jordan?"

"Only as long as it takes to see what there is to see. Of course, it is getting late so we may need to stay the night."

"Yes, of course. He looked over the group and once more at Amir. Do you have your papers signifying your status as a guide?"

Amir immediately presented his documents. The officer examined them slowly, occasionally looking back at Amir.

"Very well, everything seems in order. Let me admonish you to not spend any more time in Jordan than necessary. These are dangerous times and we want you to remain safe. Now follow me and I will get you on your way."

In no time they were back on the road and entering Jordan. Amir handled the Jordanian security crossing easily enough once he handed over the bribe money that Yaunt had provided.

They stopped in Shunat Nimrim for water and a short comfort break. Amir took the opportunity to check in with Lanzig and report. He was instructed to contact them when they neared Ma'daba.

As they were about to pull out, another short but intense earthquake hit. Having lived in California, George knew that such increased quake activity was not a good sign. He wondered if Oliver was aware of the possible danger this pointed to.

Oliver scanned the group and knew that none of them truly realized the true nature of the danger they would soon face.

♦ ♦ ♦ ♦ ♦ ♦ ♦

Though the distance wasn't great, the way to Ma'daba was a winding and desolate road. The road snaked its way through one turn and valley after another. Within a few minutes Freddy had all the footage he needed to capture the essence of the bleak terrain. He wondered how anyone could live or survive in such an environment.

In the forward vehicle, Amir provided brief comments on some of the history of the area. On one or two occasions they passed a sign providing the distance both to Ma'daba and Jabal Nibu. It was late afternoon when Amir pointed out the exit to Mount Nebo.

He had no sooner finished, when a deep rumble shook the car. He had trouble keeping it on the road. Amir signaled for the other vehicle to pull over behind him. This quake was more intense than the others. Parked along the side of the road, both vehicles rose and fell as a wave and rumble passed by and around them. The quake continued for at least a full minute.

After the rumbling stopped, they all got out of the vehicles. Emma pointed to the dust rising from the top of Nebo. Amir grabbed a pair of binoculars to take a look.

Oliver asked, "What do you see?"

"On top of Nebo is a monastery. It seems to have collapsed."

Within a few minutes some cars and a truck came down the road from the mount.

George looked at Oliver. "Perhaps we should go see if anyone needs help. We are doctors after all."

Oliver nodded. "Let's load up and see."

♦ ♦ ♦ ♦ ♦ ♦ ♦

The earthquake left extensive destruction in Ma'daba. A large number of buildings had collapsed and many others suffered major damage. Dust along with cries of agony filled the air.

A wall came down on one of Nidal's men and crushed him. The rest of their group had only scratches from falling debris. Yaunt was shocked as he looked down the street and saw the measure of desvastation. He was no humanitarian, but he was quieted by the death and destruction around him. This wasn't a distant news story, but actual life experience. He looked over at Osgood. The man seemed completely unmoved. His cold disinterest only reinforced Yaunt's opinion of him as a heartless soul.

As the dust began to settle, Osgood barked out orders. "Nidal, get your men together. Lanzig, contact Amir. I want to know their status."

Nidal and Lanzig were surprised at Osgood's inattention to the surrounding circumstances.

Osgood noted their hesitancy. "What? Our mission has not changed. Evaluate our status so that we can proceed. Hurry!"

The two men obeyed, shaking their heads.

♦ ♦ ♦ ♦ ♦ ♦ ♦

The two vehicles weaved up the damaged road and reached the top of the mount. The Franciscan Monastery built in 1932 to preserve the site was completely destroyed. The famous large brazen serpent was also down. A tourist bus was on its side and several of its passengers were attending to some of the injured. George and Oliver got out of their vehicles and immediately began rendering aid. Luckily, first aid kits from the bus and the monastery were found. There were several injured, but no dead.

Freddy was walking around getting footage. Emma handed out available water while Snoop added cheer and smiles to those they helped. Brandon and Amir went around asking and answering questions. Within an hour, the situation on the mount was under a measure of control.

Oliver and George took a break as they surveyed the situation. The sun was setting and darkness was not far behind.

"Well, O.B., what's the plan?"

He looked toward Ma'daba. It was clear that the city had taken a hard hit. There was no sign of power, only occasional auto lights. The sky was clear enough that he could see over to the Israeli side. Lights were visible toward Jericho.

"Well, from the looks of things, I say we stay here for tonight. I'm sure the authorities are doing all they can. We have some supplies."

"Thanks to your list. How did you know?"

Oliver smiled. "I didn't know about this. I only knew that we needed to have the items with us."

"Ok, but how did you know?"

"You won't like my answer."

"It's the 'God thing' again, isn't it?"

"Yes, it's the 'God thing'. I told you that you wouldn't like it."

"Yeah, but I will say that I'm glad you knew."

Oliver put his arm around his friend. "Tonight may be a long night. Stay close to Emma."

With that he patted George on the back and walked away.

◆ ◆ ◆ ◆ ◆ ◆ ◆

Amir found a place among some trees away from the others. He pulled out the satellite phone Yaunt had provided. He made the call.

Yanut felt the phone vibrate in his pocket and pulled it out. He saw that it was Amir and waved Lanzig over as he answered it.

"Amir, report."

"We are all atop Jabal Nibu. We are staying here tonight."

"Is the doctor or anyone else injured?"

"No, Mr. Yaunt, sir. The two doctors are treating the injured, but none of our group is hurt. Do you have any instructions?"

"Not at this time. Call me back in an hour or if anything significant happens. Understood?"

"Yes sir."

Yaunt hung up and looked at Lanzig. He told him everything and they walked over to tell Osgood.

Osgood wasted no time in deciding what to do next. He barked his orders.

"I want to go there. Have Nidal and twenty of his best men join us. I need to know what they are doing there. We'll get close enough to observe but we need to approach without being seen. Launch a drone. I want to know what happens until we get there. We leave immediately."

"Yes, Herr Osgood."

Lanzig turned to assemble the group. Within a few minutes they were making their way through the dark and battered streets.

♦ ♦ ♦ ♦ ♦ ♦ ♦

With everyone settling in, Oliver took a walk along the northeastern portion of the mount. Emma and Snoop watched him walk off. Snoop nodded to her and they curiously followed after him. He wasn't hard to follow since he was using a flashlight.

Oliver stopped at a place where the mount began to drop off and sat down. It wasn't long before he heard something.

"Don't stay back there. Come on up."

Emma sheepishly whispered. "How did you know we were here?"

"I'd know my friends' footsteps anywhere."

"I am sorry if we are disturbing you, Oliver."

"Yes, Uncle Ollie, if you would rather us leave, we understand."

"No, you're fine. I simply wanted to sit out here and look at the sky. With all the lights out, the stars are extra brilliant."

"Yes indeed, Oliver, they certainly are bright tonight."

"It reminds me of sitting out on top of the mountain on the Island."

"Uncle Ollie, was it as wonderful as Snoop describes it to me?"

"Absolutely and more so. It was a place and a world that tested the imagination."

"So there really were talking animals everywhere?"

Oliver smiled and nodded. "And every one of them knew their place in the Story and heard the voice of the Creator."

Snoop looked up at Emma. "This is true. I can still hear His voice when He desires it. But I must say that the noise in this world shouts so loud that it often drowns it out."

"Uncle Ollie, what is He like? I mean... you actually spoke to Him."

"You're reading the Bible like I told you, right?"

"Yes."

"What did you see when you read about Him?"

She thought a second. "Someone kind, someone strong, and someone who always knows the right thing to say."

"That's very good. You see, He's already teaching you. He doesn't have to be visibly present to speak to you or to reveal Himself."

"This is true, Emma." It was Snoop. "For although I cannot read the words, Oliver has often read them to me. And the beauty, strength, and truth of the Maker are all there."

"Uncle Ollie, from what you told me, your journey to meet Him was hard and painful. Why did it come so easy for me?"

Oliver's eyes clouded a bit. "Oh, dear Emmy, I think that speaks more about the hardness of my heart than anything else. I see in you what I saw in Mary. You both have willing hearts. I resisted His reaching out to me. But you embraced Him and were captured by His touch."

Snoop cuddled up to Emma. "This is true, Emma. And in that, you honor His name."

"But I know so little."

Oliver chuckled. "It's like the old saying. 'It's not what you know, but who you know'. And the 'Who' in this case, is the most important 'Who' there is."

Snoop slowly nodded. "Truly"

Oliver whispered to himself. "Truly."

♦ ♦ ♦ ♦ ♦ ♦ ♦

A tiny drone no bigger than a small mouse was already focusing its infrared camera onto the mount. Li was guiding the drone through an initial flyover scan of the site. He could see people gathering around a toppled bus and around the ruins of the monastery. He also noticed two adults and a small creature on the northeastern rim.

He asked Lanzig over the radio, "The doctor has a creature that accompanies him, doesn't he?"

"Yes, a ferret."

Li spoke to Osgood, who sat in the seat in front of him. "Mr. Osgood, I think I have located the doctor. He and his creature along with a female are on the northeastern portion of the mountain."

"What are they doing?"

"They seem to simply be sitting."

"Excellent. Keep an eye on them." He then asked the driver, "How long until we arrive."

"We should be there in about five minutes. Driving without light and using only night vision goggles keeps our speed down. After the earthquake, I'm unsure about road conditions."

"Very well. It sounds like the good doctor isn't going anywhere soon."

◆ ◆ ◆ ◆ ◆ ◆ ◆

Oliver enjoyed listening to Snoop teach Emma a new song. Just above the tune he thought he heard a small buzzing sound. But in the darkness, he couldn't tell where it was coming from.

As he scanned the horizon something else caught his attention in his peripheral vision. He turned back and saw it. About three quarters down the slope was a soft light on the side of the mountain.

Suddenly his heart began beating fast. He couldn't explain why, but he knew that he had to go to the place where the light was coming from.

Emma noticed Oliver's attention and demeanor had changed. "What is it, Uncle Ollie?"

"Look down the slope. See that faint glow on the side of the mountain."

She followed his pointing finger. "Yeah. It's like a small fire or light up against the mountain. I wonder what it is?"

Oliver didn't answer. He simply looked at it and knew. He stared intently at the glow. After a few minutes he turned to Emma.

"I'm going down there. Now listen to me carefully. Under absolutely no circumstance is anyone to go down there. Do you understand?"

The intensity in his voice frightened Emma a little.

"What is it, Uncle Ollie?"

"I'm not sure. But I know I must go there and that it's dangerous for anyone else to do so."

"Dangerous? How?"

"Listen carefully. You remember how I said that I might give you instructions, which may seem strange at the time? I also said that when I give you these instructions that you must trust me and do as I say. Well, this is one of those times."

Snoop looked up to Emma. "This is from the Maker, Emma. You must listen to Oliver. It is for our protection. Is this not so, Oliver?"

"Yes, good friend. Now, stay with her. You may watch from here, but you must not come down with me."

With that, Oliver started his walk down the slope.

♦ ♦ ♦ ♦ ♦ ♦ ♦

Li saw Oliver walking down the mount. "Sir, we have some movement. It seems the doctor has left his friends and is walking down the northeastern slope."

Osgood looked at the driver. "Get us as close as you can to the northern base of the mountain."

"Is there any place in particular he is heading?"

Li maneuvered the drone to scan the area. "Nothing comes up on infrared, sir."

"Very well. Keep an eye on him. I want to know where he is. We'll be at the base of the mount shortly."

Oliver stopped when he heard the buzz again. He smiled and nodded. He knew they were watching.

TWENTY TWO

Oliver could clearly see the light up ahead. As he got closer he smiled when he recognized it. Just like on the Island.

◆ ◆ ◆ ◆ ◆ ◆ ◆

All five vehicles pulled to a stop at the northern base of the mount. Nidal and his men gathered around him waiting for orders. Li, Yaunt, Lanzig and Osgood set up the drone viewing monitor on the hood of the lead vehicle. Li tracked the drone with Osgood standing next to him. Yaunt and Lanzig stepped back to talk.

They spoke softly. Lanzig watched Osgood to see if he could hear them.

"Hermann, what do you think this is all about?"

"I'm not sure. One thing's for certain, he's obsessed with this doctor. I've rarely seen him like this."

"He's been like this for the past week. He's always unpredictable, but you're right, this is more than usual."

Neither of them spoke for a few minutes.

Lanzig smiled. "He doesn't even notice us. All he can focus on is the doctor."

Yaunt nodded. "How long have you known Osgood?"

He took a deep breath before answering.

"I have worked for Osgood and his father for over forty-five years."

"Really? What was his father like?"

"Older. And yet, the son has perfected what the father began."

Just then Osgood shouted. "Lanzig, where are you? Come here immediately."

◆ ◆ ◆ ◆ ◆ ◆ ◆

Oliver stopped several feet from the mouth of a cave. A distinct soft light came out from it. From the light he could tell that the cave was newly opened. The light seemed to dance around the entrance in the form of a swirling glowing fog. His heart beat fast as he remembered. He whispered to himself. "Shekinah."

◆ ◆ ◆ ◆ ◆ ◆ ◆

Li looked down at the viewer of the drone's camera. He then picked up some binoculars and looked back up the mount. He shook his head.

Lanzig came up behind Osgood. "Is there a problem?"

Li responded, "Well sir, this is very puzzling. The drone's infrared clearly picks up the doctor by the side of the mountain. He has stopped. But the drone picks up nothing else. When I look through my binoculars I can also clearly see a light coming out of a cave. But the infrared doesn't pick up any light signature, even with thermal infrared."

"You're sure? Did you check the setting?"

"Twice."

Lanzig looked at the drone's viewer. He took the binoculars for himself. He saw the light coming from the cave.

Lanzig tried to think of an explanation.

"This shouldn't happen. If it's visible, we should detect it on some level of the non-visible scale."

Li interrupted. "Sir, the doctor seems to be entering the cave."

♦ ♦ ♦ ♦ ♦ ♦ ♦

Oliver approached the cave. His heart was racing. As he reached the mouth of the cave, he reached out to touch the light. Just like on the Island, the light had substance and danced through his fingers. Energy coursed up his arms and tickled his neck. He softly laughed, remembering his many days being on the top of the mountain in the garden. He took a deep breath and stepped into the cave.

♦ ♦ ♦ ♦ ♦ ♦ ♦

Osgood thought for a second before barking out orders.

"I need eyes to see what the doctor is doing and what's in that cave."

Li wasted no time. "I will go."

Lanzig immediately spoke. "Li, are you sure? What about your hand."

Osgood saw the point. He shouted out. "Nidal, come here!"

Nidal ran and stopped in front of Osgood.

"Select six of your best men. Arm them well. They will accompany Li up the mountain."

"Right away, Osgood, sir."

Lanzig wondered about the plan, but realized that the doctor was likely unarmed.

Osgood spoke directly to Li. "Listen to me, Li. The doctor is in there to get something."

"Get what?"

"I'm not sure. But, whatever it is, I want it. Let nothing stop you from getting it. Once you have it, dispose of the doctor. He is of no more use to us. Do you understand?"

Li smiled as he looked down at his bandaged hand. "I will settle the matter, sir. Have no doubt about it."

Lanzig added. "Li, take care. There are things here that defy explanation. Fulfill your mission but use caution."

"The doctor surprised me once. It will not happen again."

Li checked his weapons and Nidal and his men joined him.
"Do they understand English?" Li asked.
"Yes."
"Very well. Let's go."

♦ ♦ ♦ ♦ ♦ ♦ ♦

The glowing cloud filled the entrance. As he walked into the cave, he could not even see the outside darkness behind him. Oliver took three steps in when a voice spoke.

"Remove your shoes before you come any further."

Fear and excitement gripped him as he quickly obeyed the voice.

"You may now come in."

As he walked further the cloud began to thin out but the light grew brighter. He turned a corner in the cave and there he stood.

♦ ♦ ♦ ♦ ♦ ♦ ♦

Li and the six men were having some difficulty moving up the mount. The quake had loosened the ground. This, in turn, affected their footing. Several times they had to stop when one of them slipped and fell. This only added to Li's frustration. It seemed the harder they pressed, the more often someone fell.

♦ ♦ ♦ ♦ ♦ ♦ ♦

Oliver squinted as he looked at the tall glowing figure standing in front of him. "Keeper?"

"I am a keeper of this place, that is true. But I am not the one to whom you refer. My brother is elsewhere, but he sends his greetings."

"What is this place?"

"This is the tomb of an ancient great one, a deliverer of his people. I am sent to guard and protect what is placed here."

"And yet, I am brought here."

"True. And now you must enter further. I will stand guard."

Oliver cautiously walked passed the imposing guardian, who fixed his gaze on the exit. The deeper into the cave he walked, the more the light intensified. The very stones seemed to sparkle and almost move in a harmonious rhythm. He came around another corner and there He stood.

◆ ◆ ◆ ◆ ◆ ◆ ◆

Osgood, Lanzig, and Yaunt watched the drone monitor. Osgood cursed as he saw the men continue to fall and make slow progress to the cave. Nidal watched over their shoulders.

Osgood's words spewed with vitriol. "Why are they falling so much? What's wrong with your men?"

"Herr Osgood, I believe that just as the quake opened up the cave, the ground all around it has become unstable. If there is another quake, it could even collapse underneath us and them."

That thought had not occurred to him. Osgood looked around. He pressed his hands hard against his forehead trying to suppress his rage from exploding. He had to know what was in the cave.

"Get the drone down there and maneuver it into the cave."

"It may be difficult since I can't detect the cave's location on the sensors."

Osgood thought for a second and then called Li on his communicator.

"Li, can you hear me?"

Breathing hard, Li responded. "Yes sir, I can hear you."

"Stop where you are and cast a light toward the cave. I want to take the drone into the cave, but we can't see it."

"Understood."

Lanzig adjusted the controls and started the drone in a slow descent. He spotted the team and the beam of light pointed at the mountain. The beam didn't reflect on the mountainside or any cave entrance. It appeared to simply stop as if its light was cut off at a given point. The best he could do was move to that point.

The drone was within five to six feet of the cave entrance when it was suddenly destroyed. A flash of flame, fire, or something immensely bright totally obliterated it.

Li stood in place stunned and the men around him fell back. The bright flash even caught the attention of Emma and Snoop at the top of the mountain. Down at the base of the mount, they all saw a bright light on the viewer and the echo of an explosion.

Osgood shouted on the communicator. "Li, what happened? We've lost the drone's feed."

"Herr Osgood, you have lost the drone."

"What do you mean?"

"It's been destroyed."

"How?"

"A bright flash, fire, or something shot out of the cave and vaporized it. Nothing even seemed to fall to the ground."

Osgood turned to Lanzig. "I thought you said the doctor wasn't armed?"

"He wasn't...he isn't."

"Then what did it?" His voice was almost hysterical.

"I DON'T KNOW." Lanzig practically growled out the words.

"AHHHH!" Osgood shoved him aside and stomped away.

Li called out, "What are your orders, sir?"

"Hold your position for right now. Observe the cave entrance but stay where you are."

"Affirmative."

◆ ◆ ◆ ◆ ◆ ◆ ◆

Oliver faintly heard the sound behind him. His complete attention fixed on the One standing in front of him. It only took a second to fall to his knees.

"My Lord." Though the words were spoken softly, there was measured excitement in his voice.

"Arise, Oliver. We have much to discuss."

The Lord took hold of Oliver's arm and helped him up. Even after fifteen years under His instruction, Oliver's heart always fluttered at His touch.

"Master, what brings You here?"

"Why you, of course. You followed My instructions very well. Even though I intentionally left out certain information, you trusted Me. This is important now and will be in the future."

"But why to this place?"

The Lord chuckled. "Always thorough. It's a wonderful trait in you, Oliver. Only never allow it to undermine you fully trusting what I tell you."

Oliver blushed at the compliment. "Yes sir."

"As to the question, this is a special place. It is here that I laid to rest one of My mighty servants. Like the Island, it has remained hidden and at times guarded, awaiting a future purpose."

Oliver whispered to himself. "Moses."

"Yes, very good. The bones of My servant Moses are not far from here. And they will remain undisturbed until the resurrection."

"Then why am I here?"

"Because you are like My servant, Moses. You shall be My Moshe. For like him, you were brought out of the water and rescued for My purpose. You and another will be My witnesses in these last days before I return."

"The other witness?"

"Yes, you will meet him very soon. He shall be My voice and you shall display My power. And together you will bear witness to My Story and My coming."

"Power?"

"When My servant Moses delivered the people from the hands of bondage, it was by My power. And you too, shall wield this power."

The Lord turned and reached for something leaning against the wall of the cave. It was a long and weathered wooden staff.

"With this Rod, My servant Moses displayed My power before the world. You shall do the same. Kneel before me, Oliver."

Oliver quickly obeyed. He trembled as if the ground beneath was moving. His eyes looked down and the ground around him began to glow. The Shekinah thickened. He felt the Rod touch his shoulder.

"You have been known as Oliver Branch Cohen. But now you are My Moshe. And by My power and with this Rod you shall be My witness. Fear no man or power, for until your task is complete, I shall protect you. Hear and obey My voice always. My Moshe, I love you. Truly."

The Shekinah became so bright that Oliver had to place his hands over his eyes. He then felt the gentle touch of Lord's hand on his head. And yet it was as if the weight of the entire cave had fallen upon him. He collapsed.

After a few moments Moshe lifted his head. The cave was dark except for the soft receding glow of the Shekinah. The Lord was gone. Beside him was the Rod. He looked at it a second before reaching to take it. He used it to steady himself as he got up. He looked around and knew it was time to leave.

As Moshe turned the corner, he spotted the guardian facing outward in a vigilant stance. The guardian heard Moshe approaching and glanced back.

As Moshe passed by, the guardian lowered his head and spoke. "Moshe, servant of the Most High."

The guardian waited until Moshe stepped out of the cave, He then extended his arms and placed his hands onto the walls of the cave. The ground below and around the cave began to roar. The whole mountain shook in a rumbling wave. The quake surged up the mountain and down toward the lowland. The cave walls buckled and the entrance collapsed. Dust rose from the ground filling the air.

♦ ♦ ♦ ♦ ♦ ♦ ♦

Li and his men heard the initial roar and fell to the ground as the quake's wave passed by them. When he recovered, he used his night vision goggles to scan the area. Dust obscured everything. He heard a voice on his communicator.

It was Lanzig. "Li, can you hear me? Report."

"Another quake."

"Yes, I know. What about the cave and the doctor?" Lanzig was shouting.

"It's hard to tell at present. The air is full of dust, but I don't see any light coming from the cave."

"Move in closer and be careful."

"Affirmative."

The men stood bewildered. Li barked out orders. They picked up their weapons and followed Li slowly up the mountain.

♦ ♦ ♦ ♦ ♦ ♦ ♦

Down at the base of the mountain the quake had left its mark.

Fissures had opened up and half swallowed some of the vehicles and damaged the tires on the others. Osgood's anger intensified. With all of his money and power, he was unaccustomed to being thwarted to such a degree. He could almost feel the presence of his master physically gripping his body as if to punish him.

Lanzig and Yaunt watched from a distance. Osgood gripped his head and gritted out the words, "It's not my fault."

TWENTY THREE

Li and his men slowly made their way up the slope. The thick dust made any night vision impossible. The ground around them gave way easily and they fell frequently. It took them a good forty minutes to reach their destination. The dust had settled somewhat and they used lights to scan the area. The location of the cave eluded them. He spread the men out but still there was no trace of a cave.

With the dusty haze gone, Li used his night vision goggles to search a wide swath when something caught his attention. Almost to the top of the mountain he spotted a lone figure walking with a staff.

He immediately called in. "Herr Lanzig, come in."

"Yes Li, what is it?"

"There is no trace of the cave. The quake must have collapsed the entrance. But I spotted the doctor climbing up the mountain. He's practically at the top. What are your instructions?"

Osgood heard the communicator and came running and screaming.

"Go get the doctor! I'm sure he has what he retrieved from the cave. I want it!"

"What about the others?"

"Eliminate them. I want no witnesses! Understood?"

"Understood."

♦ ♦ ♦ ♦ ♦ ♦ ♦

The quake woke up everyone on the top of the mountain. George quickly assessed the injured. He looked around for Emma and called Brandon, Freddy, and Amir to help him find her. They found her and Snoop at the northeastern edge.

George immediately asked. "Where's Oliver?"

"Dad, he went down the slope. He's been gone for a good while now. We saw some lights down there and then the quake hit. That's all we know."

Snoop leaned into Emma and whispered. "Do not be fearful. All is well. He will return soon."

Emma wondered how he knew.

Just then they all heard footsteps coming from below.

As Moshe crowned the top, they all stood silent as Brandon shined a light on him. Emma gasped.

He stood there looking at them without saying a word. He was … different. With the exception of a few streaks of brown, his hair was snow white. He also looked older, much older than the fifteen years of his absence. The one exception was his eyes. They were as bright and young as before. In his right hand was a large staff about seven feet in length.

They looked at each other and then again at him.

Snoop again leaned into Emma and whispered. "He is Moshe. That is his name now."

Emma whispered back. "What?"

"The Maker has given him a new name. His name is Moshe."

When she heard him say it a second time, she felt a shiver grip her. She knew it was true. She walked up to him and lowered her head.

"Moshe."

He responded. "You listen and believe."

He placed his hand on her head and whispered. "The Lord shines His favor on you."

Moshe looked at the others who stood in shocked silence.

229

Moshe spoke. "Friends, danger is on its way. Gather everyone together near the buses."

The force of his instructions moved them to action.

Hearing Moshe, Amir approached him. Standing before him he lowered his head.

"Good sir, I perceive that you are a holy man. I am not a good man, but the ones who follow you are evil men. I know this. I have no doubt that they will harm everyone here to get what they want. They will do the same to me once they know I have betrayed them. I ask or deserve nothing, but I cannot watch so many innocent suffer because of me."

Moshe smiled. "You have done well, Amir. Do not fear. Their evil will not succeed. Now go and join the others. Soon you will witness the power of the Living God. The time will come when you must truly decide. Now go."

Amir ran to catch up with the others. Moshe looked heavenward. He then gripped the Rod tightly. "Thy will be done."

♦ ♦ ♦ ♦ ♦ ♦ ♦

The first distant rays of morning were visible as Li and his men crested the top. He quickly assessed the area. In the distance he saw the toppled bus and a group of people gathered around it. He used his binoculars to get a better look. He called in.

"Herr Lanzig, I have reached the top and have spotted a group gathered near a toppled bus. I don't see the doctor, but I know he is here."

They spread out and approached with their weapons drawn. A few women began weeping. Li spotted some of the group he recognized, but not the doctor.

As he neared, Li shouted out. "We mean no one any harm. We only want Dr. Cohen. If he comes forward and comes with us, the rest of you are safe from harm."

Moshe stepped forward with the Rod in his hand. George reached to stop him, but Emma grabbed her father's arm and shook her head.

"Your lies are of no use here. If you turn around and go back, it is you who will not be harmed."

Li laughed. "And who are you, old man?"

"I am the one you seek."

Li took a step closer and looked intently at him. He was shocked to see that Moshe was telling the truth. He raised his weapon at him and shouted louder.

"Old man, doctor, or whoever you are, your tricks will not save you this time! Come with me now and the others will not suffer."

"And your lies will not disguise your evil intentions. I warn you for the last time, return to your master. Beg now for mercy for the time of mercy is ending here."

Li screamed out. "Shut up or everyone dies!" He turned to his men. "At my command, kill everyone."

As they lifted their weapons, Moshe lifted the Rod. It happened in an instant, but seemed to occur in slow motion. A flash of lightening fire streaked from the Rod. It reached out to all of Li's men and then to Li. It engulfed and consumed them. When the light vanished, they were gone. Not even a trace of their weapons remained.

Emma fell to her knees. George and Brandon stood still with their eyes and mouths wide open. Amir fell face down to the ground. Freddy stood stunned and then perturbed that he hadn't had a camera with him. The rest of those watching had varied reactions.

Snoop made his way to his friend. He looked up raising his paws and began to sing.

Today I see and sing again
To the Living God,
That once again the world may know
That He alone is Lord.

Maker of all
Both here and above,
The Story declares it is true.
That even the Lie will be silenced
And all will confess it anew.
He alone is Lord
He alone is Lord.

Evermore we proclaim it,
He alone is Lord.

Moshe sank to his knees and joined Snoop. As they repeated the song, Emma joined them.

George and all the others listened, still processing what they had witnessed. Just then the ground and the clouds rumbled together and everyone became silent."

♦ ♦ ♦ ♦ ♦ ♦ ♦

Lanzig and the others had seen a light flash and the sound of an explosion from the top of the mountain. He wondered if his associate had succeeded. Without transportation or word, all they could do was wait. Osgood was almost uncontrollable in his fits of rage. Lanzig had never seen him so unhinged. It bordered on madness.

♦ ♦ ♦ ♦ ♦ ♦ ♦

As the shock wore off, Moshe moved among the injured. He extended the Rod to the injured and touched them. One by one they were healed. Wounds would vanish and bones were instantly mended. Snoop and Emma followed him and cheered with every person's instantaneous healing. George followed, skeptical but amazed. Freddy was busy filming the whole event. He and Brandon traded glances.

After he has finished, Moshe gave them instructions.

"George, get our group together. We leave for Ma'daba."

"What about these people?"

"They are safe and we will let someone know that they are here. But we must go."

♦ ♦ ♦ ♦ ♦ ♦ ♦

After an hour and no word, Osgood would wait no longer.

"Lanzig, send someone else up there. Get at least one of these vehicles working. And where is the SAT phone?"

Lanzig summoned Nidal. "Select a few of your quickest men and send them up. All we want is information."

"Yes, right away." Nidal responded.

Lanzig turned back to Osgood. "Herr Osgood, we are already working on the vehicle problem. We should have something within the hour."

Osgood's only answer was a frustrated growl.

♦ ♦ ♦ ♦ ♦ ♦ ♦

They had to travel at a slow speed due to the damaged roads. As they reached the base of the mountain, Moshe noticed a group about a mile off the road. He sighed. Emma noticed them as well.

"Look, some people are down there. I wonder if they need some help?"

Moshe answered without looking. "They do not need our help. Proceed to Ma'daba."

♦ ♦ ♦ ♦ ♦ ♦ ♦

Yaunt noticed the vehicles coming down the mountain road. Lanzig spotted them and used some binoculars.

"That's the doctor's group. I can see Amir. Why didn't he inform me?" His anger simmered. "If he has betrayed me. . ."

Lanzig watched the group as they passed around a bend and were out of sight. He thought a second.

Addressing Yaunt, "Get the second drone out. We must not lose them. Osgood wants the SAT phone. I'll be right back."

When Lanzig reached Osgood he was pacing and yelling at no one in particular.

"The phone, sir."

"It's about time. Go on, I'll handle this."

Lanzig simmered as he stomped away.

Osgood walked away from anyone's hearing and made his call.

"Give me General Kasim. I don't care what he is doing. Tell him Herr Osgood wants to speak to him immediately. I'll hold."

It only took a minute and the general was on the line.

"Ah, Herr Osgood, to what do I owe the honor?"

"Enough with the niceties. I have need of some of your army."

"That is a very tall order, my friend."

"We are not friends. But you are in my debt. So let me tell you what I want. I want at least one hundred heavily armed soldiers and a fully armed helicopter."

"I'm not sure."

Osgood shouted. "I don't want excuses! You know the arrangement we have. I am calling the debt. Death and torture for you and your family would surely follow if any government officials discovered our arrangement."

The general yielded. "And if I get you this, then my debt is paid?"

"Yes, yes of course."

"And when and where do you need this?"

"Get them immediately to Ma'daba. Have the helicopter pick a few of us up at the base of Mount Nebo. Tell whoever is in charge that they will receive their orders from me."

Kasim consented with a long exhale. Osgood hung up.

♦ ♦ ♦ ♦ ♦ ♦ ♦

Amir drove the lead vehicle. Moshe, Emma, and Snoop were his passengers. George, Brandon, and Freddy followed behind them.

Brandon was in the front seat and turned to George.

"George, what is going on? Can you explain to me what we saw? And why does your daughter call him Moshe?

George waited a moment. "Well, you saw the change in Oliver's appearance. She said that Moshe is Oliver's new name. She said it's the name God has given him."

Brandon's face said it all.

"I know, I know. It doesn't make sense to me either, but that's what she said. As far as his changed appearance, the fire and healing coming from his stick, rod, or whatever, I have no answer. I can't explain it, can you?"

Brandon looked at them. He didn't have an answer. He wasn't ready to admit the possibility of God or miracles. He simply didn't have a plausible explanation. He turned and looked ahead, wondering what he had gotten himself into.

♦ ♦ ♦ ♦ ♦ ♦ ♦

Amir asked. "Sir, where exactly are we going?"

"Are you familiar with Ma'daba?"

"Yes sir. I have family there. Although perhaps, they will not claim me. They are good and gentle people."

"Get us to the southwest edge of the city."

Amir smiled. "That is the area where they live."

Moshe looked at him. "I'm not at all surprised. In fact, take us to where they live."

"Are you sure?"

"Yes, Amir, I am. I don't believe it's an accident that you are here among us."

Amir looked puzzled. Knowing his past, he wondered what his relatives would think when they saw him again. They would be right to condemn him. But would they?

Several years had passed since Amir had seen some of his family. He took a route on Al Waton Al Arabi St. which somewhat looped the city. Many people were walking around, displaced by the destruction of the quake. He wondered how his relatives had fared.

When he arrived at the house he was surprised to see his uncle and many others sitting outside the house as if enjoying a leisured conversation. He pulled up next to the house. Amir was the first to get out. He started walking toward the house.

His uncle, Omar, immediately recognized him. Amir was shocked to see his uncle almost run to greet him.

When he reached Amir, Omar firmly embraced him. Kissing both his cheeks, Omar was beginning to tear up.

"Amir, we were told you were coming and here you are."

"You were told? By whom?"

"By our visitor, of course." Omar pointed back to a man Amir didn't recognize sitting next to his cousin and aunt.

"Come, he is waiting for your friends. Tell them to come."

Amir was too stunned to argue. He waved for the group to come join him.

As Moshe and the others walked toward the group, the guest stood up. He walked passed Omar and Amir and went straight to Moshe. He stopped in front of him and smiled.

"So, you are finally here."

George and Emma watched the two of them.

Emma was the first to comment. "Dad, is it just me? Except for the white hair, they look like they could be brothers."

Snoop, who was on Emma's shoulder also commented. "Moshe never told me he had a brother."

Moshe looked intently at the man in front of him.

"We've never met. My name is Eli Branch Cohen."

"Eli? But... but you were killed."

"Yes, or so everyone thought. It seems that you are not the only one God brings back from the 'should-be dead'."

"And so, here we are..."

"Yes, ... here we are."

The cousins embraced and wept.

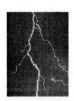

TWENTY FOUR

Eli spent over an hour explaining to Moshe, God's miraculous rescue of his life and all of the events bringing him to this place. (*see Book 3 of the Story*). Moshe then shared his journey to the Island (*see the Island, Book 1 of the Story*) and his rescue and coming to be there.

As the two shared their stories, all the others listened. Omar and his family both wept and cheered. Emma sat back amazed to hear the seeds of her faith validated as she cuddled Snoop in her arms. Snoop listened and clapped his paws throughout the narratives. Others watched Snoop, either perplexed or amused. Eli looked at Snoop, smiling and sharing a private wink. Freddy kept himself from thinking too much about what he was hearing by concentrating on filming. George and Brandon traded looks ranging from skepticism to self-doubt. Amir quietly listened with his head lowered. He sat next to his uncle who repeatedly patted him on the back. He felt guilty and out of place, but the hope he sensed from the stories kept him in his seat.

When they had finished, both Eli and Moshe rose from their seats. They turned and thanked Omar and his family. They respectfully declined offers for food. Their intentions were unanimous. They had to leave right away.

Moshe turned to Amir. "Amir, it is no longer necessary for you to come with us. You may go with us if you wish."

Amir looked at his smiling uncle and aunt. His heart was torn. He wanted to continue enjoying the new connection with his family. But he also had many questions and knew they could only be answered if he left. His uncle patted his back once more and nodded.

Amir looked directly at Moshe. "I will go with you, sir."

"Then let's go."

And with that, they group left, continuing on a road leading to the south.

◆ ◆ ◆ ◆ ◆ ◆ ◆

Yaunt had followed the group's journey and subsequent stop outside of Ma'daba. When they sat around and talked, he landed the drone to save power. He placed the drone in solar powered standby on a nearby housetop and kept watch.

The army helicopter arrived within the hour and they left for a staging area east of the city. Osgood was told that the soldiers were on their way from Amman and would arrive within the hour. He rubbed his hands under the churning sound of the helicopter. Lanzig wondered what wicked scheme Osgood was cooking up. When they landed, Lanzig had his answer.

Osgood began shouting right away. "Yaunt, what are they doing now?"

"They are simply sitting around talking."

"What about Amir?"

"He has refused to answer my calls. The signal I am receiving indicates he has turned off his phone."

Osgood scowled. "The fool has chosen poorly. When this is finished both he and his family will pay."

Osgood thought for a second. "From its position, can you get a clear image?"

Yaunt smiled. "Sir, I can practically read their lips."

"Good, show me the doctor."

As he zoomed in and scanned the group he was confused. "Sir, look for yourself. I'm not certain about which one is the doctor."

"What do you mean? You've met him, correct?"

"Yes sir. I see someone that resembles the doctor, but he has a beard and different clothing. And there's another dressed like the doctor, except he's older and has white hair."

"Let me see."

Lanzig leaned over and looked on as well.

"Focus in on the white haired man. He's sitting next to the girl and the animal. My guess would be with him. He's obviously disguised."

Just then Moshe turned and looked directly into the camera and smiled.

It gave Yaunt a start. "That's him. I can tell by that grin. How does he do that? It's like he knows I'm watching."

Osgood leaned in. "Focus in closer. See if there is anything unusual in his possession."

Yaunt did a slow pan. "Outside of his appearance I don't see anything. Well, except for the long stick he's holding on to."

"Focus in on the stick."

The high definition image provided brilliant details. The rod was dark wood, aged and weathered. It was not merely a piece of wood picked up from the side of the road. Everything about it said – ancient relic.

Narrowed eyes accompanied an evil grin. The stirring within told him what he needed to know.

"That's it! That's what he brought out of the cave. That long stick is what I'm talking about. When this all comes down, I don't care what it takes. I want that stick. Also, no witnesses."

Lanzig responded first. "Well, Herr Osgood, as long as they are in among those people we cannot act."

Osgood shouted, "What!"

"What I am saying is that these are all Jordanian citizens. I don't believe the soldiers will harm their own people without some cause. I suggest we wait until they leave and then act."

Osgood wanted to come back hard, but he saw the logic of Lanzig's words. "Yes, I suppose you are right. How long did you say on the soldiers?"

"Within the hour."

"Very well. I need to be alone. Message my phone when they arrive or if anything changes."

Without waiting for a response, Osgood walked away to an adjacent building.

Yaunt was beginning to sense reluctance in Lanzig. "What's troubling you, Hermann? I know we seem to have lost Li, but it's unlike you to be reticent."

Lanzig had seen the look of an opportunist many times before. With Li absent, he realized the error of telling or trusting Yaunt too much. He knew he could handle Yaunt if need be. But there was something troubling him.

"Yaunt, I have been in this business a long time. I have seen... a lot. But there are some things about all of this that I'm having trouble explaining."

"What in particular?"

"To start off, you have seen them. These are not trained individuals. And yet, at the hotel and now on the mountain, they bested and possibly eliminated Li and the others. You've watched them, they aren't carrying weapons. How do you explain that?"

Yaunt scratched his chin and nodded.

"And what's with the doctor's appearance? First he comes back looking like he hasn't aged and now he looks older than he should. Can you explain that?"

Yaunt then added. "And he seems to know when we are

watching him. Add to that Osgood's obsession with this… stick, staff, rod, or whatever it is."

Lanzig nodded. "In my line of work, understanding who or what you are up against is vital to success. And with this doctor, I don't know. And that concerns me."

♦ ♦ ♦ ♦ ♦ ♦ ♦

Osgood had purchased several buildings on the spot for the staging area. He found an empty storage room in one of the buildings. He closed the door behind him and lit three small dark candles. More than any other time, he needed contact. He sat on the floor of the room and began his chant. Unlike other times, a response came quickly. The smoke began to coalesce in one corner. All reflective light from the corner was gone as if sucked into a dark hole. Osgood swayed and continued chanting at a faster pace. Soon the blackened corner expanded to fill half the room. Then came the deep ominous guttural voice.

"You have found it?"

With eyes closed, Osgood answered. "Yes, Master."

"What the man possesses has unimaginable power. Spare nothing or no one to obtain it."

"As you wish, Master."

"And when you have taken it, destroy it."

Osgood opened his eyes in surprise. "But why, Master? With such power I can do great things in your name."

"If you do not destroy it, it will destroy you. Its power is beyond your ability to control. It must be destroyed so the enemy cannot use it."

"But…"

"SILENCE!" The force of the voice pushed him back. "You must do as I say. It has remained hidden for centuries, protected from our hands. It is brought out now for a purpose, a purpose that must fail. Destroy it!"

EC Lartigue

Osgood felt betrayed. After desiring it so badly he was now losing the opportunity to use its power. His failure to respond drew instant reaction. The darkness moved toward him and enveloped him. Engulfed in an ink-black shroud, Osgood felt a vice grip on his throat.

He was choking under the grip and a sulfuric breath. "You worthless pretender, how dare you defy me? I own you just like I owned your father before you."

Suddenly fiery eyes within the cloud formed and bore down on Osgood. He was helpless as he trembled in terror.

"Forgive me, Master. I am yours to command. Whatever you say, I will do. I am yours."

The dark hand that held him threw him hard to the ground. He lay open-mouthed as the impact knocked the air out of his lungs. The black smoke swirled over him and formed a whirlpool that forced itself into his body. He jerked under the brute force of the invasion. His body lay motionless for a moment. Slowly he opened his eyes. The fear was gone. It was replaced by an odious scowl. He let out a low and cavernous laugh.

When he finally got up, he examined his hands and flexed his arms. He felt power surging through him. It was unlike any drug-induced stimulant he had ever experienced. He lifted his fists into the air and screamed, "Yes!"

He growled once through gritted teeth and then stretched his neck muscles. When he walked out of the room, he practically tore the door off its hinges as he flung it open. He was ready to destroy.

♦ ♦ ♦ ♦ ♦ ♦ ♦

Amir followed Eli's directions. They left the highway and traveled down some seldom-used roads. Fortunately, the roads, though old, were manageable at a moderate speed. And yet, Amir was having his doubts.

"No offense, sir, but where are we going?"

"This road will take us to the highway on the eastern shore of

242

the Dead Sea."

"We could have taken the highway north from Ma'daba."

Eli smiled. "Yes, I know. But we need to get to the south. That way would have cost us too much time."

"Yes, of course, but what is the hurry?"

Eli looked at Moshe before answering. "We are being pursued."

The look on their faces made Emma a bit nervous. She said nothing. She merely took a deep breath and stroked Snoop's back and hummed.

The people in the other vehicle had similar questions but didn't have anyone to ask. They simply followed and wondered.

♦ ♦ ♦ ♦ ♦ ♦ ♦

The troops were arriving when Osgood returned. Both Yaunt and Lanzig noticed but didn't know what to make of the change in his demeanor. He no longer bordered on madness. Instead, he had the look of hard strength, daring anyone to defy him.

A Jordanian colonel walked up to them and spotted Osgood.

"Colonel Tahir, by orders of General Hasim, I am at your command, sir."

Osgood grinned at the officer. "Very good, Colonel. How many men do you have with you?"

"I have one hundred and fifty heavily armed men and our transportation is purposed for quick attack. What is our mission?"

Osgood snickered and turned to Yaunt who was holding the drone monitor and looked ready to speak.

"What is it?" Osgood barked.

"Sir, while you were gone, they left. They are traveling south along some unmarked roads. It appears they are heading for the Dead Sea highway."

"Show me on a map view."

Yaunt adjusted the viewer and turned it to Osgood. He inspected it and grinned. He turned to the colonel.

"Colonel, come with me on the helicopter. Add as many men as it can carry. We will head them off from the south. The others can then move in from the north. We will trap them between us."

"Very well, sir. I will make it so."

Osgood turned to Yaunt and Lanzig. "You two join the other troops. Let me know when you have reached the highway. That will assure me that they are trapped between us and can't escape. Understood?"

They both nodded. Lanzig had a question.

"Herr Osgood, what do you plan to do to the group?"

His eyes narrowed and then widened accompanied by a wicked grin. "They will all die, victims of an unfortunate military accident. They were mistaken for Jewish spies. Ha!" He turned and walked toward the helicopter.

♦ ♦ ♦ ♦ ♦ ♦ ♦

Some clouds were moving in by the time they reached the highway and headed south. The usual brilliant turquoise sea looked dull under the graying sky. A distant thunder echoed across the valley. Eli looked back at Moshe and they shared something unspoken. They had not traveled far south when they heard the unmistakable sound of a helicopter. It zoomed passed them low and fast. Even with a quick glance, it was obviously an armed military type. Both vehicles slowed as the helicopter decelerated and took a position one hundred yards east of the highway. It hovered in the distanced position, keeping pace with their vehicles.

Emma could not keep silent any longer. "Uncle… I mean Moshe, what does this mean?"

Before he could answer, his phone rang. Brandon asked the very same question.

"Well, it seems that we are being watched. We will not provoke any action. We will continue south and see what they intend. I know this may sound hollow, but remember the mountain and fear not."

Snoop pulled on Emma's shirt to get her attention. She looked down.

"Do not be afraid, Emma. Whatever intentions evil may have, the time is not yet. We will be safe. Watch and see."

The innocent look in Snoop's eyes eased her racing heart. She nodded.

For thirty minutes they continued south. The helicopter kept its distance and pace. The sky continued to darken with flashes of lightening visible behind them to the north.

◆ ◆ ◆ ◆ ◆ ◆ ◆

Osgood clarified his instructions to the colonel. Finally, the call from Yaunt came. They had reached the highway and were heading south. The trap was set.

Osgood gave the colonel the signal. The helicopter increased its speed and moved south at least two miles ahead of the vehicles. It then turned and placed itself squarely over the highway. It hovered until they spotted the vehicles. Two missiles immediately launched. In mere seconds they struck and destroyed the road two hundred yards in front of the craft. Where the highway had been was now a hole twenty feet wide and at least ten feet deep. The coming vehicles immediately stopped.

Eli nodded. "Well, I guess we're not going south anymore. Turn around Amir, and take us north."

The helicopter again took up a position one hundred feet to the east and a half-mile behind them. As they drove north, the storm moved south. Occasional lightening loomed large in the distance. Within thirty minutes they would all come together.

TWENTY FIVE

Amir's hands were sweating as he looked in the rearview and continued to see the helicopter.

"Sirs, you do realize that if they choose to act against us, no one will know of it. We will likely be dumped into the sea."

Eli touched his shoulder. "Amir, do you believe in God?"

"Allah is…"

"No, no, I am not talking about Allah. I am talking about the true and living God. He sent His Son, Jesus. His hand is with us today. We are His servants. And today we will not be handed over to these evil men. Instead, today you will witness the hand of the Living God deliver us and you will know that He Is."

Emma listened with quivering lips as she swallowed the lump in her throat.

The sky continued to darken as the clouds churned. Lightening flashed within the shadowy ceiling as it slowly moved ever lower.

Amir turned on his headlights. In the far distance he saw a long line of headlights coming from the north. He looked over to Eli.

"They have trapped us, sir."

Eli turned back to Moshe who had just opened his eyes from a prayer.

Moshe waited a moment. "Stop the car."

As soon as it stopped Moshe got out. He looked back at the helicopter and at the sky. He raised the Rod above his head. Suddenly a flash of lightening shot from the cloud and struck the helicopter's tail rotor.

Branches of sparks flew in all directions. The pilot put it into a controlled spin and crash-landed twenty feet east of the highway. All of the occupants immediately exited the craft. Within two minutes it exploded and sent them all to the ground.

Moshe got back into the car. "Drive on."

Amir's hands were shaking as he sped away. He looked at the fire in the rearview mirror, hoping no shots would be coming their way. Everyone in the other vehicle was too stunned to say anything. Brandon's hands were shaking as he tried to concentrate on the road.

They pressed on for about ten minutes. The lights in the distance were still at least ten miles away. Moshe tapped Amir on the shoulder.

"Up ahead the ground is level. First, I want you to turn off your headlights and stop. I will get out and tell the others to do the same and follow us. I then want you to turn off the road and drive toward the sea."

"Toward the sea?"

Moshe nodded. Amir shrugged his shoulders and obeyed.

He stopped, turned off the lights and Moshe got out. When Moshe returned, he tapped Amir on the shoulder again.

"Now, do as I said. When we've gone a bit you may turn your lights back on. I don't want you driving into the sea."

"Of course not, sir. What do I do when we get near the water?"

Eli smiled and answered. "Stop." They all chuckled.

It only took two minutes to reach the sea. They stopped and all got out.

Moshe and Eli walked over to the water's edge. They placed their hands on each other's shoulders and bowed to pray. It was only a short prayer and then they turned to the others.

Eli spoke. "Today begins our work. We are witnesses of the Living God and of His Son Jesus. No hand coming against us will succeed until our work is completed. So that you will know that the LORD, He is God, behold His power."

Moshe took a step forward. With both hands he raised and extended the Rod perpendicular to the ground. He then quickly brought it down.

Simultaneously, the wall cloud above them fell like a blanket across the entire valley. A thick fog surrounded them while the area immediately around them remained clear.

◆ ◆ ◆ ◆ ◆ ◆ ◆

The convoy screeched to a halt when the fog bank collapsed around them. Some of the men yelled and all of them felt a measure of fear. They continued their progress, only at a very slow pace. They had traveled for about thirty minutes when they spotted someone walking on the highway ahead. It was the Osgood, the colonel and several men.

When they stopped, Yaunt was the first to get out.

"Herr Osgood, what happened?"

Osgood's voice seemed strained. "This freakish storm. The helicopter was struck by lightening and we crashed about a few miles back."

"What about the doctor and his group?"

"You passed them!" Osgood shouted.

"That's not possible. We passed no one."

"They turned off the road and headed toward the sea. You didn't see them because of the fog. They turned off their lights. But we definitely saw them turn off. Now let's go. Have some men walk ahead of us. Even in this fog, they should spot the tire tracks."

Yaunt stood there without saying anything.

Osgood shouted. "I said, let's go! They can't go far. They're still trapped."

Yaunt ran back to the convoy and gave instructions. It took some time to turn the convoy around. They continued their search.

♦ ♦ ♦ ♦ ♦ ♦ ♦

When the fog descended the whole group huddled close and looked over to Eli and Moshe. All of them were in shock except Snoop. He was bouncing and clapping while standing on Emma's shoulders. The fog silenced the air and all they could hear was the waves on the shore.

Brandon finally spoke up for the others. He voiced their shared question.

"So what do we do now?"

Both Eli and Moshe looked over their shoulders and back again.

Eli pointed to the sea. "We cross over."

They all looked at each other as Snoop once again clapped.

Moshe turned and walked up to the shore. He took the Rod and lowered it toward the lapping waves. Before it touched water the sea retreated from the Rod and the wind began to blow. Moshe raised the Rod in front of him and stepped forward on what had previously been the water's edge. As he walked forward, the fog parted and moved away from him on either side. He kept walking until he was out of sight.

Eli spoke to the group. "Get into the vehicles. Amir, follow Moshe. The drop off is very gentle before it levels off. Turn on your lights. I want you all to see. Let's go."

♦ ♦ ♦ ♦ ♦ ♦ ♦

Visibility for the troop's convoy was down to about fifty feet. They traveled about five miles when they discovered tire tracks leading off the road. The convoy followed the trail. The fog suddenly thinned out when they reached a slight drop off. It was there the convoy stopped. Lanzig got out of the lead vehicle to inspect the way ahead.

Lanzig was getting up from his knees when Osgood joined him. Yaunt and the colonel were right behind him.

"Why have we stopped?"

Sandy soil dribbled through Lanzig's fingers. "I don't like the look of this."

"The look of what?"

Lanzig turned to Osgood. "The shore of the Dead Sea begins right here. See the car tracks going down right into what should be deep water. Where did the water go? And look ahead, the fog is clear up ahead but thick and dark on both sides. It's like there is a tunnel through the fog and the water. How is this possible?"

The colonel listened and wondered. He turned and shouted. "Turn off the vehicles!"

With the motors quiet, they all listened. Beyond the fog bank, they could hear it. It was the sound of water churning.

♦ ♦ ♦ ♦ ♦ ♦ ♦

Moshe moved at a walking pace. He sometimes had to walk around some rock formations. The two vehicles moved slowly behind him. With the Rod raised, Moshe walked on. The fog and waters parted ahead of him with every step and every turn. Freddy got out of the car and began filming as he walked. He wondered to himself how what he was seeing was even possible. Everyone else was silent except Snoop. He stuck his head out the window and continued clapping. In light of what they were experiencing, Snoop's actions suddenly didn't seem strange anymore.

♦ ♦ ♦ ♦ ♦ ♦ ♦

"Well, Herr Osgood, can you explain to me what is happening here? Where has the water gone? Or is it gone? You can hear it as well as I can. And why is there a tunnel in the fog and dry ground? This is not possible"

The colonel listened and doubt began to grow in his mind as well. Fear was also beginning to move through the normally hardened troops. Osgood could see that he was losing control.

He shouted with all his might. "These are merely weather anomalies! The ones we seek are using this opportunity to escape. I understand your reluctance. But I will reward anyone who will follow me and go after them."

He paused a second and continued. "One million world currency units of your choice to anyone who will go with me. And another one million when we get them."

The colonel asked Yaunt. "Can he afford such a price?"

"Oh yes, he's worth billions."

The colonel thought for a second. "Make it two million."

Osgood looked at him and smiled. "Two million it is. And then another million when it is done."

The colonel raised his rifle and shouted to his men. "Come men, do not fear. Let us go in the strength and protection of Allah. He will reward us greatly."

While there was a paused caution, the confidence of their colonel and the idea of such a reward stirred many of them. Eighty men stepped forward and joined the colonel.

The colonel looked at those who did not respond. "You will not be punished but neither will you share in the reward. So stay and receive nothing and we will go and gain everything."

The colonel turned to Osgood and saluted.

Osgood grinned and pulled Lanzig aside. "Well, Herr Lanzig, surely you will not be shamed by these mere conscripts."

Lanzig looked back out toward the fog bank before answering. "You may convince the greedy, Herr Osgood. But I fight and destroy what I understand. This is beyond that. In all of my years, I have never seen or even heard of such things as what we are witnessing. This is not possible. I sense a trap."

"Ha! A trap? What do you mean?"

"I cannot explain it, but there is something about this doctor that smacks of a power beyond … beyond explanation."

Osgood shot back shouting. "POWER! You know nothing of power." His eyes practically bulged out of their sockets. His face contorted to almost beastly proportions. "I am power!"

With one hand he lifted Lanzig and tossed him into the air as if he were a small object. He was thrown five feet into the air and twelve feet away. He landed with a jarring thud and moaned as he rolled to a stop.

Osgood then raised his fists into the air. Bolts of electrical flashes streaked out from them and toward Lanzig who lay on the ground shaking.

Osgood looked directly at Lanzig and spoke in a deep growling voice. "I will deal with you fully when I return."

He then turned to Yaunt. "And what about you? Will you defy me as well?"

Yaunt trembled in terror. "No, Master."

Osgood turned to the colonel. "I've had enough of this doctor and his tricks. Let's go spill some blood."

An evil presence suddenly invaded the colonel and his men. He smirked and raised his weapon. "Allah Akbar."

In a frenzied rush all but a dozen of the troops ran to the vehicles and loaded up. They were shouting and firing shots into the air as the vehicles bolted to pursue their prey.

Lanzig looked up just as they sped away down into the fog tunnel and out of sight.

He lowered his head and whispered to himself, "The Dead Sea."

TWENTY SIX

As they neared the western shore, the fog began to lift in a widening vista. They could see several cars parked on the western highway, stranded by the fog. Many people were standing on the edge of what had been the shoreline. Moshe was within fifty yards of the shore. He had found a path that provided a less than drastic rise to the shore.

Some of the people on the shore saw the white-haired Moshe and ran to assist him assuming he was old and in distress. People from the road joined those on the shore. They all watched two vehicles driving up out of the seabed. Once the cars were on shore, Eli joined Moshe who stood looking out to the east.

Eli turned and shouted to the crowd. "People of Israel and all those gathered, today you bear witness that again the hand of God moves among you. Know that the LORD, He is God."

Moshe raised the Rod above his head. Holding the Rod in his right hand, he spread his arms wide apart. Immediately the fog bank began to part and lift like a giant curtain. People fell to their knees and gasped. As light flooded the valley, the sight was phenomenal.

The Dead Sea was parted and walls of water a thousand feet high rose from the seabed.

♦ ♦ ♦ ♦ ♦ ♦ ♦

When the fog suddenly lifted, the drivers were shocked at the sights around them. Several of the military vehicles crashed into each other. Others flipped over, spilling the passengers. Some of the soldiers lay crushed under overturned vehicles. In the entire calamity, the whole convoy stopped. Those not killed in the chaos, looked on in terror at the towering walls of water on either side of them. Some of them screamed and many began running toward the western shore.

The colonel regained his wits and shouted for the driver to make for the shoreline. The distance to the shore was a mere two miles. And yet, the charging vehicles collided with one another as they vied for position.

♦ ♦ ♦ ♦ ♦ ♦ ♦

Looking at the vehicles in the distance, Moshe lowered the Rod and held it by his side. Suddenly, fire leaped from the Rod and shot out toward their pursuers. The fire struck the tires and all of them swerved out of control. The twisting force of the vehicles threw dozens of men in various directions. All of the military vehicles were stopped about a mile from the shore.

Osgood had slammed into the dashboard and was bleeding from his forehead. He wiped the blood from his eyes as he cursed and screamed, pushing away the dead soldier leaning against him. He kicked the door open and surveyed the scene. He looked toward the western shore and among the crowd he saw the lone white-haired figure. He let out an animal scream as he spotted and picked up a weapon.

Off to his left he heard Yaunt screaming out to him. He turned and spotted him pinned under two soldiers in a twisted wreck. Osgood shrugged his shoulders, directing his focus to the shore. He looked at his weapon. The distance was too far to make a shot at the man on the shore. He broke into a run as his rage inflamed every part of his being.

◆ ◆ ◆ ◆ ◆ ◆ ◆

Moshe slowly lowered his head as if weighed down by grief. He looked back at his group. Emma was on her knees with tears trailing down her cheeks. Snoop stood beside her and softly patted her side. George stood in shock as he surveyed the magnitude of the entire scene. Amir was face down on the ground as if afraid to look up. Brandon stood beside Freddy, pointing and instructing him where to aim his camera.

Eli stepped beside Moshe and placed his hand on his shoulder. "It must be done."

Moshe looked at Eli and knew he was right. He turned to face the sea. He lifted the Rod high in one hand and spread his arms wide.

He softly whispered, "Truly."

In a quick motion, he brought his arms together and dropped the tip of the Rod down to the ground.

◆ ◆ ◆ ◆ ◆ ◆ ◆

Several of the remaining soldiers on the eastern shore had rendered aid to Lanzig. They all drew in a quick breath when the fog lifted and they saw the parted waters. Many of the men had begun to pray or wail out loud. They had all watched as flashes lit up in the far distance. But then came a terrifying rumbling sound.

◆ ◆ ◆ ◆ ◆ ◆ ◆

Immediately after the Rod touched the ground, the land shook. Beginning on the eastern end, the north and south walls of water started to collapse. The sheer volume of the crumbling walls of water sent a shockwave moving to the west. The force of the shockwave reached the fleeing soldiers before the sound. They were all knocked down right before the terrific sound slammed them once again. All of them looked back. Many of them screamed in horror as they saw walls of water crashing down and racing toward them.

Yaunt yelled out helplessly as he watched the approaching death.

Osgood dropped his weapon as he quickly got up, bolting for the shore. His mind, could not comprehend the futility of any attempt to escape. Some of the soldiers surrendered. They fell down and some shot themselves rather than face the oncoming destruction.

Even in all of this, Osgood's fear was replaced with a fury that seemed to give him speed. His rage so fully deceived him that he now believed he would still succeed and make it to shore before the waters overtook him. Fury engulfed him as he screamed out to Moshe threats of death and destruction. He was so completely overtaken in his madness that he didn't even realize the moment he was swallowed up. The waves crushed and swept him down so deep that his body was impaled and buried, never to be seen again.

◆ ◆ ◆ ◆ ◆ ◆ ◆

A thick saline mist filled the air as the waters proceeded to find their equilibrium. Everyone on shore shut their eyes tight. They waited for the sting of the mist to subside. Many bodies were seen floating and drifting to either shore.

On the eastern shore, Lanzig and the few remaining soldiers watched in silent horror. No one had words to express what they had witnessed. After a time, they helped Lanzig up and they all started walking north on the lonely highway. Two hours later, a tourist bus picked them up. Informed of the road's condition ahead, the driver turned around. On the long ride back, Lanzig wondered how he would explain what he had seen. Would anyone believe what he himself had trouble accepting.

◆ ◆ ◆ ◆ ◆ ◆ ◆

Moshe fell to his knees. He wept as Eli stood beside him.

Snoop made his way to his friend's side and began to hum a soft tune eventually adding the words.

Mighty to rescue
all who will come.

Free for the taking
To any who call.

But mighty in justice
And who can withstand
The power of heaven's
Unstoppable hand.
Run then for rescue
The hour is at hand.
For stories are ending,
And moments are short.
The Coming approaches
Decisions are made
For rescue or judgment
For freedom or woe.

Moshe looked at the Rod in his hand. He turned to Eli.

"I was trained to ease pain and save lives. Now my hands have brought death. I ah…" His voice trembled.

Eli looked at his fellow servant.

"It was not you. Never suppose that it is you who wields the power of God. It is not, nor will it ever be at your disposal. It is we who move at the bidding of God and are at His disposal. We are sent to declare and display as witnesses concerning Who He Is. This is but the beginning. Men will rarely perceive the events taking place from the perspective of God's working. Therefore, they will miss altogether the Story. They see only shades and parts. Yet, all the while their hearts are colored by the Lie. It saddens me to think how many more will refuse and reject the Story. All we can do is let Him use us to rescue as many as possible before it's too late."

Snoop nodded. "Truly."

Brandon and Freddy followed Amir to their vehicle. George

placed his arm around Emma as they walked slowly behind them. Snoop wasted no time and caught up with them.

Eli reached down and helped Moshe up from his knees.

"Come on, brother, we still have a trip to make before nightfall."

The spectators parted to allow Eli and Moshe to pass. Some looked at them in fear, while others desired to reach out and touch them. Many exchanged whispered comments. Some had taken pictures but wondered if anyone would believe they were real.

Before the group drove off a person took a picture of the vehicles.

Amir started the car and asked, "Where are we going, sir?"

Eli thought for a second. "South to the Negev."

EPILOGUE

They made their way out of the valley and up toward Arad where they stopped for fuel. Eli directed them to an unregistered village between Arad and Be'er Sheva. The little community had about forty houses scattered along the backside of a ridgeline hidden from the highway. The road was bumpy but passable. They stopped in front of one of the houses.

Moshe tapped Eli on the shoulder. "What is this place?"

"My home. At least it has been for these many years. Let's get inside. We'll clean up, have some tea, and then we will all talk."

♦ ♦ ♦ ♦ ♦ ♦ ♦

After tea and a small meal, Eli introduced everyone to their hosts.

"I wish you all to meet the two people God has used to care for and protect me these many years."

An elderly Bedouin couple stepped forward.

"This is Ibrahim and his wife, Minera. Later, I will tell you of our story together. For now, simply know that we are safe here and that they extend their hospitality to all of you."

The couple bowed their heads slightly and then left.

Eli continued. "When I left here several days ago, I told them I was bringing someone back with me. I didn't realize there would be so many, but no problem. There are places for all of us to sleep. But for now, let us talk."

When Freddy picked up his camera, Eli raised his hand. "As I begin to talk, I ask that none of this be recorded. It is all written in my journal, which any of you can read later. But I want no recording.

Freddy nodded in agreement and set down his camera.

For the next hour Eli kept everyone mesmerized as he told his story (*see Book 3, the Story*).

When he finished, Snoop clapped and flipped in the air. Everyone laughed as they watched his aerobatics.

Everyone now turned to Moshe. He had the Rod lying across his lap. He placed it on the floor next to him and took a deep breath. He looked over to Brandon.

"Well, Brandon, I promised you a story. And I'm about to give it to you. I hesitated before because I doubted whether you would believe me. I hope that after what you have witnessed today you can see it differently. As I think back, it truly is a miracle that I am sitting here tonight sharing this. But here it is."

And for the next three hours, he meticulously told his adventure. (*See the Island, Book 1, the Story*).

They hardly even moved until Moshe completed the narrative.

It so mesmerized Freddy, he had not even asked if he could film it. A few times he looked at Brandon who was battling between skepticism and dealing with the reality of what he had witnessed. Freddy had his own battles. Neither of them could settle the argument within themselves about what they had seen. All they could do was listen and scratch their heads.

For most of the telling, Amir sat with his head down. A few times he wiped away tears, hoping no one would see. Without raising his head, he whispered a prayer. When he had finished, he fell completely face down and wept hard. His whole body shook as the rescue of heaven cleansed the heart of a thief.

As Emma listened, she laughed, she cried, and she cheered. She would often close her eyes and try to imagine what it must have been like on the Island.

Several times during the telling, Snoop would join Moshe and sing together the songs of the Island. It was during one of last songs that it happened.

George would later describe it as a coming light. The darkness that had strangled his heart was being pierced. It felt like waking up from a long sleep. And then came the voice. It was singing along with Snoop and Moshe. Then it spoke his name and whispered words meant for him alone.

George trembled. All of the excuses melted away.

He looked up and whispered three words, "I believe You."

He immediately fell face down. He saw his failures and the darkness of his soul. He pleaded in his heart for forgiveness. He then watched as it was all washed away. He wept hard as the tragedy of his life was swept away and replaced with light.

Emma knew the moment it happened. She watched her father fall to the ground. It took her breath away. When George's sobs softened to whimpers, she kneeled beside him. She gently placed her hand on his back.

George felt her hand. He slowly arose and turned to her. They could hardly see each other through the tears. He wrapped his arms around her.

"Emmy, I'm so sorry…I'm so, so sorry."

"It's ok, Daddy, it's ok."

Moshe stopped his telling as he watched his friend find his rescue. He raised his head and gave thanks.

In the shadows of the back doorway, Ibrahim and Minera raised hands and also gave thanks.

When the telling was finished, Eli bowed his head and prayed.

"Oh LORD of heaven and earth. Your Story lives, for You live.

In this humble place we give thanks and call on You to complete what You have begun. May we be faithful unto the end. For Your glory and Honor. In the name of our Savior and Lord Jesus, Amen."

Snoop whispered, "Truly."

The hosts began to give instructions for the evening.

Emma wanted to run up and hug her uncle, but instead she held on to her father. She looked up at Moshe.

"When you told your story, a part of me wished so badly that I could have seen it."

"You shall one day."

"I know."

Moshe suddenly felt a breeze come across his cheek. It made him tremble slightly. He looked over to Eli as if to signal him. Eli nodded and came over.

Moshe then looked at George and Emma. "I want you two to go with us outside. I ..." He got choked up and couldn't finish the phrase. He looked down at Snoop and smiled.

And so Eli, Moshe, George, Emma and Snoop walked out. They followed Moshe away from the house and up the ridge a short distance. He then turned to them.

"We are to wait here."

Emma wondered out loud. "What are we waiting for?"

"Patience, my dear."

It wasn't long and a cool fresh breeze came down the ridge. Snoop immediately lifted his head and let it flow across his furry face. They heard footsteps coming down the ridge. Two tall men walked toward them. Both of the men moved down steady and strong. They had no problem keeping balance coming down the steep path.

When they came into view, Snoop let out a squeal and leaped into the arms of one of them and perched himself on his shoulder.

Moshe whispered. "The Keeper."

Emma's eyes widened and she fell to her knees. George only stood staring.

"Get up, young one, and do not fear."

Moshe walked up to the Keeper and wrapped his arms around his towering friend.

Eli looked at the other man standing behind the Keeper. He lowered his head and whispered, "Shamer." His old friend had come as well.

Moshe released his grip and looked up. "It is so good to see you again, my friend. Earlier I smelled it in the breeze and I knew. You carry the very fragrance of our Lord. But why have you come?"

He looked up at Snoop. "I have come for the little one."

Emma reacted. "What? Why?"

"He has finished his task. He is not meant for this world. His family and friends are waiting for him."

"But...but will I ever see him again?"

"Yes, Emma, you shall, later. We shall all see each other again."

Moshe reached up for Snoop who leapt into his arms. He looked down at him.

"Well, my friend, it seems we part company for awhile. Greet all of our friends and give them my love."

Moshe began to choke up. "And find Mary. Tell her..." It took him a moment before he could continue. "Tell her I love her dearly. Sing her one of our songs and tell her... tell her I will see her soon."

Snoop's eyes were moist. He tilted his head to one side and smiled. "Oh Moshe, I shall find her. I will sing her the songs of your rescue and the songs of your strength in the Maker. And we will wait for you. We are all kept in the Maker's love. Truly."

George listened in wonder, like a child on Christmas morning.

Moshe stroked Snoop's head. Snoop purred as he reached up and touched his hand.

Emma was now at Moshe's side. She tugged on his shirt. He turned to her.

She reached up. "May I?"

He handed Snoop over to her. She looked down at him. She could barely see as tears filled her eyes.

"I have known you for so little time and yet I feel…"

"It is the Maker's love you feel, Emma. It is what we share and what is always with us. The Maker has a great adventure for you in the coming days. Listen and learn. You and your father are children of rescue. He would have you share His Story."

George heard the words and knew.

Emma whispered a sigh.

"Oh Snoop, I will miss you dearly. I want to hear more of the songs."

"Oh Emma, you can. All you have to do is be still and listen. He sings them always. They speak of Him and He sings them to our hearts. Trust me, you will hear them and you will sing them."

She felt a tap on her shoulder. It was the Keeper.

"It is time. We must go. Trust the words of the little one. His songs are true."

He reached down and took Snoop in his arms. Snoop got up on his hinds and waved to them all. The Keeper and his companion gestured farewell with their hands. And instantly they vanished.

Emma and George gasped at the suddenness while Eli and Moshe smiled.

George asked. "Is it always like that?"

Both Moshe and Eli answered simultaneously. "Yes." They both laughed.

George put his arms around Emma. "Emmy, tomorrow we go home."

"What?"

"Yes." He choked up a bit. "We need to tell your Mom."

"Oh, Daddy." She wrapped her arms around her dad and he lifted her off her feet.

Eli allowed them to celebrate before he spoke.

"You two go on back and find Minera. She has places for you."

As they walked away they heard George whistling a soft tune. When they were out of sight, Eli put his arm on Moshe's shoulder. They both looked out toward the southwest. Sprinkled across hillsides on the horizon were flickers of lights from scattered villages and cities. In the distance they heard several military jets streaking to their destinations.

"Well, my brother, here we are, together at last. the Story has brought us both here and will take us to … well … well, that's still to be told. And we will tell it, the two of us together."

Moshe responded. "Truly."

A SHORT WORD FROM THE AUTHOR

When looking at the three books, it is "the Story" that connects them. The three books are meant to stand as separate, yet connected, narratives. And yet, as mentioned in the original Prologue, it is "the Story" that sits central in the collection. This will be most clearly expressed in the third and final book. The tentative title for the third book is "The Battle of the Witnesses."

Now back to "the Story." It is my desire that the reader understand what "the Story" is saying. All three books, and thus "the Story," are expressed in a simple poem.

> *Before the Beginning, was the Story.*
> *But then a Lie was declared and believed.*
> *But in the end,*
> *Everyone will know and understand the Story.*

In a late section of the first book, this poem is explained.

"**The Story**" in it simplest form is this: "*I Am.*" This is the self-revealed name of God. God is Who He has revealed Himself to be and the fullness of all that this entails. Words alone fail to express the completeness of His fullness. But we use words because to do otherwise would leave us saying nothing. And as someone said, "We speak because we do not wish to remain silent."

The Lie, and all lies derive from this original Lie, is this: "*No, He isn't.*"

In the end, everyone will know and understand that "He Is!" All other stories fall within "The Story." We are all passing narratives either believing "the Story" or accepting "the Lie."

The Story begins with Him. The Story ends with Him.

He is the Story.

Special Preview

The Battle of the Witnesses
The Story, Book 3

The Chronicle of Eli

The first indication of trouble was the dogs.

A single dog barking broke the deadly stillness of the late night. It wasn't long before several more joined in. But then it all changed. One dog after another went from a deep bark to a high pitched painful yelping. One by one they each went silent. In the distance a long lone howl echoed down the alleys.

Then came the shots. It was like fireworks, but different. The sound of the dogs had stirred Armand Cohen. But when he heard the shots, he sensed that danger was coming.

He immediately woke his wife, Emily. They both listened. They heard more shots and then the screaming began. He went to the window and heard it coming from down the street. Lights in some houses were coming on only to be followed by more shots and screams. Houses were on fire.

Emily's voice was trembling. "I thought we were safe here."

They had lived in the diplomatic compound for over a year. The

Lebanese government constantly assured them that they were safe. But in a world going mad, such assurances were more wishful thinking than guarantees.

Personal weapons were strictly forbidden. The State Department had provided protection, but at night it was minimal. Depending on the strength of the attackers, the two men downstairs might only delay disaster.

Armand's mind raced for a plan. With each minute his options were dwindling. The security men downstairs yelled out to them.

"Ambassador Cohen, remain upstairs! The perimeter has been compromised. Try to stay calm. We have called for help. It should be here soon. Lock yourselves in your room."

Emily was practically frantic. "Armand! Eli!"

Armand raced down the hall and went to Eli's bedroom. He decided not to turn on any lights. He saw his young son soundly sleeping. His nightlight dimly lit the floor. At eight years old, the boy loved his baseball nightlight.

Armand softly shook his son's shoulder. Eli barely stirred. Armand didn't want to make any needless noise, so he gently picked Eli up and wrapped him in a light blanket. He quickly made his way to their bedroom.

When he reached their room, he placed Eli on the bed.

More shots and screams. They were getting closer.

The noises woke Eli. He rubbed his eyes trying to see his surroundings. The only light in the room came from the closet, which was half open.

"Mom, Dad, what am I doing in your room? How did I get here?"

His dad placed his finger over his lips to silence him. Eli saw the distress in his mom's eyes. The sound of a nearby explosion shook the windows. Without delay, his mom bolted to sit on the bed next to him. She wrapped her arms around him. He felt her trembling. The fear immediately transferred to him. He began to softly cry.

Armand was trying to remain calm, but feared he might buckle.

He remembered his training. Panic is the enemy of survival. He looked at his wife and son and sensed a coming inevitability.

The shots were now very close. He went over to the window and dared a peek. In the distance he could spot emergency lights. Help was on its way. He also saw the house next door on fire. He realized that help would not arrive in time. He had decisions to make.

"I want you both to go into the closet and close the door."

"Darling, no."

Armand swallowed hard and nodded yes. From the look in his eyes, she almost fainted. The touch of Eli's hands on her arm shocked her back. She softly sobbed as she took Eli by the hand and they walked to the closet.

"Get into the deepest corner. And, no matter what, don't come out."

"Daddy!" Eli was struggling to get free from his mom's grip.

"Son, go with Mommy. Please. And pray."

Eli lowered his head and yielded.

They went into the closet. When they closed the door, the darkness engulfed them.

The downstairs was rocked by an explosion that blew the front door directly into the body of one of the guards. He was dead before he hit the ground. The other guard fired his weapon, but was quickly dispatched by the charging figures in black.

Six hooded men blasted through the entrance with weapons sweeping the room for any other resistance. The presence of guards told them they were at the right house. After they cleared all of the downstairs, the leader pointed up the stairs.

He directed three of the men. "No prisoners."

They grinned and nodded.

Weapons in the ready, they slowly walked up the stairs.

Armand had heard it all. He knew they were coming. He had always wondered what he would feel like if and when such a time came. The training had said one thing. He now realized something more. He slowly moved to his knees.

"Lord, I have always put my trust in You. Now comes my last test. I am in Your hands. Keep me safe in You."

Emily held Eli tight. "Pray, darling, pray."

"I am Mommy. I am."

Shots sprayed the door and easily tore through it. Among the many shots, several found their mark on Armand's kneeling body. He softly fell to the ground. He never felt a thing.

Emily heard the shots. She trembled so intensely she imagined the ground, and not her, was moving. She then heard Eli's soft prayer. Calmness suddenly poured over her. She began to faintly hum a tune her sister-in-law had taught her. Tears gently rolled down her cheeks.

The closet door flew open and the light came on. A dark hooded figure stepped in. It didn't take him long to find them. He grabbed Emily and yanked her to her feet.

Eli screamed. 'Mommy!"

"Stay in there, boy, don't move," the man yelled.

As she was dragged into the bedroom, she called out to Eli. "Keep praying, honey."

"Yes, Mommy."

The man threw her to the ground. She lightly screamed, more out of the pain than of fear. The man looked down at her.

"Well, infidel, do have anything to say before you die?"

Emily's gentle eyes looked at her captor and softly spoke.

"The Lord is my shepherd."

"He cannot protect you, so die, infidel."

One quick shot dispatched her. Her serene smile disturbed and then angered the man.

One of the others interrupted his thoughts.

"What about the boy?"

"Yes. We will make him see his worthless parents before he meets his fate." They both laughed.

Eli silently prayed and then began to hum the little tune his mother had sung moments before.

All three of the men grinned as they took a step toward the closet.

Suddenly, a bright light threw them back and they tripped over the bodies on the ground. In the fall, they dropped their weapons. When they looked up, they had to shield their eyes from the intense brilliance seeming to emanate from the closet.

It took them a moment to adjust to the light. When they did, they saw a man standing at the closet door. But what sort of man was he?

He was at least seven feet tall. Dressed like some peasant shepherd, he stood looking at them with his arms crossed. His eyes were strong and fearless but he carried no weapon.

When they realized that he was weaponless, they looked at each other and grinned. They each reached for the weapons and rose to their feet.

The tall figure extended his right arm and opened his hand toward them. Fire shot out. The flames divided and flew toward each of the men. The fire struck and ignited their weapons. The flames quickly traveled down the rifles and flowed like a fiery river across their arms. The blaze then grew and engulfed their entire bodies. The men screamed as they ran in various directions. They ran into furniture and soon the whole room was ablaze.

The tall figure turned and entered the closet. He extended his hand toward Eli.

"Come on, my son. We must leave this place. Cover your eyes."

The deep calmness in his voice evacuated any fear from the young lad.

The tall man wrapped Eli in his cloak. He lifted Eli up and carried him out of the room, now fully overtaken in flames.

Downstairs the leader had heard the shots. He and the others were pillaging the house, assuming that his men had done their work.

He heard footsteps coming down the stairs. He was shocked to see the tall figure coming down carrying the boy. He screamed out to his men to come as he raised his weapon toward the man.

Like before, the tall figure needed only to raise his hand. The same fate overcame all of the murderers downstairs. Likewise, their flaming bodies caught the remainder of the house on fire.

With the fading sounds of their screams, Eli fainted in the arms of his rescuer.

The next thing he remembered was the sound of sheep and the smell of a stable. He looked up and saw the man. He was sitting by a fire. He was softly humming a tune. It was the same tune he had heard his mother sing.

The First Book in the Epic Trilogy

The Island taps into a thirst
for a sense of wonder and something to believe in.

Read an excerpt of this book and order it on eclwriter.com

ABOUT THE AUTHOR

EC Lartigue is currently the Missions Pastor at a church in the Tulsa, Oklahoma area. His senior Pastor describes him as 'a pastor with a poet's heart and a storyteller's mind'. His work has taken him to countries across the globe on mission with God. He has seen that more than anything else, 'story' translates across cultures and generations. And the greatest 'Story' of all is the Gospel. Communicating that 'Story', is his passion.

His prayer is that the reader enjoy the adventure of story, especially the one God desires to write in their lives. For only God writes great non-fiction.